Heir Of Jaxinor

Jaxinor Chronicles #1

Michelle L. Levigne

Hard Shell Word Factory

ISBN: 0-7599-3527-0
Trade Paperback
Published June 2005

© 2005 Michelle L. Levigne
eBook ISBN: 0-7599-3526-2
Published May 2005

Hard Shell Word Factory
PO Box 161
Amherst Jct. WI 54407
books@hardshell.com
www.hardshell.com
Cover art © 2005
All rights reserved.

All characters in this book have no existence outside the imagination of the author, and have no relation whatever to anyone bearing the same name or names. These characters are not even distantly inspired by any individual known or unknown to the author, and all incidents are pure invention

Prologue

THE SWORD HIT the slate paving with a wooden clatter. Andrixine followed it a heartbeat later, her bruised knees making a sodden thud that echoed dully in the old creamery-turned-practice room.

"I hate this," she grated between clenched teeth, refusing to gasp like a cow in labor despite the racing of her heart and the sweat that blinded her. A vision of her warrior friends among the Sword Sisters mocking her weakness stabbed at her heart and mind. Her shoulders shook as she braced herself stiff-armed against the floor; palms slid on sweat-slicked stone.

"You have been out of your sickbed only five days, daughter." Brother Klee picked up her practice sword and carried it to the wall rack holding other blunted wooden weapons. "Enough for today."

"No. I have to keep working." Andrixine flinched as her voice banged off the stone walls. "Please?"

For a moment, the two simply looked at each other, volumes of communication passing between the emaciated noblewoman and the tall monk with silver in his dark hair and beard. She shuddered, her fine trousers and linen shirt drenched in sweat from a mere ten minutes of sword drills. He breathed normally, his dark blue robe barely disturbed. Andrixine sat back on her heels. Her warrior braids, thin twists of dark hair bound with the silver cord reserved for nobles, swung free of the clips that held them out of her face. A gasping laugh escaped her, and she raked more sweat-drenched strands of hair out of her too-pale face.

"You lasted ten strokes longer than yesterday. The regimen is intended to make you stronger, not send you back to your sickbed." He held out a hand to help her stand. "If you exhaust yourself, how shall you stay awake during your contemplation time in the chapel?"

"This is like no training regimen I've ever known." Andrixine wobbled as she regained her legs. "You say it's meant for kings and Oathbound warriors—why use it on me?"

"We have no training programs for noble maidens who will inherit their fathers' estates," Brother Klee said with a smile. That earned him a snort from the exhausted, noble maiden leaning on his arm. His smile faded. "You must know, we believe you were poisoned."

"Who would poison me? Who would hate Lord Edrix Faxinor enough to attack his heir?" She shuddered and twisted free of his support, to stagger to the bench next to the door.

"Not your father, Andrixine. You. Who profits if you do not inherit?"

"Lorien doesn't want the estates. She'd be a troubadour if she could. Or spend her life in Court, dancing and dictating fashion. None of the boys want the bother. They want to be soldiers. Not that I blame them," she mused, nodding. "I would give anything to take my oath of celibacy and join the Sword Sisters."

"Anything but Faxinor, you mean. You were born to serve, Andrixine Faxinor. Your heart is loyal, and you know your duty clearly. You are a true servant of Yomnian, and you will always put the right ahead of your own desires and dreams. That is why we chose to give you this training regimen reserved for those entering holy service." His dark eyes mesmerized her. "Despite your summers training with the maiden warriors, you are still an innocent at heart. You think too well of the entire world, despite knowing enemies wait to destroy Reshor. Think, Andrixine. Your illness came on you too suddenly, too severely to be mere disease. What happened just before you fell ill?"

She stared at the monk, sensing she knew the answer already but that it was one she wished to keep hidden even from herself.

"We were on a tour, Mother and Alysyn and I. We visited Uncle Maxil at Henchvery. He was angry at me, like always."

"Why?" he snapped, like the Captain of the Guard at Faxinor Castle, drilling a new recruit.

"I refused to marry Feril. Again. He was furious. Icy furious, so you could only see it in his eyes." She closed her eyes as the scene played itself in her memory.

Feril, her sneering, greasy, overweight cousin, pouting because she refused to consider him a suitor. Her uncle, dark and regal, drawing his dignity around himself like a cloak as his manners turned cold.

"Then what happened?"

"We left the next day. Alysyn fell ill, and we stopped at Maysford. I was so worried about her, and certain Feril would try some nasty trick in revenge, and so glad to be heading home, I didn't pay attention to how badly I felt." She opened her eyes. "Is it only good fortune that when trouble strikes my family, Snowy Mount is close by to help us?"

"Yomnian's hand is on you, just as it was on your parents when they fled Sendorland to save their lives. Snowy Mount has always been and always will be a refuge for those in need, a haven for those who devote their lives to contemplation and study and healing, an anchor for those who give their lives to Yomnian by serving others. Your mother brought you here to the mountains to heal because she trusts us implicitly."

"Even so close to the border with Sendorland," Andrixine murmured. "Isn't she afraid someone will learn Arriena of Traxslan is here, and send someone to kill her?"

"Who would send word, in the middle of winter? Who would care that Lady Faxinor was once a noblewoman of Sendorland? Who would want to take revenge?"

"Uncle Maxil would love to send her back to her nasty relatives," she said, going very still. "Brother Klee, my uncle hates me because I won't marry his son. He hates my sisters and brothers, because seven of us stand between Feril and Faxinor becoming his inheritance. But he would never kill us. His wife, Gersta of Henchvery, would gladly murder to get what she wanted, but she's been dead fourteen years now."

"Andrixine, heir of Faxinor, hear me," Brother Klee intoned, pulling himself up straight and tall, so she could see the warrior hidden inside the peaceful, silvered monk. "You are touched by Yomnian's hand. You are a faithful servant of the All-Creator, and that alone makes you a target of evil forces. You should have died of that poison, but you did not. Put aside the words of men and false loyalties that blind you. Listen with your heart and with the spirit Yomnian put within you, and you will know the truth, and the true path to follow."

She stared into his dark eyes, shivering as she had done when illness racked her body and wasted away her muscle, and delirium kept her mind prisoner.

For three long heartbeats, the bearded monk vanished. *The man who stood before her had Brother Klee's eyes and wide shoulders, but he was clean-shaven and thirty years younger. Instead of the simple blue robe of a holy scholar, he wore battle-scarred leathers and shining chain mail. His warrior braids were long and dark, bound with the red of an Oathbound warrior and the blue of holy service. He held a naked sword in his right hand, the scabbard in his left.*

The scabbard was a dull ivory color, like bone, the fine designs dark with the grime of years—maybe blood. Andrixine sensed she should recognize the sword by the scabbard alone.

The sword's blade looked clear as crystal and seemed to swallow up all the light and send it back tripled, blinding, fractured into thousands of razor sharp pieces. The pieces struck at her eyes, penetrating her mind and spirit, sending terror through her that she had never known, even in the worst of her fever dreams.

Andrixine cried out and jerked free of the vision. Shuddering, she pressed her fists into her eyes.

"Daughter?" Brother Klee dropped onto the bench next to her and put an arm around her shoulders. "What is it?"

Andrixine shook her head. How could she tell him? He would think she had relapsed.

She knew that sword, if only because it had haunted her dreams nearly every night since she had regained her right mind. Maybe even before that.

Andrixine's hand itched to grasp the pommel, and her arm ached to test the weight and balance of the blade. If Yomnian's spirit touched her, as Brother Klee said, was this a warning or a quest she had been given? Or a delusion sent by dark spirits, to blind her to the path she should follow in life?

She was Andrixine Faxinor, heir and first-born of Lord Edrix Faxinor. She was destined to care for the Faxinor estates, to make a high-born marriage and provide herself with a suitable heir. Her duties required she train soldiers to protect Reshor whenever King Rafnar called for them. Her duties would not let her go free, to live the life of a warrior maiden in holy service with the Sword Sisters.

She most certainly could not follow a vision quest for a sword that called to the depths of her very soul.

"Nothing," she finally whispered. "I'm just tired. My head aches a little."

"Your heart aches as well," Brother Klee said. "You know what I have said is true. You have enemies, and they will not go away no matter how much good will you bestow on the world."

"No." She opened her eyes and tried to smile at him. "They will not. Thank you for making me see."

PART ONE
Snowy Mount

Chapter One

"GLAD TO BE heading home?" Jultar asked. The white-haired warlord smiled at his apprentice and arched his back. "Or is it just my old bones soaking in the sun for a change?"

"Glad and soaking, sir," Kalsan answered with laughter thickening his voice.

The band of warriors rode their horses two-by-two across the spring-green Kandrigori Plain. Sunshine soaked through thin shirts, warming muscles made tight by a cold winter navigating the mountain range between Sendorland and Reshor. Ten warrior spies were few against the soldiers patrolling the barrier between two unfriendly countries, yet small enough to avoid notice and to find crucial information which ambassadors and envoys missed.

Kalsan frowned despite the luxurious warmth. The two years of spying had been harsh, and he had earned his warrior status ten times over. Soon he would trade his green apprentice cord for the red of an Oathbound warrior in Yomnian's holy service. He welcomed spring, delighted to return home to Reshor—but knowing war approached took the sparkle from the sunshine.

Jultar of Rayeen, the toughest, most cunning of King Rafnar's warlords, had been chosen to lead the spying party. Kalsan of Hestrin, with no hope of ever inheriting the Hestrin estates, had chosen to train as a warrior late in his teens, and he was lucky to have Jultar choose him as his apprentice. He was proud to serve his king and country. However, the news of impending war, which their band carried, dampened his joy. All winter he had warmed himself with memories of the pretty girls he had met on the journey to the mountains. Knowing war approached pushed thoughts of stolen kisses and dancing in village squares far to the back of his mind.

"It's for King Rafnar to handle now," Jultar said, leaning closer to his apprentice so his long, white braids bound with silver and red cord swung in the breeze. He reached out and tugged on Kalsan's thin dark braid. "You've earned these and the right to be named full warrior at solstice. A warrior knows when to carry his burden without stinting and when to lay it down. Lay it down, boy. Rafnar can handle the burden, and Yomnian is able to bear all. Trust Yomnian if you cannot trust the king."

"Yes, sir." Kalsan grinned, knowing his master called him "boy" to tease him. He was twenty-seven and taller than half the seasoned warriors riding behind him. Kalsan reached down and stroked the scabbard of his sword. He was a warrior.

Maybe not an Oathbound warrior like Jultar's band, but someday. Kalsan read the holy writ and prayed and tried to live in physical and mental purity. Two winters of privation had been good training, teaching him discipline and just how much he could live without. Yet he wondered if he would ever attain the spiritual depth to hear Yomnian's call on his life.

What should he become when he took his vows? Simply a warrior, ready to ride out at the king's call? Or a warrior scholar? Or a warrior priest? *Could* he put Yomnian and Reshor ahead of his dreams of adventure and glory? Perhaps he didn't want to reach the capital because then he would have to choose, and Kalsan had no idea what to choose.

Visions of the girls he had danced with and kissed haunted him during his morning prayers. Visions of a faceless, slim maiden carrying a burning sword haunted his sleep. Was that Yomnian's call, or one of those strange metaphors that only a seer or Renunciate scholar could interpret?

Kalsan shook those troubling thoughts from his mind, even if only temporarily. He glanced over his shoulder, taking in the reassuring, familiar sight of the war band: browned by the elements; dressed in leathers and rough cloth; each man armed, in good health and riding their horses as if man and beast were one.

Behind them lay the mountains, ahead lay the Blue Shadows Forest. They would skirt Snowy Mount with its seers, healers and scholars. They might pause a day to catch up on gossip and get a feel for the thoughts and emotions of the common people before starting down the long spider web of trade roads. Two weeks of hard, fast travel eastward on the King's Highway would take them to King Rafnar in Cereston. Then, Kalsan knew with relief sparkling in his gray eyes—then he could lay down his burden.

"MY HAIR IS turning red." Andrixine began to laugh, but the rasping in her voice killed her humor. She tossed the long, sun-brightened brown braid over her shoulder and swallowed hard, daring her throat to keep hurting.

Brother Klee had warned her the fever damage to her voice might never fully leave. She hadn't minded that she would never be able to sing because she had never been musically inclined. Laughing was a different matter. Now it was gone, stolen by the threads of pain that ran through her chest and around her throat when she tried to laugh.

Andrixine swallowed hard, feeling the ache become a tight knot through her body. The glorious sunshine and the colors of springtime in Blue Shadows Forest faded. The joy of wearing trousers again and riding her blood bay stallion, Grennel, did not pulse as warmly as a moment before.

Winter had passed in the struggle to regain her health and strength. Andrixine had thrived on the strict exercises and spiritual training Brother Klee imposed on her.

After praying and struggling to think logically, Andrixine knew the healers at Snowy Mount were right; she had been poisoned. But what should she do? Would the enemy continue to strike at her, or someone else in her family? How could she protect them?

"Keep silent," Brother Klee had counseled. "Pretend you suspect nothing and use the confidence of your enemies as your shield and their trap. Gather evidence they cannot deny."

"I will find out, and they will pay," she whispered. Andrixine knew it was petty, but she vowed to enjoy punishing the ones who had taken her laughter.

"Did you say something, dear?" her mother called, leaning out of the canopied wagon. She held four-year-old Alysyn on her lap. The little girl giggled and swatted at Grennel's tail, so conveniently swaying within her grasp.

"Nothing, Mother. Talking to myself."

"Eager to get home?" Lady Arriena Faxinor brushed a pale blue scarf aside, revealing the elaborate braids woven into her golden hair.

"Not half as much as you are." Self-consciously, Andrixine adjusted the single braid hanging down her back to her saddle. Her lack of head covering told the world she was unmarried. Her thin, silver-wrapped warrior braids could not halt the social assault that signal provoked.

Until she wore the marriage band on her wrist and bound her hair up at the back of her head, the world would see her unmarried condition and her estate before they saw the trained warrior—or the girl hungry for a sense of reason and understanding in her life. Andrixine hated the restless feeling, the sense of something more waiting for her to do and to be, if only she could hear Yomnian's voice. Prayer and contemplation and reading holy writ only calmed her for a little while, never fully healed the spiritual "itch" and hunger.

If she could join the maiden warriors and dedicate her life to service, would she be free of this restlessness? Would the purple cord of a Sword Sister in her braids free her from unwanted attentions? She could only dream the answer was yes; as heir of Lord Edrix Faxinor, her life was not hers to live as she pleased.

"Your brothers and sister have likely driven your father and the servants to distraction," Lady Arriena continued with a sigh that was part laughter.

"And half dismantled the castle?" she added.

"But that is half the pleasure of returning. The surprise of seeing how much damage they didn't do, and putting it all back together."

Andrixine smiled. She truly was eager to get home, too, to see her siblings and fit back into the daily routine of Faxinor Castle. Her guilt at keeping her mother so far from home through fall and winter overshadowed her own joy at homecoming.

Lady Arriena Faxinor was an oddity in her devotion to her children. She never gave them over to wet nurses from birth, like most grand ladies, and cared for her offspring with as much devotion as any peasant woman. Lord Edrix Faxinor complained it was a waste of money to hire more than one nurse for their children. But he said it with a smile in his lady's hearing, and they always laughed together.

Andrixine wondered how she would feel about her own children someday. As heir of Faxinor, it was her duty to continue the bloodline, dispense justice and manage the family estates. She did not need to know war craft, only to understand enough to gather soldiers when the king called.

Some said she had gone too far in her devotion to duty when she earned her warrior braids. What use were they in a time of peace? But Lady Arriena had been born in Sendorland, and she had taught her children that no matter how loudly Sendorland spoke peace, it always plotted treachery. Its people hated Reshor's prosperity and individual freedoms. Sendorland believed its holy mission was to turn Reshor into a grim shadow of itself.

Andrixine grew up knowing war would come and trained simply to protect her mother. The men of Sendorland feared a prophecy that a woman carrying a bright sword would begin their downfall. Andrixine liked to imagine the discomfort the sight of her warrior braids would give her mother's vindictive Traxslan relatives.

Thought of her braids made her smile. She reached up and stroked the thin twist of hair and silver cord on either side of her face, hanging from temples to waist. They kept people from looking further and seeing the gauntness of her face, the wide, Faxinor bones which illness had revealed. Tanned and healthy now, back in the saddle and not jolting along in the wagon with the other women, Andrixine wanted no pity from anyone. She leaned slightly to the left to catch the flash of Grennel's white socks. They shimmered, matching the white blaze down his nose. As if he knew his rider admired him, the stallion pranced for a few steps. She laughed and patted his neck.

"Andrixine?" Lady Arriena leaned a little further out from her seat in the wagon. Alysyn giggled as sunbeams caught her eyes and danced across her hands.

"Yes, Mother?" She nudged Grennel, and the stallion slowed his pace so they could speak face to face.

"I said, your father won't recognize you when we get home."

"No, I've finally lost all my baby fat—and Alysyn found it." Andrixine leaned over to tug on her little sister's red-gold curls. Alysyn laughed and tried to catch her sister's lean, brown hand with her chubby pink ones.

"Baby fat." Lady Arriena gave a most unladylike snort. That meant the maidservants were asleep in the afternoon heat trapped under the wagon's canopy. The two menservants riding ahead of them nodded off in their saddles. "You've lost what little figure you had. The only thing to show you're a woman is your hair."

"Mother..." Andrixine sighed. "I promise I will look like a woman when the need arises." She smiled when she realized she actually looked forward to dressing up and dancing.

If only she didn't have to dance with earnest young suitors who were more interested in an estate than a bride. She couldn't even enjoy a simple dance at a harvest festival anymore without someone listing the qualifications of her partner as marriage material.

"Your father's last letter reached me before we set off yesterday morning," Lady Arriena said, a glow in her eyes. Andrixine longed to know such feelings for herself. "He's planning a grand festival to welcome us home."

"And help me choose a husband?"

"Andrixine...I wish I could say you will be as happy as your father and I, but I won't lie to you. Duty sometimes precludes personal dreams. You need a husband."

"Like a brood mare needs—forgive me, I shouldn't have said that."

"But in a way, it is true. If only you could conquer this task as easily as you did sword craft." Lady Arriena sighed, but Andrixine thought she heard a hint of laughter in her voice.

"It took practice, hard work and pain, Mother."

"It takes practice, hard work, patience and pain to bring about a true, satisfying marriage."

"You caught me out on that one, I must admit. Even those blessed to marry for love, like you and Father, have to work for your happiness." A glance ahead showed lights gleaming through the first shadows of dusk. "We're approaching the inn."

"Not soon enough. How you can stand that saddle all day long, I do not know. I lost all my stamina this winter, with no estate to tend. I ache from this wagon, despite the cushions."

"Practice, Mother." Andrixine grinned and set her heels into her horse's sides, escaping before her mother could respond.

How, she wondered, could her mother say she had lost her stamina, when she had rolled up her sleeves and helped the Renunciates at Snowy Mount all winter long? Lady Arriena knew from her Sendorland life what it truly meant to be idle and useless, and she refused to be that way or allow her children to grow up to be drones.

As Andrixine reached the head of their procession, the trail curved and entered a clearing. An inn sprawled from one edge to the other, with bitter black smoke curling up from two chimneys. The building seemed to sink into the ground as trees encroached from all sides. The inn yard had been churned into sharp ruts and pits. Andrixine dismounted to lead Grennel around the obstacle course. Her nose twitched as the mixed odors of animals and cesspool reached her on a shift in the breeze. The hairs rose on the back of her neck, and she wished she could turn around and urge everyone to leave.

If she were by herself she could find a tree to put at her back, Grennel beside her and a fire before her. With three maids, two menservants and her mother and sister to tend, such a tactic was impossible.

"Why are we going this way?" she asked Jasper, the boy groom coming up behind her. His square, brown face, shadowed by a thatch of black hair, wrinkled in displeasure. She felt better seeing he didn't like this place any better than she.

"Your uncle advised us this was a better route, M'Lady." He shook his head, looking around again. "This is a longer trail home, but he said it would be safer and easier on the ladies." He bowed his head, ducking away from her studying glance.

Andrixine fought a smile at the boy's shyness. She remembered hauling him from the duck pond with her brothers. When had the realization of her station and womanhood hit him?

"I don't like the looks of this place. Play the scout when you bed the horses down, will you?"

"Yes, M'Lady." Light touched his black eyes, though he fought to retain a serious expression.

"Good. Until my father's soldiers meet us, we're depending on you and Tamas." She put Grennel's reins into his hands, then turned to meet the wagon as it came to a stop before the inn door.

She didn't doubt this route was safer; they had seen no one since they turned off the King's Highway just past Maysford. It was just like her Uncle Maxil's spite to send them down a deserted trail with bad inns. He was probably still seething because Andrixine had refused repeatedly to marry his oldest son, Feril.

What if her uncle *was* the one who had tried to poison her? The timing was right. She had fallen ill immediately after the visit to his home. Andrixine damped that thought, knowing it unworthy and disloyal to her father's family. Maxil's dead wife, Gersta was more likely to use poison to get her way, but she had died birthing dull-witted Aldis. Maxil might dislike his brother's children because they blocked his inheriting Faxinor, but he wouldn't resort to murder.

Andrixine's first sight of the innkeeper and his wife worsened her impressions of the place and made her wish she could speak her mind to her uncle. Both looked hungry, despite their bloated faces and forms. Their dull brown hair lay in tangled, greasy clumps across their foreheads and down their necks. Both had dusty brown eyes, and their pale faces were blotched with bad cooking and filthy living. Their tattered clothes were once rich garments, and Andrixine wondered where they got the originals. Cast-offs from grateful, charitable guests? Or stolen from guests who fled the squalid conditions?

"Only for one night," Lady Arriena murmured as her daughter helped her down from the wagon.

"Is my face that readable?" she replied as quietly.

"I know you, sweetling. Your father and I endured rough living when we were young, but never as foul as this." She swept the yard with one more wincing glance, then straightened her shoulders. She put on the smile saved for trying situations and turned to face their hosts.

ANDRIXINE SAT ON the narrow, splintered ledge of the window, dressed only in her long-sleeved gray shirt. The dream of the sword had awakened her again.

The sword hung in a sling of golden cloth. The blade possessed a clarity like glass. White, blue and gold light radiated from the blade. Its bone scabbard lay next to it, aged with years and wear. The sword hung over a simple cot, from the ceiling of a small stone room with nothing but a trunk and pegs in the walls that held dark blue Renunciate robes.

Brother Klee had swords, but they were wooden. The only real, metal swords at Snowy Mount had been her sword, inherited from her grandfather, and the swords Tamas and Jasper carried. The regimen of her healing had included sword craft, archery and horsemanship, but the arrows had been blunted, and the only spirited horse had been Grennel. If Brother Klee had fighting swords, she knew he would have shared them with her.

Andrixine knew why she dreamed of swords—she longed for any excuse to avoid choosing a husband. The rough life of a Sword Sister was a pleasure tour compared to long hours of holding court, dancing and listening to pretty speeches.

She took a deep, cool breath of the night air. With the fires banked for the night, the air smelled more wholesome. She didn't mind the aroma from the stables and the pig and hen yards. The animal smell was natural; the effluvium of unwashed furniture and bedding could have been avoided, and was therefore intolerable. All during dinner, she could taste the grease and grime in the air. Andrixine couldn't imagine how such shoddy housekeepers stayed in business. Mentally complaining about their disgusting hosts occupied her thoughts until her mind drifted into a sleepy haze.

She slid into a dream of summer training with the Sword Sisters near Faxinor Castle. *Andrixine stood on the practice field, battering friends with a wooden sword that turned real. She stopped, horrified as she drew blood—and the young women gathered around her turned into filthy, leering men who reached out greedy hands for her. Andrixine swung hard, and the sword burst out with blinding light, incinerating her attackers.*

Andrixine jerked awake in the windowsill, for a moment hearing the thuds of swords hacking into flesh, the cries of dying men and women shrieking in fear.

All was quiet in the room; her mother lay in one narrow, lumpy bed and Alysyn in the other. Andrixine had taken her baby sister to sleep with her to allow their mother a decent night's rest.

Something banged softly in the yard below her window. Andrixine felt a sudden chill and reached for her trousers. She cast a glance at both sleepers. Neither stirred. She heard nothing from the room where the maids slept. She crept back to the window, tucking her long shirt inside her trousers.

Unnatural silence reigned. She listened for the animals in the stables as she put on her belt and fastened her knife in place. If all was well, the animals would not listen with the same wariness she felt. Andrixine gave one tug to her belt and knelt before the window.

Chilled, she stared at the shapes and shadows of a dozen men creeping through thin patches in the forest several hundred yards from the inn. They carried weapons: swords, spears and ropes.

"Mother." She placed her hand over her mother's mouth. "Mother, listen." Andrixine couldn't see her expression. "Men are surrounding the inn. Get dressed." She took her hand away and stepped back to take her sword from under the bed. She already knew what to do. She would slip down to the stables and wake Jasper and Tamas and bring them to protect their party before the approaching men reached the inn.

"Rixy..." Alysyn moaned, waking. She rolled over and looked at the two poised between the beds. "Me go."

"I can't take you, poppet. It's dangerous. Bad men are coming."

"Me go," the child insisted, louder.

"I can't take her," she appealed to her mother.

"It might be better. What if you can't get back?"

"We'll all go together, then."

"Small numbers are easier to hide. I have to wake the maids. You go first." Lady Arriena managed a brave smile.

Andrixine bit back a rebuttal. She felt the fear her mother hid. She nodded and snatched up the shawl that had been covering the child in lieu of the dingy bedclothes.

"Help me make a sling," she said, flinging the cloth over one shoulder. Quickly, her mother helped her tie it so the largest part hung at her waist. "You have to be quiet, Alysyn. Understand?" Andrixine waited for one quick nod from the child and snatched her from the bed, depositing her in the sling so her legs straddled her sister's waist. She hesitated only a moment, then put her sword into her mother's hands. Andrixine knew she could outrun any ruffian, even with Alysyn's weight in her arms.

"Yomnian guard you," Lady Arriena whispered, squeezing her daughter's shoulder. Then she reached for her clothes.

"And you," Andrixine breathed, before stepping to the door.

The floor felt gritty under her bare feet, but Andrixine didn't dare take time for her boots. She shivered as she slipped down the stairs. The ancient wood creaked under her steps but not loudly enough to warn anyone listening. She hoped.

The main room was a cavern of sour smelling darkness. She kept to the wall when she reached the ground, following it to the door into the owners' private rooms. Sour smells rose to wrap around her head as her feet slipped on something soft and slick. Andrixine refused to speculate on what it was. She opened the door—and found herself in an empty room. Some bits of trash, broken furniture, an empty bed visible in the moonlight, but no people. They had fled without warning their guests.

Shadows filled the yard between the inn and the stable where the grooms slept when she crept outside. She breathed a prayer and ducked down to make the dash in the open. Andrixine wished her shirt was black, not gray.

Grennel recognized her scent as she stepped into the stable, and nickered. To her relief, no other horse responded. She searched for an empty stall. Jasper had said at dinner there was no loft for them to sleep in.

"Jasper, Tamas?" She held her breath, afraid of silence that meant the grooms had been killed already.

"M'Lady?" There was a stirring in the hay, and Jasper's wide, tanned face appeared in the thin beam of moonlight slanting through a hole in the roof.

She opened her mouth, to be stopped as a shriek shattered the false peace of the night. It sounded like Cedes, the maid hired a week ago from Maysford. A wagon horse answered the scream, rearing up in his stall and coming down to the floor with a crunch of hooves on rotten wood.

"Attack?" Tamas growled. He rose, brushing hay off his clothes and rubbing one hand over his balding pate.

"Give me a sword. I have to go back for my mother." Andrixine didn't wait when she spotted the scabbards hanging on a protruding nail on the wall, but yanked the sword from the one closest. It fit her grasp awkwardly.

Andrixine strode from the stable into shadows. Alysyn's weight was negligible among all her other burdens. With her free hand, she stroked the child's head. Alysyn stirred the tiniest bit, and Andrixine prayed the child had fallen asleep again.

She couldn't go back for her mother until Alysyn was safely hidden. Turning her back on the sounds of feet banging on wood and doors or possibly bodies thudding against walls, she ran into the forest until her breath caught in her lungs. Was she far enough in?

Breathing a silent prayer, she untied the shawl sling, wrapped it around Alysyn and tucked her sister into the shelter of a thick cluster of bushes. Andrixine hesitated, flinching when another scream rang from the inn. That wasn't her mother—it couldn't be her mother.

She unsheathed the sword as she ran, knowing such a move invited danger. All she needed was to trip and fall on the blade. What good would she do her mother and sister then? Such thoughts vanished as she reached the inn clearing.

Light flared, tearing the darkness to shreds. Andrixine skidded to a stop, debris crumbling under her bare feet, and stared as the roof of the inn burst into flames. The faint breeze couldn't help the fire eat through thatching and wood with such ease. The whole building had to be rotten and dry where it wasn't clotted with grease and filth, made for a fire.

Andrixine moved around the side of the inn, heading for the main door. And froze.

An ugly, scarred ruffian shuddered on top of Cedes, crushing her into the rocky ground. The girl stared at the sky, mouth open in a silent scream. Another man held her shoulders down, but even Andrixine could see there was no need. Cedes had no fight left in her. Her skin was snowy contrast to her dark, luxurious hair. She was naked, red lines and bruises showing where the men had battered her into submission, then cut and ripped her clothes off her.

Andrixine stared as the man lifted himself off Cedes, laughing, and tugged up his trousers. The girl's blood spattered his legs. His companion got up and pulled his own trousers down to his knees, laughing. He was already blood-smeared, going back for more.

Andrixine looked at the sword in her hand and nearly dropped it. Her stomach twisted. She remembered the taunts Feril had flung at her over the years. He said her warrior's training was only play-acting; she could not face battle without freezing. Andrixine felt sick at the thought that he might be right.

"No," she whispered. "Yomnian, help me!" Her whisper turned into a shout as she flung herself from the bushes.

The man with a long scar from his right temple to his jaw and along his chin froze, kneeling between Cedes' legs. The other drew his sword and came at Andrixine, swinging. Cedes didn't move, didn't even hear her.

Yomnian, guide my hand, Andrixine prayed.

Commander Jeshra's voice rang in her memory, and Andrixine could almost feel the silver-haired Sword Sister's hand guiding her sword arm. *Remember every victim, child, and let your love for them guide you—not the hate you feel for their abusers. Yomnian gave you skill. Use it to honor the All-Creator, not to entertain the Dark Spirits.*

The ruffian brought his sword down hard. Andrixine sidestepped easily. Her strengths were in agility and tricky slashes, not brute muscle. She caught the last of the swing with her guard and twisted, guiding the stroke back to him. He stumbled, eyes wide and choked. Andrixine grinned. Good—her moves and skill frightened him.

She slashed upwards, letting herself go down almost to one knee, aiming for his belly. Bleating, the ruffian backed up, tripping in a deep rut. Andrixine followed through, slashing his arm just above the elbow before he could bring up his sword.

The scene repeated: Andrixine attacking, the man retreating, taking another cut, then managing to defend against worse injury.

Something was wrong. Andrixine wiped sweaty hair from her face and glanced over her shoulder. Listening for the gasps of her opponent to track him, she scanned the clearing.

Cedes' white body was a violation of the shadows. White, and red with blood glistening bright at her throat.

The scarred man had slaughtered Cedes and fled.

A pebble crunched in the dry mud under a boot. Andrixine felt the breeze from an arm swinging up in attack.

Her fever-scarred throat burned as she snarled and spun on her bare heel. Scooping low, putting all her anger into her arm, she slashed low and lunged up.

Everything stopped. Even the background crackling of the fire seemed to halt for three eternal heartbeats. The ruffian's sword clattered to the ground. Eyes wide, face pale, he dropped his head to stare at Andrixine's sword one-third buried in his chest, caught where ribs met breastbone. Below the catching point, his belly slowly spilled opened, gutted like a pig.

Gagging, Andrixine pulled back her sword and fled. The smell of his blood was bitter, and the spatters scorched her sword hand. Her legs trembled. She didn't hear him clatter to the ground, didn't feel the rough ground tearing her feet as she ran for the burning inn and darted inside.

Thick, choking, blinding smoke hung from the ceiling, dropping lower with every step she took. Andrixine crouched low as she approached the stairs.

Flames danced down from the ceiling, reaching for her as she gained the upper floor. She paused, listening. No sound came from her mother's room but the harsh crackle as the fire ate its way down the walls.

She pushed the door open with the point of the sword, praying to see her mother crouched in the corner, sword raised and ready. Clothes were strewn on the floor, the trunk overturned and slashed. The beds were toppled, the frames smashed and the webbing cut. No sign of her mother.

In the next room, Andrixine found the same. She stepped further inside and beyond one bed found another maid; Lily, with her head nearly separated from her body. Her body was naked and bruised and bleeding, like Cedes. If Lady Arriena wasn't there, was she unharmed? Why rape two young women, and carry away an older woman...unless they knew she was noble? Would they leave her mother unharmed, for the sake of ransom? If they caught Andrixine, would they spare her for the sake of ransom?

Dream fragments told Andrixine that would not happen, if these men caught her. She refused to follow through on that thought, which stabbed with nausea as bad as what she had suffered that winter past. Quickly, she snatched at her braid and held it off her neck as she pulled out her knife. Her hair sliced off easily and fell in silence. She refused to look at the gleaming new carpet on the filthy floor. The hair left on her head hung in a ragged fringe to her shoulders. Her warrior braids felt unnaturally long.

With one last look around, she hurried down the stairs. Despite the smoke billowing past her, the flames threatening just yards away, she paused in the doorway to the inn yard and searched the clearing. No one else moved within sight. Why had the ruffians come and gone so quickly? All the tales she had heard from traveling swordmasters and Kangan, Captain of the Guard at Faxinor Castle, told her those men had come for a specific purpose, found what they wanted and fled. But what? Not just a noblewoman to ransom?

Then there was no more time. Cold prickles of warning touched her back, making her dart from the doorway. Scant seconds later, the roof fell in with a roar and a shower of sparks.

Her mother was gone. Where were Tamas and Jasper? Had the fight moved down the cart trail while she fought Cedes' rapist?

Andrixine knew she couldn't catch up with them, even if she could find the trail in the dark and smoke. Her eyes filled with tears, and she brushed them angrily away. Alysyn was her sole responsibility now. Fighting her churning stomach, she headed into the woods to find her sister.

Chapter Two

MORNING BROUGHT NEW pain. Her back ached from crouching in the damp shadows. Her eyes burned from smoke and staring into the darkness. Her chest ached, echoes of days struggling to breathe that winter past. Andrixine had stayed awake and flinched at the slightest sound all night. Alysyn slept through the commotion with only a few murmurs and twitches, and Andrixine feared when day came she would look at the child and see she was ill or dead. The only warmth she had all night had come from Alysyn cuddled close against her, but to her sleep-deprived mind, that was no comfort.

She crouched in the shelter of thick bushes as growing light cut through the smoke and morning mist, showing them truly alone as far as the eye could see. The quiet unraveled beneath the normal sounds of life in the forest. Animals chirped and clicked and sang, oblivious to the smoking ruin in their midst. Andrixine took that as a good sign.

"Rixy." Alysyn stirred and rubbed at her eyes with both fists, as she did every morning. "Hungry. Where Mamma?"

"Mamma—" Andrixine choked. Her throat burned from more than smoke. "Mamma had to go on ahead of us, poppet." She shifted the child on her lap. "We'll catch up with her in a few days, all right?"

"Hungry," Alysyn repeated. Andrixine hoped that was a sign of acceptance. "Cold, too."

"I know." She closed her eyes. Now that she knew they truly were alone, fatigue battered her defenses. A scant second later, she stiffened.

Were those hoof beats? Andrixine clutched Alysyn closer, slipping her hand over the child's mouth before she could protest. Yes, definitely hoof beats coming down the trail.

The soldiers coming from Faxinor to meet them were still three days away, at the earliest. So who approached now?

She had dropped her sword. That realization panicked her more than the approach of riders. Andrixine dragged her hands through the forest litter, nearly crying out in relief when her hands touched cold metal and rawhide strips. She gripped it tight, lifting it to test the strength in her arm. It wasn't her grandfather's sword, her inheritance, but it would have to do.

One horse. It stopped when it reached the clearing and snorted, loud in the silence surrounding the smoking ruins. Then, it moved into the trees toward her.

"Gwenny!" Alysyn crowed, twisting around in her sister's arms as the horse reached their hiding place.

"Grennel?" Andrixine whispered, afraid to trust her eyes. Her own horse, singed by fire, bare of all tack. Through blurring eyes, she saw a dark shape reach from the shadows. A soft muzzle and oat-scented breath touched her face. Grennel snorted and nudged her shoulder.

"He hungry too, Rixy," Alysyn announced.

"Well, he'll just have to scavenge with us, that's all," she sputtered through a few tears. Andrixine knew crying was a waste, but she felt better for it. She scrambled to her feet, clutching Alysyn close. Grennel stepped back, eyes fastened on her in loyal waiting and obedience. She had never loved him more than now. With Grennel as sentry, Andrixine could search for supplies and not worry about her back.

She had kept herself awake thinking over her situation. The first task was to scavenge the ruins to outfit herself and Alysyn, then look for help. She couldn't wait for the Faxinor soldiers to appear. Snowy Mount was the closest haven—Andrixine didn't trust Maysford, a half day's ride closer. Walking, with Alysyn to slow her, she had estimated a week. Grennel's wide back and strong legs would cut the travel to less than a day.

She would go to Snowy Mount, leave Alysyn where she would be safe, get help, return to meet her father's soldiers and lead them in rescue of her mother.

She hoped. She prayed.

Andrixine moved to the stable, sending up yet another prayer she would find supplies in the unburned building. If the marauders hadn't been as intent on pillage as on rape, she might find a saddle. Grain, saddlebags and water skins were too much to hope for, but she let herself hope.

"Alysyn, stay here and watch Grennel for me." Andrixine saw the first sign of pouting. "It's a game. We're playing soldiers. You have to be my guard while I search the stables."

"Play guard?" The child's eyes lit. She nearly kicked Andrixine in the thigh in her eagerness to be put down and stand at the foot of a tree on the edge of the clearing.

The straight, hard line of Andrixine's mouth relaxed a bit as she walked across the littered yard to the stable. Some aching tension left her shoulders.

A dark shape filling the stable doorway transformed when she came closer, becoming Jasper and Tamas sprawled in a bloody heap. Flies buzzed over the dried, sticky black puddles around the bodies. Jasper had fallen first, his throat slashed, his sword hand lopped off. Tamas had fallen face down on top of him.

Andrixine retreated into details to keep from feeling. A wandering armsmaster had told her about the sensation when he stayed at Faxinor Castle during a winter storm. The man was wizened and bent, hair silver against his ebony skin. His eyes held the power of a long life lived well. He told her how in stress, a man's mind could divide, concentrating on details, steps and plans, leaving the hate, fear and sorrow for later, for safer times. Andrixine understood now.

"Wait a little," she whispered to the faithful servants. Andrixine looked away and stepped past their bodies.

She searched the stalls. After what she had seen, the unexpected bounty of full grain sacks and Grennel's own tack didn't delight her. Jasper's coat fit her, but his boots were too big. She stuffed rags into them. She appropriated the extra clothes of both men. Thinking of Cedes and Lily, Andrixine shuddered and knew she didn't dare dress as a woman until she was safely home.

There was a wine skin, half full; a satchel full of dried fruit and nuts; another with half a loaf of bread and a hunk of orange-gold cheese large enough for breakfast and lunch. These she took outside immediately, with the clothes.

"Watch these for me," she ordered Alysyn, setting down the first bundles. "This is breakfast," she added, before the child could ask the question that had to be uppermost on her stomach.

Andrixine gave her a handful of raisins and tore off a piece of bread. Poised between tears and laughter, she watched Alysyn stuff the food into her mouth like a starving puppy. Alysyn would have refused dry bread and raisins at home.

"It's only the beginning of changes, poppet," she whispered and turned back to the stable.

When she had removed everything usable, she battered at the creaky supports until the roof fell. Andrixine dug in the pouch that Tamas once carried, flint and steel mixed with tobacco and pipe. She struck sparks against the rotten, dried thatch until it caught fire. There had been too much fire already, but she refused to leave the bodies for forest animals to devour and could spare no time to bury them.

Alysyn was too busy playing with the clothes to notice the fire until it had crawled over the whole of the fallen stable. She toddled over to investigate, but Andrixine was ready and caught her.

"You're still the guard, remember? You have to watch and make sure no one comes when they see our fire, understand?" She used as calm a tone as she could manage, shaking her finger in the child's face as their father did to make a point. Alysyn laughed and tried to snatch at Andrixine's finger and nodded.

While the fire burned, Andrixine made a quick inspection of the premises. The Sword Sisters had taught her to read the ground but she had never tested her training before. She had also never seen a real, life-or-death attack until now. The dull blade of a practice sword could break bones and leave bruises, but she had not been prepared for the blood and the stinking gush of innards.

She found wagon tracks and the prints of the horses used to draw it. Her father's signet, three crosses connected at their base, was plain in the prints of the horseshoes. Someone had taken the time to get into the stable and harness the horses to the wagon. That bespoke a plan. The marauders had taken all the horses, but only Grennel had escaped.

Cedes lay where the men had used and killed her, untouched by the fire. Andrixine turned her eyes away and fought a wave of sickness. A few deep breaths helped her regain the calculating, unfeeling state of mind that let her function. She gathered up the body and carried it to the funeral pyre. The flesh was cold and slack and lighter than she imagined Cedes had been in life. Andrixine turned away quickly once the body touched the flames.

After a moment of thought, fighting her need for revenge no matter how petty, Andrixine brought over the body of the man she had killed. She dragged him to the fire, letting Commander Jeshra's voice fill her mind.

We serve Yomnian, children, and must be greater than our own desires and emotions. Show mercy to your enemies, and grace. Remember, it is Yomnian's honor we protect and not our own.

She found no other bodies. The innkeeper and his wife had escaped. Her mother and the maid Glynnys were captives. Lily had been consumed in the flames last night.

The silence around the inn woke Andrixine to her exposed position. Even if no one had come for the flames last night, someone would see the smoke now. Until she and her sister were safe at Snowy Mount, Andrixine had no idea who would be friend or foe.

"Alysyn, we're leaving," Andrixine said, after shaking herself back into action. She picked up Jasper's coat and put it on. "Ready?"

"Game all done?" The little girl frowned. She was a strange

picture, wearing only her white shift stained with grass and ashes, her golden-red curls tangled, face dirty and smeared with raisins and dry crumbs. Where, Andrixine wondered, had Lady Arriena's pretty baby gone?

"No, not for many days I think." She hunkered down on her haunches, letting her aching eyes close a few seconds. "It's changing, though. See how my hair is all gone?" She waited until Alysyn nodded. "I'm going to pretend to be a boy. You have to tell anybody who asks that I'm your brother, Drixus. Understand?"

"Drixus," the child chirped. She laughed, reaching out for her sister's warrior braids.

"We're playing make-believe that I'm a boy and we're on a pilgrimage to Snowy Mount."

"Birds there?"

"Yes, the birds will still be there—if you're good, all the trip back." She smiled wearily; Alysyn had loved to watch the birds flying around the bell tower. Andrixine longed for the peace and safety of the scholar's retreat more for her soul's sake than for her body's ease. "Now, you gather up all those clothes while I saddle Grennel."

When she bent to lift the saddle onto the stallion's back, she saw the blood dried on her hand and arm. The inn's well was filled with ash and rubble from the fire. She would have to find a stream or spring to wash in along the trail. When they met up with people, Andrixine didn't want uncomfortable questions about the blood on her hands and clothes.

"Alysyn, time to go!" she called, to stop her thoughts.

Andrixine took a torn shirt, wrapping its body between the child's legs and around, like a diaper, using the arms to tie Alysyn to her. She could ride astride and hold onto the pommel, and Andrixine wouldn't have to worry about her falling off if they had to gallop. She wrapped the shawl over and around Alysyn's legs, for modesty. Andrixine hoped she would hear her mother scold about modesty again.

KALSAN JERKED BACKWARDS, painfully aware of his twisting ankle. He bit his lip to fight the ache and brought his arm up, blocking Brenden's downward blow.

The forest clearing rang with swords clashing, sweet in the cool morning air. A roar rose from the other warriors. Sweat dripping in his eyes, Kalsan grinned and leaped forward in attack. Brenden's dusky skin and startling green eyes glowed.

"Enough!" Jultar slammed a staff down between them, managing to smack both men across their bare, sweating shoulders.

Laughter replaced grunts and gasps and clashing swords. Kalsan stepped back, letting his sword arm hang limp. Four paces away, Brenden met his gaze and broke out in a wide grin.

"Better and better," he said, bowing, letting his silver hair flop. "Master, we'd best leave the boy behind when we report to the king. Every warlord will clamor to take him. All our hard work will be wasted. He's earned his beard, but he won't grow it among us."

"Perhaps," Jultar said. His smile was serene, but his eyes sparkled with mischief.

"Word, Master?" Kalsan asked. He wiped his face and reached for his shirt hanging on a branch.

"We will warn our king in time. No more than that," the warlord said, raising his hands to silence the questions spilling from his men's lips. Jultar had risen before dawn to ride to Snowy Mount and inquire of the seers among the holy scholars.

"Do we have time to stop at Maysford for the night?" Rogan asked, his voice a mocking whine of complaint.

"Yes, we do. Real baths and hot food," Jultar said, as his warriors laughed. "And pretty girls," he added, looking at Kalsan.

"Which one is it this time?" Brenden called, his voice muffled as he pulled on his shirt. "Not the tavern keeper's daughter, I hope. She was nearly betrothed to Brick, the smith. It's bad luck to anger a man who makes swords."

"I promise you," Kalsan said, feeling his face warm at the teasing. "I will leave Vinya alone. There are plenty of other pretty girls to dance with in Maysford."

Jultar's words had stilled many questions and worries in his mind. Kalsan could think about stolen kisses and pretty girls again.

AFTER THREE HOURS riding due north, the sun went from warm to uncomfortably hot and bright, making the air sticky. Andrixine felt it beating on her unprotected neck. Tears stung her eyes for the loss of her long, glossy hair.

"Rixy, want down," Alysyn said, beginning to squirm.

"We can't stop right now, I'm looking for a spring so we can wash."

"Down now. Need the nessi," she insisted, her voice pained.

"All right." Andrixine halted Grennel, wrapped an arm around her and swung out of the saddle. Once on the ground, she tugged on the knot of the shirt's arms to release the girl. When Alysyn needed the necessary, she had to use it immediately.

Alysyn toddled into the woods for the nearest convenient tree. Andrixine was relieved her sister didn't need help. One more demand would break her. She leaned against Grennel's flank and closed her eyes. Now that she stood still, sleep leaped at her like a huge, smothering animal.

Grennel snorted, his muscles quivering under her hand. She struggled alert and turned, blinking, trying to see down the curving, shadow-speckled trail where he looked. His ears pricked forward, swiveling to catch sounds that escaped her dulled ears. Andrixine glanced toward the trees, just making out the top of Alysyn's curly head, then back down the trail. She saw nothing but green and shadows and slanting pillars of sun.

She heard whistling. That meant someone who knew the trail so well he had no fear. Or, someone with enough confidence in his sword arm he feared no one. She reached for her sword and rubbed again at the more stubborn bloodstains on her hands.

Alysyn stepped from the trees as a man came around a bend in the trail. She saw nothing and came directly to Andrixine, holding out her arms to be lifted into the saddle.

"In a moment, poppet. We have a visitor." Andrixine handed the rag shirt to the child and moved her closer to Grennel. The stallion would protect her sister and not step on her.

"Hallooo!" the approaching figure shouted. He picked up his pace. "Well met. Where are you coming from?"

"The inn, about three hours back." Andrixine knew her mind wasn't up to subterfuge.

"By the looks of you, the night wasn't pleasant," he said, grinning at her disheveled, weary state.

"It was attacked in the night. My sister and I barely escaped with our lives."

"Attacked?" The man stopped short. He was close enough to be seen clearly. All brown—hair, beard, clothes, and tanned skin. He carried a sack slung over one shoulder and a short sword at his belt. "Any other survivors?"

"There was a lady and her maid. They're missing with the innkeeper and his wife. I assume they were taken for ransom."

"Yes, likely." The man looked her and Alysyn up and down with quick, sharp eyes. "Is there much left?" He stopped when Grennel snorted at him.

"Both the inn and the stable burned."

"You salvaged plenty." He gestured at Grennel and the bundles tied to his saddle. Another step, hand outstretched, and he stopped when Grennel bit at him.

"Only what belonged to us."

"Belonged?" He snorted. "A fine stallion like this, belonging to a filthy boy like you?"

"Try to take him and find the truth," she answered, softening her voice as her father did when he faced a potentially dangerous opponent.

"Perhaps I will." He smiled. "I doubt those braids belong to you any more than the horse. They must both be earned." He shrugged, using the motion to fling his sack from his shoulder and whip the sword from its scabbard.

Andrixine leaped in attack, drawing her sword before he could lunge. He let out a roar of shock at her quickness. Andrixine slashed at him. He ducked and stumbled backwards, his arms flung outward to save his balance.

She advanced, a double-hand grip on her sword for extra weight when she swung. He yelped and managed to bring his sword back around to block a stab at his chest. The swords rang against each other, sending a shock of contact up Andrixine's weary arms. Her whole body ached, but she pressed on. This was no drill where she could slow the pace until she gained her second wind.

He stumbled over a boulder hidden by grass and weeds to land on his back across the top, grunting, the wind knocked from him. Andrixine came down with a hard stroke, making the sword an axe. He brought up his knees and rolled off. Her sword hit the rock with a loud clang, followed by a snapping crack. Grennel echoed the sound with a scream and lunged forward, teeth bared at the man as he leaped to his feet again.

Andrixine's mouth dropped open in a silent cry of dismay as she stared at the broken blade. The vibration went up her arms, joining the throbbing in her head. She leaped backwards, raising the stump of the blade in defense—but her attacker had fled. Grennel took two more steps after the man, then snorted and turned back to her.

Alysyn shrieked. Andrixine ran to her, stomach twisted in knots of fear. But when she reached her and snatched the child up in her arms, the little girl screamed laughter.

"You won!" Alysyn wriggled in her arms, beating on her shoulders with tiny slaps of delight.

"Poppet," she whispered. It occurred to her to be grateful she hadn't had to kill the man.

They had to get away before he realized she had broken her sword, and returned. Even with Grennel so willing to defend her, she couldn't let that happen. She stuck the stump and broken blade into the scabbard to at least look like she could defend herself.

"Hold on tight now," she ordered as she swung up into the saddle, Alysyn still in her arms.

She tied the shirt around the child as they rode at a slow trot. Then, securely fastened together, she sent Grennel into a gallop. The wind beat at her face, and the trees rushed past. Andrixine sent up a prayer of gratitude that her attacker had fled in the opposite direction.

Noon came and went, and they rode. Andrixine gave Alysyn an occasional mouthful of wine and some cheese, and cracked nuts for her on the saddle with the handle of her knife. She forced herself to eat bread and cheese; she needed food despite her stomach's protests.

When the sun touched the tops of the trees straight ahead down the narrow slit of the trail, Andrixine decided it was time for a true rest. If she remembered landmarks correctly, Maysford was only an hour or so further down the trail. She knew what a picture they made. If anyone recognized Grennel or Alysyn, they might recognize her despite her short hair and filthy clothes. Until she reached Snowy Mount, no one must know she and Alysyn had survived. A certainty filled her that someone had attacked *her* family, specifically. Brother Klee and the healers at Snowy Mount believed she had been poisoned. Could it be the same enemy, willing to destroy their entire traveling party to get at her? But why? And who?

She slowed their trot to look and get her bearings. Grennel snorted and stepped off the trail. She tightened the reins, prepared to fight him as he moved into the underbrush and shadows. Then the idiocy of it washed over her. The stallion had shown such good sense so far, why couldn't she trust him now? She knew she had to find a hiding place soon, rest until night, then continue down the trail and hope no one would see them.

"What Gwenny doing?" Alysyn murmured around a nutmeat in her mouth.

"I don't know, sweetling." Pity for the child flooded her, and Andrixine didn't know whether to laugh or cry. Her sister had played the "game" all day with a vengeance, staying quiet when she usually chattered about everything. Alysyn had to be sore from the long hours in the saddle, despite the padding.

"Need the nessi, Rixy."

"Me, too. Let's find a spring. I want to wash and drink. Grennel needs a drink, too. Do you want a bath?"

"Want Mamma."

"Mamma wants you, too." Andrixine swallowed a sigh. She knew her luck had been too good for too long. "But we have to follow the rules of the game before we can go home. You don't want to cheat, do you?"

"No." She sounded uncertain.

Grennel halted, stopping whatever she might have said next. He snorted and shook his head, turning to watch them with one eye. Andrixine straightened in the saddle and looked around. Saplings and bushes surrounded them. The stallion had found an animal trail into the forest. She patted his neck in approval.

"Just a little longer," she said to horse and child. "Hold on, poppet." She untied her sister before dismounting, leaving Alysyn in the saddle. Her legs felt boneless and she clung to the stirrup without shame. When the ground steadied under her feet, she brought Alysyn down. "Now for you, my valiant soldier," she whispered, turning to Grennel.

Her fingers wanted to tangle as she struggled to remove saddle and blanket. The stallion stood still, never twitching a muscle until she had all his tack removed. He nosed Andrixine when she moved a step away from him. She looked down the length of his flank. His normally glossy coat was rough with sweat and dirt and burrs, worse than a plow horse. She knew what he deserved, but her whole body cried out in protest at the thought.

"Alysyn..." Andrixine shook her head. She couldn't ask her sister, even if the child could have reached high enough to groom the stallion. Lord Edrix raised his children to be responsible for their possessions. After such a hard day, it would be cruel to leave Grennel hot and dirty and not groom him.

"Thirsty." Alysyn tried to tug the wineskin free of the traveling hook on the saddle.

"That's right. See if you can find a spring, will you?" She dug through the bag hanging from the saddle until she found the water skin and gave it to her sister. As the child trotted off, she added, "Don't go too far. If you think you're lost, call for me."

She watched the girl move through the underbrush until she was only a blur of dirty white smock and reddish curls. She breathed a sigh of weariness, then turned to Grennel.

She had to take off her boots and remove some rags packed in around her feet to have something to rub down the stallion. Not until she stood in her bare feet did she realize how hot they had been. Andrixine reveled in the cool dirt and grass under her feet as she groomed the stallion. The sensation soothed, giving promise of rest.

The exercise and rhythm of working on the horse's coat helped loosen tense muscles, and she soon approached a quiet state in her mind—half exhaustion and half a sense of accomplishment. The frantic, wordless prayers that had buzzed inside her head all day finally quieted. The three of them were safe, they had food, they had purpose, they had a safe place to rest; they had a plan. The present was provided for and the future, she sensed, would be taken care of just as well.

Andrixine pressed on, refusing to let her eyes close until Alysyn came back and they were totally secure in their hiding place. As she rubbed, she tried to form her thoughts into something more coherent than she had managed all day, a prayer mixed with a plan. She knew Yomnian would understand what she needed and wanted to say, even if she couldn't seem to put the words together.

Grennel was nearly done, only two legs waiting, when Alysyn stumbled back through the bushes. Andrixine kept working.

"Did you get the water?"

"Bath," Alysyn pronounced. There was pride in her voice and something tight, perhaps angry.

"Bath?" She turned.

The child was dripping wet. Little drops gathered at the ends of her ringlets and fell to her shoulders or the ground with tiny plops. Alysyn held up the sloshing water skin, grinning.

"Oh, very good." Andrixine took the skin, then knelt and hugged the child. "You smell good, too. Poppet, you play the game so well, I'll ask Father to give you a pony when we get home, so you can learn to ride. Would you like that?"

"Pony? Like Gwenny?" Alysyn flung her arms around her sister's neck.

"Maybe not like Grennel, but close." Andrixine untangled herself and saw a flicker of anger. "What's wrong?"

"Bad people."

"What bad people?" She brushed a damp curl out of the child's face, wondering where she was going to find a comb.

"At the water. I was good like Mamma said. I said hello and cur—coo—" Alysyn gave an angry little sigh and demonstrated her bobbing curtsey. "They won't talk to me."

"At the water? Show me."

Andrixine reached for the sword still attached to the saddle at her feet, forgetting it was broken until she felt the unbalanced scabbard. Perhaps the sight of the sheathed sword would be enough protection. Taking Alysyn's hand, she gestured for her to lead on.

The spring lay only a dozen steps down the trail. The smell of water had likely made Grennel stop here. Andrixine knew she would never have found the spot otherwise.

Two filthy, rag-clad forms sprawled against a tree a few paces from where the spring bubbled up into a natural cavity in the ground. Andrixine paused at the edge of the clearing, holding Alysyn's hand to keep her back. The quiet felt wrong. No birds sang close by.

"Alysyn, go to Grennel. Now," she added, forestalling any protest. Andrixine waited until the sound of her sister's footsteps faded away. "Well, and how did you get here?" she whispered, stepping around the spring to the bodies of the innkeeper and his wife.

They had been stabbed, the dark stains of blood hardly visible in their grease-blackened rags. Both wore staring surprise on their death-frozen faces. No struggle, no fear, no anger. Andrixine didn't like the possible explanation.

She knelt next to the man and gingerly examined the body, hoping for some clue. The cold of death didn't bother her here, as it had when she carried Cedes to her funeral pyre. Under the body she found a gold coin.

"That explains a lot, doesn't it?" she said to the corpses.

KALSAN RELEASED THE hands of the village girl as the music ended and stepped back to sweep her a bow. She was tiny and blonde, smelled of apple blossoms, and her hands were soft where he held them in the spins and side-steps of the dance.

He couldn't remember her name, and that bothered him. He smiled at her, but when she smiled, inviting another dance, he found he didn't have the stomach for it. Three dances in the square outside the tavern had been enough.

Around him, other Maysford girls danced with sweethearts and travelers, the music provided by a harp, drum, flute and lute. Night fell in a splash of gold and purple sunset, edged with a silver and rose twilight. The air smelled of civilization—roasted meats, hot cider, bread and cherry pastries. He had a real bed tonight, a full stomach and a clean body for the first time in two weeks.

Kalsan didn't know why he felt so restless, why nothing satisfied for very long.

Maybe it was the sight of the tavern keeper's daughter with a love knot of blue thread twined into her jet-black curls. She was promised to Brick, the smith. Kalsan hadn't expected her to wait, so why did it bother him?

Maybe not losing her, he suspected, but the happiness and pride in Brick's face when the tall, red-haired blacksmith came to claim his sweetheart for the first dance.

Maybe the restlessness came from dreams of the maiden with the sword. He recognized her from the sense of longing, the soft humming like a harp in the air when she touched the edges of his dreams. Sometimes he saw her eyes, dark with sorrow, and it tore him apart to know she could be hurt. Kalsan had an impression of dark auburn hair, a slim body and little else. He wanted to find her. Maybe that longing poisoned his careless enjoyment of any pretty girl who would dance and laugh and kiss among shadows.

"Tired, lad?" Jultar asked, as Kalsan approached the well in the middle of the cobbled village square. The warlord had settled down on the bench that circled the well, out of the traffic of the dance yet close enough to watch.

"I don't know." Kalsan managed a chuckle as he settled down at his master's feet.

"Not tired of civilized living already, are you?"

"Some parts, maybe." He gestured at the dancers. Kalsan had always trusted Jultar with thoughts he couldn't share with anyone else. "The last few months, all I wanted was to dance with a pretty girl when we returned to Reshor. Why does it bore me?"

"You want more than just *any* pretty girl in your arms, or any sweet lips to kiss, I think."

"Master?" He turned, twisting a kink into his neck as he tried to see Jultar. Over his years of apprenticeship, he had come to believe the warlord could do anything—but could he see into another's misty dreams, too?

"Think on it, lad," the older man said with a chuckle.

Chapter Three

ANDRIXINE WOKE STIFF and muddle-headed, blinking into the shadows, smelling the hot, green, bitter odors of plants that had baked all day in the heat. She lay still, wondering where she was, how she had come to be there.

Her cheek hurt. She sat up and rubbed it. In the shadows, she saw a knob of root where her head had rested on bare dirt. The torn saddle blanket underneath her had bunched up and moved toward her feet.

"Alysyn?" she whispered, her voice a croak of panic and renewed harsh aching.

Andrixine crawled across the tiny shelter of leafy branches she had fashioned against the afternoon heat. Her head ached with the effort of memory. Then her hand came down on the soft warmth of her sister's arm. She followed the arm to the rest of the body and gathered the child up against her shoulder.

"Wake up, poppet. Time to go." She rubbed Alysyn's back.

From the color of the slice of sky seen through the branches, it was not too far into the evening. Her sense of time had not failed, even in her aching stupor; she had awakened when she wanted. Andrixine breathed a prayer of thanks as she crawled from the shelter.

Grennel greeted her with a snort, coming up behind her to nuzzle the back of her neck. Andrixine smiled at the familiar, comforting touch. She jostled Alysyn a little to hurry her waking. As she took deep breaths of the cooler air, she tried to study their surroundings. Nothing stirred beyond the expected sounds of the forest animals in transition from day to night.

"Rixy?" Alysyn scrubbed her eyes with her fists. "Hungry."

Andrixine felt like laughing. "Go on to the spring and drink and wash up. We'll eat on the way." She set the child down and patted her behind to get her moving.

"Those bad people gone?" she asked with a frown.

"Yes, I sent them away."

Andrixine had dragged the dead bodies further into the forest and left them where scavengers could feed and no passing travelers would be offended by sight or smell. Traitors didn't deserve the courtesy of burial; she had little energy to spare. She pocketed the gold coin for proof. Gold coins were not easily obtained except by nobility and warlords.

"I need a new sword, Grennel," she said, turning to the horse. He snorted, bobbing his head, eyes closing in pleasure as she rubbed the sensitive spot between his eyes. "It's a long journey home, and we saw how people react to my owning you. If I can't defend myself, they'll cut off my warrior braids and take you." She slipped an arm around the stallion's neck and pressed her face against his warm, scratchy coat.

Threads of dreams returned, triggered by her words. Andrixine kept her eyes closed, willing the memory clearer.

Brother Klee stood at the head of a line of cloaked and armored figures that stretched to the horizon. He carried a sword. A ghostly sword, emitting a light of its own. The sword from her dreams. The holy man held it out to her and knelt.

"Yomnian, are you speaking to me?" she whispered.

She had Grennel saddled when Alysyn came back, her face rosy from enthusiastic scrubbing. Andrixine gave her a clean shirt to dry with and set aside another shirt to dress her. Then she went to the spring to wash herself, with fresh clothes under her arm.

The moon barely showed above the trees as they emerged onto the trail. Andrixine wrapped her arm around Alysyn, hugging her sister with sudden jubilation. The child giggled, straining against the cloth that bound them together in the saddle.

Alysyn looked up, her head hitting against her sister's breastbone. "Mamma doesn't let me stay awake when it's dark. Why?"

"Because little girls need their sleep."

"But the dark is pretty."

"I know. Enjoy it while you can, poppet." She nudged Grennel to a faster trot. "Remember, we're still playing a game. Can you be quiet like a kitten until we stop again?" She smiled when her sister bobbed her head in answer, off rhythm from Grennel's pace.

Andrixine settled into the horse's stride. If they had no more trouble, they could reach Snowy Mount's gates by sunrise.

The night stayed quiet. Andrixine listened to every sound, trying to break the steady rhythm of Grennel's hoof beats. If she fell into the sound she would get drowsy. Grennel might get them to their destination if she fell asleep, but she couldn't take that chance.

The only movement came from them; the clomp of hoof beats and the creaking of saddle leather the only disruptions to the night quiet. The cool whispering breeze sifting through the trees helped her stay awake.

Alysyn fell asleep. Andrixine envied the innocent trust of the little body and mind in her care. With each league that passed under Grennel's hooves, Andrixine longed more for the shelter ahead of them. Not for clean clothes and food and safety, but to pass Alysyn's safety and well-being to more capable hands.

Those thoughts grew depressing. She studied the moon to escape, until she thought she detected movement in the shadows of its glowing surface. Andrixine blanched and turned her attention back to the forest. Imagination was all well and good, but at the back of her mind lurked the fear of things swooping down and snatching Alysyn or her or both from Grennel's saddle.

"Brother Klee will want a report," she whispered. Andrixine chuckled as Grennel's ears swiveled at the sound of her voice. "He will treat me like a soldier to make me feel better, and demand a report."

Her voice sounded odd, muffled by the thuds of Grennel's hooves. The forest vibrated with soft humming sounds. She thought she heard the questing calls of owls. Something flitted over their heads, crossing the gap of the trail, retreating into the cover of the trees before she could see. The forest went on undisturbed by their presence. It made her feel safe and very small and unimportant.

"I have to think of a report to make, Grennel. Get the news out as quickly and impersonally as I can. That's the trick in all the troubadour tales. The messenger always has a personal interest in the message, but he gives it to his master without any feeling. Then he goes outside and cries until he faints." Andrixine snorted. "I'm done with crying. Nobody is going to cry but the one responsible for this when I catch him."

Light touched her face. She blinked, then rubbed her eyes as her attention turned outward again. Grennel emerged from the forest as the light of pre-dawn touched the sky. Below them lay a shallow valley washed in the silvery light before sunrise. On the other side of the valley, where the land rose to meet the first slopes of Snowy Mount, lay the gate and walls of the holy scholars' retreat.

"Alysyn," she said, grasping her sister's shoulder to wake her. "Alysyn, poppet, wake up. We're almost there."

She laughed, her voice jolted as Grennel broke into a gallop. The stallion loved to race to the full limit of his strength in smooth, open land like this. Alysyn stirred in her arms. Andrixine wondered how the child could sleep with the thunder of Grennel's hooves and the rushing of the air whipping his mane into their faces.

"Birds," she said in her sister's ear, nearly smashing her nose against the side of her head. "You can see the birds soon. And breakfast! Porridge and milk, poppet."

They were nearly halfway across the plain, the ground starting to slope upward when Grennel began to slow. The long hours of travel told against his dependable strength. He didn't resist when Andrixine reined him to a walk.

"Hungry," Alysyn said.

"You're always hungry." She laughed, hugging the child with one arm. "We'll eat soon. And you're going to get a proper bath, too. And clean clothes. Does that sound good?"

"Cherry conserve with porridge?"

"And cherry conserve. If there's any left. You ate most of it before."

It felt like years since they had left Snowy Mount, not three days. Alysyn had eaten herself sick on cherry conserves, given by doting, elderly scholars who lost all sense of discipline when it came to sweet little curly-haired girls.

Laughter poised silent on her lips, she strained to see the gates. Something dark moved among the shadows there. She frowned and leaned forward, as if that would help her see better. Grennel picked up his pace. Whatever it was didn't bother him.

Another half mile, and the shape resolved into a figure in blue Renunciate robes coming down the path from the gates. A silver-bearded man, he stood tall with wide shoulders and a stance that spoke quiet readiness. Brother Klee always seemed to *know*. She was too tired to question how now, but grateful.

"You are not well come back, my children. I grieve at the pain that enfolds you," he said when they drew close enough to hear him. His voice held gravel so early in the morning. Tears threatened in his eyes.

Brother Klee stepped out to meet them when Andrixine reined Grennel to a stop. He held out his arms, and she gladly lowered Alysyn into his grasp. Then she dismounted, holding tightly to Grennel's reins. Brother Klee slipped his arm around her shoulders. She leaned into his support, and tears pricked her eyes as he brought them in through the gates.

"Daughter...Andrixine, let go." A touch of laughter in Brother Klee's voice startled her.

Andrixine jerked from her daze. She sat on a bench in the outer courtyard paved in silver-gray cobblestones with high walls of amber and white stone. A tiny, pock-scarred woman stood before her, trying to take Grennel's reins from her hands. She felt a hot blush grow as she opened her clenched fist and released the reins. Alysyn was gone, presumably taken away by another early riser. It felt like several great weights fell off her back at one time, knowing Grennel and her sister were both tended to now.

"How did you know we were coming?" she asked as Brother Klee tugged her to her feet. It was the only question clear in her mind. She held onto it to keep herself awake.

"My dreams. I saw you riding with fire and swords behind you and tears on your face. Were you attacked on the road?"

"At the inn." She shuddered. A sob broke out. "Brother Klee, I've killed!"

"The first blood is always the hardest," he murmured. He slipped his arm around her back again, a firmer support than before. "Do you wish to speak to the High Scholar?"

"Before anything. Please." Andrixine swallowed hard against another sob. Just a little longer, a little more iron control, then she could rest. With help so close and release in sight, she dredged up strength she didn't know she had.

Her entrance to High Scholar Lucius' private apartments was different from her last visit, when she had bade him good-bye. Remembering, she felt more sticky and dirty and tired. She longed for the flowers in her lost hair, the silken swing of her long gown, the light swishing of her slippers on the stone floor slabs. She felt embarrassed, appearing before the gentle, wise leader of the Renunciate scholars in her soiled, ragged condition. But she had to do it while her resolve was still strong, the words and memories still fresh in her mind.

"Once again, your visions prove themselves painfully accurate, Brother." The musical creaking of Lucius' voice greeted them as the door to his antechamber swung open. The elderly man's thin, bony face and wide blue eyes were a beacon of hope amid the dark wood and the forest scenes depicted in the thick wall hangings.

"Sir, I ask sanctuary for my sister, Alysyn of Faxinor and aid for myself," Andrixine blurted as Brother Klee led her inside. She had to speak before the High Scholar's compassion robbed her of her strength.

"Sanctuary?" The man stared, looking from her to Brother Klee and back again. "Lady Andrixine, do you know what you ask of us? The implications?"

"My mother's traveling party was attacked two nights ago. The innkeeper was part of the plan. I found him and his wife in the forest, murdered, but with no sign of struggle." She dug into the pouch at her belt and pulled out the gold coin. Her hand shook as she displayed it. "I found this under his body. I believe it was payment and they were murdered to keep the tale quiet. I believe these men were sent by the same person who poisoned me last fall."

"Ah, now that explains much. But Brother Klee, let the child sit. She is ready to collapse." Lucius waved at the chair directly behind Andrixine.

"She is a warrior. Her dignity is more important than her comfort." Brother Klee took more of her weight upon himself. "Continue—but hurry." The slightest smile on his lips made her head swim with relief.

"Sir, I ask permission to leave my sister here and for provisions. I must rescue my mother. I ask to borrow a sword. My own sword was broken along the way."

"Broken?" He helped her to sit now, apparently feeling the report was over.

"A man who felt Grennel was too fine for a dirty boy. He attacked me. I snapped my sword on a rock." A sheepish smile crossed her face just before a jaw-cracking yawn took over.

"We have no swords to give." The High Scholar exchanged a resigned look with Brother Klee. "You know Brother Klee always used wooden swords in practice."

"But there is another sword here. I saw it!"

"Saw it?" He raised his eyebrows. "Where?"

"In Brother Klee's quarters. An embroidered sling over his bed. The sword...it's like nothing I've ever seen."

"Brother Klee?"

"My vow of silence is unbroken." Brother Klee sighed.

"I saw it in my dreams," Andrixine admitted. She waited for either man to tell her she had hallucinated.

"Dreams, we understand too well," Lucius whispered. He closed his eyes a moment, then looked to Brother Klee. The other man nodded, stood and left the room.

"Sir, have I done wrong?" Andrixine whispered. Her bones felt light as feathers, her muscles like water.

"No, you merely obey Yomnian's will. How is your throat?"

"It burns. There was a fire and I had no rest. Where—"

"Yes, you must rest. In a little while. I must warn you before Brother Klee returns, your life is no longer your own." He tried to smile. "I wish it could be otherwise."

"Sir, I don't understand." Andrixine felt her chest tighten, squeezing her lungs.

"Lady Andrixine, heir of Faxinor, hear my words." He crossed the room to stand before her. Despite the shapeless blue robe, he wore the majesty of sacred ritual. "I have learned through my many years in holy service, if we bow willingly to Yomnian's guidance we will have joy in harsh surroundings, contentment in the midst of famine, peace in the midst of pain. Since conception, you were part of a grand plan. Prepare yourself for obedience and faith, even when you do not understand."

"I don't understand right now," she whispered, clasping her arms tight around herself. She felt more vulnerable now in the company of this ancient, holy man than when she stood in the open before the burning inn.

"A light burned in the darkness, against the darkness, piercing and shattering the cold with warmth, the black of death with the rainbow fires of life," Brother Klee intoned as he stepped back into the room.

Fire burned in his normally placid eyes. His robe hung open from neck to waist revealing a silver mail shirt that sparkled in the lamplight. Balanced between his outstretched hands lay the sword from her dreams, half emerging from its bone scabbard.

"The light became a sword," the High Scholar continued, "of prophecy and leadership. Yomnian gave it into the hands of a child." He knelt before Andrixine, his eyes meeting hers.

"The sword chooses its own," Brother Klee said, holding it out to her. "Since I entered these walls, no one has seen this sword. No one has spoken of it. It called to you in visions. My guardianship now passes to the next Sword Bearer."

He waited. The room spun under Andrixine, and she clutched at the chair as his words penetrated the haze in her mind. Bits of legend and daydreams spun dizzily through her thoughts. She should have recognized the sword from her dreams.

"The Spirit Sword?" Andrixine found the strength to stand. She nearly tripped on Lucius' robe as she struggled past him, away from the sword. "I can't." She clasped her hands behind her back. The sword stretched out arms of light for her.

"The Spirit Sword never calls a new Bearer unless there is need. I wanted to be a scholar when I was called. My duty was to lead during the Thirty Years War with Sendorland." Brother Klee paralyzed her with the intensity of his eyes.

"But...that war started over eighty years ago! Rakleer? You are Rakleer?" Andrixine thought all the air fled the room.

"I was Rakleer, once. Bearer of the Spirit Sword. Now the sword awakes and calls its new Bearer. Hail, Andrixine Faxinor."

"Our prayers go with you," the High Scholar whispered.

Andrixine fainted. She felt Brother Klee catch her, saving her from slamming her head into the wall, before everything went completely black.

ANDRIXINE SMELLED FLOWERS and clean, mountain cool air. She felt a soft mattress and thick sheets smelling of herbs.

Her body was clean, she realized. No longer itchy, sticky, sweaty, smelling of salt and blood and horse. Her muscles ached. Flexing her arms and legs experimentally, she felt the stiffness of bruises. From the sounds of birds she guessed it was day, but she didn't want to open her eyes. It felt almost too wonderful to simply lie still and let the world go on without her.

"How is your sister?" High Scholar Lucius' voice was soft, coming from another room. Vastly different from the near worshipful tones he had used before.

"Sleeping. Is Rixy sick again?" Alysyn sounded somewhat petulant. Andrixine smiled and even at that small effort, ached.

"No, she has simply gone beyond her strength. Check on her for me, will you?" There was a scraping sound, a chair moved, and then a soft creaking of wood as a body settled into it.

A shuffling of little feet approached. The mattress sagged on her left side as Alysyn climbed up onto the bed. She touched Andrixine's face. Little fingers stroked her cheek. The hand rested on her shoulder, pressing hard, then she felt a soft, wet kiss planted on her cheek. And a teardrop.

"Don't cry, poppet," she whispered. Andrixine forced her eyes open against sticky dryness. Her throat hurt, and her voice rasped.

She saw Alysyn's worried pout break into a glowing smile. The few tears glimmering in her eyes trickled down slowly. Andrixine looked up toward the ceiling. The sling of embroidered cloth from her dreams hung over the bed. The unmistakable shape of a sword pressed against the material. Memory made her head throb.

"You really better?" Alysyn whispered loudly. She scrubbed at her wet cheek, leaving a trail of biscuit crumbs.

"Just tired. Is the High Scholar outside?" A quick nod and smile were her answer. Andrixine wondered if she herself would ever be as easily reassured again. "Did Brother Alpen give you maple buns for breakfast?"

"Hot." The girl giggled with remembered delight. "He said lots for you when you feel better."

"I feel much better. Will you get some for me?" she asked, wedging her arms under herself to sit up. Andrixine barely got upright before her sister slid off the bed and ran from the room. She pushed the blankets off and slid her legs over the side of the bed. The room seemed to tilt a moment.

"Gently, daughter." Lucius stood in the doorway. "We erred by thrusting a heavy burden on you ill-prepared. You must go slowly for a while."

"Is it a sin to ask for explanation? Not justification, but simply to understand?" Andrixine balanced against the side of the bed, taking deep breaths until her head cleared.

"No." He smiled. "Perhaps it is a sin *not* to ask to understand. Blind faith is as foolish as deliberate refusal of destiny." He picked up a long robe of soft white from the chair by the door and handed it to her.

"Thank you," she murmured, slipping the robe over the loose shift she had slept in. As she tied the belt, her gaze returned to the sword hanging over the bed. "It hovers over me like a vulture."

"A guardian spirit, to keep you from deadly injury."

"The histories say some Sword Bearers *have* died in their duty," she countered.

"Do the histories say why?"

"No. Only that a new Bearer heard the call and took up the sword from the hand of the dead," she whispered.

"The Bearers died because they fell from their vows. They tried to use the power of the sword for their own purposes. You are now a person of great power, Lady Andrixine. Even King Rafnar must bow to your leadership. Yet remember, you bear the sword only as a servant, ever putting aside your own desires for the good of our land."

"For how long?"

"For as long as is necessary." He offered her his arm, bent to take her weight. "Come, you need sunshine and fresh air while you rest. And those maple buns your sister is fetching."

"Not a very good excuse, was it?"

"You knew I waited, and you wished to spare the child."

"I wished to spare us a thousand questions," Andrixine countered, a laugh leaving her lips like a bursting bubble. The sound turned to a jagged cough. Lucius supported her against his shoulder, patting her back until the spell had passed.

ANDRIXINE WENT TO the sunny porch she knew well from her

convalescence. Lucius left her with orders to rest and study. She stretched out on the cot set up in the morning sun. Next to it sat a table stacked high with scrolls, likely left by Brother Klee. The scrolls, when she examined them, spoke of the Spirit Sword, the histories, duties and thoughts of the various Bearers.

"Rakleer is alive," she whispered. That meant Brother Klee was over a century old.

According to holy writ, the sword kept him alive and strong until time to pass it to the new Bearer.

Alysyn appeared with Brother Alpen, a tall, silver-haired, rosy-faced man. Head baker for Snowy Mount, he carried a tray with breakfast enough and plenty left over. The promised maple buns still steamed, and Andrixine wondered how he had managed that feat. It wouldn't have surprised her if all the holy folk here had prophetic power. There was milk, boiled eggs and cold glazed apples. The baker put a bun into Alysyn's hand, poured a cup of milk for Andrixine, handed it to her and left in silence, his smile a benediction.

Hours passed in a drowsy haze of glancing through the parchments and nibbling, until the wide shadow of Brother Klee fell across the cot.

"You have color in your face again." He nodded, wearing his familiar, comforting smile. Where his robe parted around his throat, Andrixine saw only tanned skin and silvery white hair again. "There is a peace about you, now. Have you come to accept your destiny?"

"Every warrior dreams of finding the Spirit Sword. None of us ever consider the reality, do we?" She managed a smile and made room for him to sit next to her. "What will you do now?"

"Now that the duty has passed to you?" His gaze roved over her head. "Such a pity. Your hair was a great beauty. We must remember to have it cut to be more becoming before we leave."

"Brother Klee—should I still call you that?" The question just occurring to her damped her irritation that he had avoided her question.

"Rakleer is legend, not flesh and blood. I am Klee. Just as you are Andrixine, no matter what formality may dictate as your title, am I right?" He winked. "As for what I will do, why, I shall go with you. We must protect your family and rescue your mother. Those are duties that cannot be avoided. Along the way, I shall teach you the history and powers of the sword."

"You will? We will?" Her head felt light in relief.

"Daughter, holy writ states clearly those who search first for Yomnian's will and serve others find their own needs met." He brushed a crudely cut strand of hair out of her eyes.

"I was afraid I would have to abandon my quest," she confessed.

"No. Your performance would be hampered with such questions unanswered. This shall be a proving ground for you." Brother Klee patted her hand. "Now, while your sister is fascinated by the birds, we should study. There is much to learn, and once you regain your strength, we must take to the road. Time must not be wasted." He reached for the closest scroll on the table and unrolled it on his lap.

AFTER DINNER, WHILE Alysyn pestered the head librarian for stories, Andrixine took a moment alone to go to her room and simply stand looking at the Spirit Sword.

There was so much to learn to be a proper Bearer. During her summers of training, on overnight trips, the elder Sword Sisters would sit around the fire and tell stories of the Spirit Sword and its Bearers. They dreamed of the day a woman would again be given the duty. Despite those times, Andrixine knew only a fraction of what she needed. She had wondered often, as she did now, why a warlord was never chosen as Sword Bearer. Why her? Why now?

Her warrior training had seemed more than adequate when she thought she would hold Faxinor Castle in a time of peace. Now, everything had changed. She had to learn to hold the mountain range border between Reshor and Sendorland. Sendorland sent few troops by sea. Andrixine had to learn how to direct hundreds of warriors and their commanders. She had to know all the geography of her country and those surrounding Reshor, not just the lands around Faxinor castle. She had to learn to lead men she had never met, not just the soldiers sworn to Faxinor.

Extended lessons in protocol and court manners awaited her. Ordinarily, she was required to go to the king's court three times in her life: at her twenty-first birthday, to be acknowledge as heir; at the death of her father, to vow loyalty when she took her inheritance; and at the twenty-first birthday of her heir.

As Sword Bearer, she would spend years at court at the king's side. She now had precedence over all the warlords and nobles. If the situation warranted, she could even negate the king's orders. Despite that power, she had to tread carefully. Ceremony and ritual were her only protection against unintended enemies and hurt feelings.

Andrixine shook her head to drive those thoughts away. Why worry about the future? How could she call herself Sword Bearer when she had never even touched the Spirit Sword?

The sporadic gold threads in the sword's sling caught the lamplight, winking at her. She wanted to draw the sword free and test the balance and grip. Did the blade glow with a light of its own, or had it only been her weary imagination?

Andrixine knew nothing anyone told her would make any difference if she wasn't sure how she truly felt and believed. She had to settle her own soul before she could worry about the fate of the country. She hoped that would be accomplished before she reached Faxinor.

She had new clothes now; long, draping shirts to hide her few womanly curves and heavy pants suitable for long travel and rough wear. Brother Klee agreed she should remain with her disguise as a boy. She didn't want to be seen as a woman until she was home, the threat and enemies permanently disposed of. The first step was to meet her father's soldiers and enlist their aid in the search for her mother.

Andrixine stared at the sword. Would it do any harm to take it down and look at it? She would never practice with the sword. It would not be drawn except for ceremony and battle. To *be* the Sword Bearer was one thing. She could accept that. To wield the Spirit Sword in battle was something else entirely.

She stepped up on the bed and brought the sword out of its sling. In the lamplight, she saw faint signs of carving in the scabbard. It was of bone, with no sign of seam or joining. Age and use had stained the ivory a creamy silver. The carvings had caught dust or perhaps blood over the years, giving definition to what they depicted. Andrixine looked closely but the figures evaded her understanding.

The grip was perfect, fitting her hand as if made to order. The balance was good, even with the scabbard still on the blade. She twisted her wrist and made several experimental passes. Andrixine nodded, pleased, though she knew it could be no other way. This was the Spirit Sword, after all.

She slid the scabbard off. The blade caught the light, cutting it into rainbows. Like in her dream. The blade looked like a mixture of silver and crystal, swallowing her reflection. No matter which way she turned the blade, flat or edge, it caught the light perfectly, sending flashes into her eyes.

Her breath caught and her limbs froze. Andrixine tried to resist, but something drained all her strength. The room dissolved around her.

The forest was dim with morning light. Branches swayed softly in the breeze. Everything lay in green and black shadows, a few leaves touched with gold. The road curved to the left. A mile marker carved on a gray stone pillar stood to the right. Birds sang in the distance, muffled and sweet. Andrixine felt the soft chill of the morning breeze.

A distant rumbling resolved into the rattle and thump of a wagon moving too quickly. A flash of scarlet and blue canopy appeared among the leaves at the curve in the road. The horses careened into sight. The driver was little more than an impression of black beard, leather clothes and fierce scowl. He whipped the horses and shouted at them. A hot flash of angry panic speared her as she recognized her mother's wagon. The same horses drew it, foaming with effort, bleeding in countless spots. A whiplash came down on the right horse's back as Andrixine watched. The driver turned his head, revealing a scar down one side of his face—Cedes' rapist.

A loud snap reverberated through the air. The left rear wheel peeled off its axle. A shriek came from inside the wagon, which had its curtains lowered and tied down. The driver pulled the horses to a stop with a brutal jerk on the lead reins. He stood up in the seat and blew a raucous blast on a horn he took from his belt. Four riders came around the bend in the trail from the opposite direction.

Two ruffians tugged the wagon curtains aside, reached in and hauled out two women, flinging them to the ground while the other men began to unload the wagon. Andrixine watched her mother stumble and catch herself against a tree. Glynnys tore her dress as she hit the ground and rolled once. She lay still a moment, her shoulders heaving with sobs before dragging herself to her feet and turning her attention to her mistress.

Lady Arriena held herself still and tall, refusing to watch the men as they argued among themselves and mended the wagon. She looked weary, hungry, her clothes wrinkled, dirty with ash and wear, but she stood composed as if waiting to greet guests at a festival. Andrixine felt a pain in her chest in mingled pride and fear for her mother. To all appearances, she was merely dirty and worn with travel, unharmed but for the indignity of being a prisoner. Andrixine knew her mother could survive that.

Glynnys, however, received the abuse Lady Arriena escaped. Even as she cowered next to her mistress, one man took the time to tug on her loose, golden hair and fondle her with such familiarity, Andrixine writhed in sympathy. She was glad her own features were nothing to draw lustful attention. Cedes and Lily had not been as pretty as Glynnys by half.

The vision faded on that observation. Cedes and Lily had hair as dark or darker than Andrixine's. Lady Arriena and Glynnys, both of fair hair, had escaped. Cedes had been hired during Andrixine's convalescence.

Was the person who ordered the raid someone who didn't know about Cedes? What if Andrixine's enemy ordered the dark-haired women killed and the fair spared? It was simpler than trying to accurately describe the person targeted for death.

Andrixine blinked, and the room reappeared around her. She took a few deep breaths and raised her arms to get her blood flowing. She felt she had stood there for hours. From the angle of the light it had been minutes, maybe seconds.

She sheathed the sword and hesitated only a moment before hanging it on her belt. The weight felt right, the sword moving slightly on her hip as she left the room.

When Andrixine found Brother Klee a few minutes later, he stood alone in the orchard, trimming away branches that bore no blossoms. The knife in his hand caught the last rays of sunset, sending bright splinters into her eyes. After the brilliance she had seen in the sword, no light could ever blind her again. Though she walked softly, the man turned to face her long before she was within speaking distance.

His smile held sympathy. He studied her face a moment. "There is a new light to your eyes. Dimmer, deeper and touched with pain. The sword has spoken. What is its message?"

"My mother is alive and I know the road the raiders have taken. Due east. They are going somewhere specific. I don't think they're looking for ransom alone, or else they would head south along the more direct road for Faxinor."

Brother Klee nodded. "Then we must ride out tomorrow. You are rested?"

"We could put a few hours of riding behind us tonight."

"No. There are preparations to make, prayers offered on our behalf. Two may ride more swiftly than a troop, even with several days between them."

Chapter Four

ANDRIXINE KNELT BEFORE the altar in the chapel. She had been there since moonrise, dressed in a white robe, barefoot, holding the bare sword raised before her. Midnight approached. She felt the seconds slipping by, made keenly aware of time by the gentle, humming power of the sword in her hands. Andrixine felt a growing ache after kneeling on the cold stones for hours. Growing, but faint. The Spirit Sword gave her the strength to hold still and straight and endure. She understood now the concept of being served as she herself served.

She kept her eyes fastened on the starburst of silver and sapphires and diamonds, worked on wood, hanging over the altar. The image swam before her eyes until she blinked. She tried not to blink, tried not to do anything except concentrate on the duty awaiting her, on her vows.

After all the preparation, the instructions from both Brother Klee and High Scholar Lucius, Andrixine had expected long, sonorous chants and pompous, somber language. Her vows were deceptively simple. Lucius had read them to her as she knelt for her vigil. The time alone was meant for her to think them over, to commit them to mind and heart. Andrixine wondered if anyone had ever renounced the claim of the sword before the vows were made. History said nothing on that aspect.

Her life for Yomnian's Light.

Her body's comfort for the safety of Reshor.

Her soul to the service of Yomnian.

Her mind to the guidance of those who would follow her into battle.

Her purity of mind, heart and body, preserved as example and emblem to all the land.

Andrixine thought back to all the ballads and legends she had grown up loving. The service of the Spirit Sword was far more than any ballad or tale could convey. She felt betrayed by her former ignorance and dreams. Yet she wondered how anyone could say no to the claim of the sword on their lives.

Responsibilities and duties bound her life. She knew she had often chafed against the boundaries her position as heir had raised around her. Andrixine had wanted freedom to join the Sword-Sisters and be a maiden warrior—the Spirit Sword had now made her leader of every warrior in Reshor. She wanted freedom from the duty to marry and birth an heir. What chains of complications did the sword create now?

Andrixine knew what answer her parents would give her. She would have to marry and have a child before her duties as Sword Bearer took her to war.

She didn't want to marry. Not because of her cousin Feril's disgusting attempts at seduction. Not because the Sword Sisters taught her to hate men, as Feril claimed. Because of Cedes and Lily, the blood spilling from their bodies, the laughter of the men who had raped them.

"Oh, please, Yomnian, save me from that," Andrixine whispered. She fought nausea as her imagination displayed images of a faceless man touching her, impregnating her out of duty.

Andrixine knew marriage could be a delight. She knew her parents were still in love after seven children and twenty-two years. She knew they were happy—but how many noble marriages were? Why couldn't she be one of the blessed?

She frowned at her self-pity and blinked her eyes hard to fight tears. The light on the sword fractured into rainbows.

A green meadow, ringed by trees. Flowers and torches, banners and music and a sense of people dancing and singing and laughing. A man stood just out of her line of sight to her right. Andrixine forgot to breathe as sensations overwhelmed her.

Strongest of all were a mixture of breathless happiness and longing pulsing through her body. Just for that moment, she knew the humming pleasure of his arm around her waist, the sweet dizziness that filled her as his lips touched hers.

Gasping, Andrixine blinked, and the flicker of vision and sensation left. She felt her face burn and knew such things were not proper in Yomnian's sanctuary.

Or were they? Hadn't Yomnian given her the vision? Was it a promise? Didn't Yomnian bless the joining of male and female and the creation of new life?

Behind her the door swung open, bringing the chill of midnight air. Andrixine imagined she heard the singing of the stars in the darkness high above. The brushing of robes on the cold stones gently tugged her thoughts back to the present. The stiffness in her knees, the ache in her shoulders and elbows, the weight of the sword all clamored for her attention.

"The darkness is allowed one final moment to turn your mind from your vows," Brother Klee whispered, kneeling next to her. "Hold fast, daughter. It is soon over."

"We are come for your vows, Andrixine Faxinor, heir of Edrix Faxinor, Bearer of the Spirit Sword." High Scholar Lucius stepped around her other side.

His simple blue, hooded robe had changed to one of blazing white embroidered with silver, belted with silver and sapphires. A gleaming royal blue cloak hung from his shoulders. She trembled, but not from the ache and weariness in her body.

"Purify me, Holy Teacher, for the service I now take at peril of my soul and mind and body," she whispered. Andrixine swallowed hard against a choking sensation that threatened to steal her voice altogether. What did it all mean, her visions and fears and thoughts this night? Distraction or blessing? She found she couldn't wait until morning, when she and Brother Klee would be on the road with nothing to do but talk and study.

KALSAN WOKE TO the sound of neighing. For a moment, he thought he was asleep by the side of the road, in a wayhouse. Or worse, he was asleep in the stable when he should have been guarding the horses.

He woke more, feeling the rush-filled mattress under him, the warmth of the blanket over his bare back. No, they were in the small, comfortable inn at Worland's Forge. Enough room here to sleep two to a bed. Some inns were so crowded they had often crammed three or four to a bed.

Why were the horses still stamping and neighing? Not as loud as in his dreams, but enough to wake him.

Kenden hadn't even moved on his side of the bed. The two men snoring softly in the other bed in the room showed no signs of waking. Kalsan sat up, grumbling silently. Why should the other men wake? The horses were his responsibility.

He was awake enough and sensible enough not to let his boots make any stomping echoes as he slid into them and left the room. Kalsan crept down the stairs and out into the inn yard.

The tang of cooling metal from the nearby forge gave a pleasant bite to the air. The blacksmith had re-shod two horses that afternoon when they stopped early, and put new edges on their swords and knives. This stop would have been more pleasant if the village were larger, with more pretty girls to flirt with. The inn connected to the blacksmith's shop and stables wasn't big enough for dancing, only large enough to let villagers gather to talk.

Kalsan stopped his grumbling when several horses let out squeals as though someone were hitting them in the confines of their stalls.

The warriors were the only ones in the inn that night. Kalsan wondered about that, and wondered if a trap had been laid for travelers. He considered going back into the inn for a sword or to awaken someone to accompany him.

Two shadows crept through the dark slash between stable door and wall. Kalsan stepped into shadows and held still. His lungs were formidable. Even if the warriors ignored the stomps and snorts of the horses, they wouldn't sleep through his shout.

After a few seconds, the shadows moved out into the moonlight, resolving into two dirty young men creeping around the back of the stables with their backs to him. Kalsan watched, waiting, holding his breath until they left his sight. He counted to twenty. The horses fell silent.

Kalsan slowly crossed the yard of packed dirt, straining his senses for the first sign of the horses' tormentors returning. The night was quiet but for gusts of wind picking up bits of straw or leaves and rustling tree branches beyond the stables. At the stable door he paused and looked back at the shadow-black and moon-white yard. Nothing moved but him. He shivered once and wished he had put on his shirt.

The horses nickered, sensing his presence. Kalsan found flint and steel and lit the stable lantern. It was better he lose another half hour of sleep than to come down in the morning and find something had been stolen or the horses harmed. Better to know now, with some chance of finding the culprits.

He checked Jultar's gray warhorse first. Nothing wrong. No lather of upset on the horse's flanks. All the gear was in place, hanging on its pegs where Kalsan had left it.

Kalsan went down the line, checking each horse and its gear, giving one a few reassuring strokes or murmuring to another, or putting more water in a trough for another. He saved Fala, his honey-colored mare for last. She just looked at him with big, dark eyes and snorted when he asked her if she was all right.

"I'm a nervous fool, is that it?" he murmured and leaned against the mare's warm side. She snorted and turned her head back far enough to lip his shoulder, then nudge him away. "Oh, am I disturbing my lady's sleep?" Kalsan asked with a chuckle. He gave her an affectionate slap and stepped away. "I'll see you in the morning, you thankless wench."

He was still chuckling when he stepped through the stable door. Kalsan turned to push it closed, then realized he still held the lantern. He stepped around the door to put it back on its shelf and blow it out when he caught movement from the corner of his eye. Black shadows leaped on him from the darkness.

"Alert!" he shouted, emptying his lungs to the night.

Turning, he swung the lit lantern at his attackers. The shadows weren't there. Cold prickled up his bare back, and Kalsan turned, recognizing the decoy too late. He glimpsed a hand, a rock, and another hand clenched in a fist coming up fast against his face.

His head echoed, dull and loud inside and the stars in the night sky multiplied ten-fold. Kalsan shouted again and swung the lantern, trying to catch someone as his knees buckled. The stone hit the back of his head. He felt the skin split, the blood gush hot on his chill, bare skin. The world tilted up around him and swallowed him into blackness.

"HE'S WAKING, SIR," a soft, creaking, old woman's voice said.

It sent sharp-edged echoes bouncing around inside Kalsan's head, breaking the blackness into blinding white streaks. He moaned, and the sound reverberated inside his head and moved down into his stomach.

"Easy, lad," Jultar said. His wide, calloused hand rested warm and heavy on Kalsan's shoulder. "You've taken quite a blow. No, don't sit," he ordered, when Kalsan tried to sit up before he had even opened his eyes.

"Horses?" Kalsan asked. He nearly smiled when the sound didn't aggravate the throbbing spears behind his eyes.

He opened his eyes and found himself in his room. His face warmed when he realized the shadows behind his master were the other warriors, all watching him.

"The horses are fine, lad." Jultar stepped back and seemed to notice the other men for the first time. "He's not dead yet, you vultures. Get you back to your sleep."

Kalsan turned his head to find the woman as the men chuckled or murmured comments and began to disperse. He recognized the innkeeper's mother, a tiny woman all in gray and faded brown, hair and eyes and clothes. She smiled at him and stepped back to fill a pottery cup for him from a copper pitcher.

"You drink this slowly," she cautioned, handing it to him. "Blows like you took can make your stomach unfriendly."

"Here lad, let me help," Kenden said, stepping from the shadows at the end of the bed. He moved around behind the woman and helped Kalsan sit up.

Kalsan's head swam, but the dizziness didn't move down into his stomach as he had feared. He had taken a nasty fall when he was only fourteen, trying to break one of his uncle's stallions. He had been unable to eat for two days, and his vision had been doubled for nearly that long. This injury wouldn't keep him out of the saddle, and he was grateful.

The cup held watered wine. Kalsan found his mouth dry, and his stomach clamored for the weak bitterness. He sipped the first half of the cup, then drained the rest in two gulps.

"I guess you're feeling better," Kenden said with a chuckle. He squeezed Kalsan's shoulder.

"Can you tell us what happened?" Jultar said. He and the other two occupants of the room had stayed.

"The horses were upset. I went down to check on them and saw someone—no, two people, leaving the stable. When I went in and checked the horses, they were fine." Kalsan smiled his thanks when the woman filled his cup again. "Nothing stolen, none hurt. They attacked when I came out. Punched me in the face and then a rock to my head." He reached up gingerly and touched the back of his head. A thick poultice covered in linen didn't stop the sharp pain when he probed the wound.

"That's not all the damage," the warlord said. He ran one hand down a braid and slowly shook his head.

"My—" Kalsan looked down at his own warrior braids. They were his greatest pride since he had been permitted to use the green cord of apprenticeship.

Someone had cut off the right braid just below shoulder length. His quill-thin braids used to hang to his elbows. He checked, and the left braid was still long, though a few rough, frayed spots showed where someone had hacked at it.

"We were going to cut it to match," Kenden said, "but thought you'd want to know, first."

"Why?" Kalsan said, a rasp in his voice.

"It's a childish prank," Jultar said.

"They nearly took my head off!"

"Aye, but see it as a compliment." The warlord stepped toward the door. "They were afraid to face you in a fair fight, so they took the coward's way. Now, get you some rest, lad. We're here for another day while I seek out some news. Use the time wisely and rest your head."

Nodding to the other men in the room, he stepped through the door and vanished down the hall.

"What news can there be?" Kalsan grumbled. "Thank you, Aunt," he hurried to say as the innkeeper's mother gathered up her bandages and herbs and stepped toward the door.

"Worland's Forge is home to Hernon the Horseman," Xandar said as he stretched out on the other bed and crossed his arms under his head. "People say Hernon knows everything because his horses tell him. He's due back tomorrow."

"So we just sit here?" Kalsan fingered his longer braid. The ripple of fury spreading through him wiped away the ache.

"We look for an idiot sporting a trophy of black hair and green cord," Kenden suggested. Removing his knife from the sheath on his belt, he offered it to Kalsan with a bow.

"Cowards," he grumbled and took the knife. Kalsan closed his eyes as he started sawing at the longer braid. It galled him to have to cut it, but having shorter braids would be easier than having two of disparate lengths. Someone would ask the story behind the differences. He couldn't take that.

Chapter Five

"ME GO!" ALYSYN wailed, struggling against Brother Alpen's grasp. It was hard for such a tall man to hold such a small, wriggling child.

Andrixine understood his difficulty and sympathized. She had often fought to keep Alysyn from trotting into dangerous or dirty places. The trouble was that Alysyn moved like a hummingbird.

"Poppet, be still!" Andrixine called across the stone courtyard. She sighed and straightened up from adjusting Grennel's stirrups and strode across the paving stones. Alysyn broke free and raced to meet her.

"Me go, too!" she repeated, tears threatening. When Andrixine caught her up in her arms, she clung to her older sister's shirt with both fists, tight enough to nearly dig holes in the thick material.

"I thought you liked Brother Alpen and Sister Trinian and High Scholar Lucius and watching the birds," Andrixine said, trying to put a soft, sad note in her voice. It was hard when she felt only frustration.

"Do, but—"

"If you don't play the game the right way, how can I let you play some other time?"

"Still the game?" The disbelief in her voice nearly brought a smile to her sister's lips.

"It's still the game. You were a very good guard, remember? You have to stay here and help guard against the enemy, just like you did when we were in the forest. I'm going to ask Father for a pony for you, remember?"

"Painted black, like Gwenny?"

"No, not painted black," Andrixine said with a sigh. That had perhaps been the most painful part of the masquerade.

Nearly as hard as cutting her hair, but just as expedient, had been the task of dying Grennel's beautiful red coat a dull black and hacking at his silken mane to change his silhouette. Andrixine had nearly cried as she watched Brother Tabor daub the black, sticky stain to his white blaze and stockings. She felt betrayed when Grennel gave no sign that he minded.

"What color?" Alysyn demanded, tears drying before they fell.

"I remember a white baby born to Klarinda Endring's pony last spring. I'll ask to buy it from her. *If* you do your job well. Understand?" she added, setting Alysyn down again.

"Keep guard, like in the forest." She nodded twice, then bestowed her sunny smile on her sister.

"Give me a kiss for luck, poppet?" Andrixine said, kneeling and opening her arms. She stayed there ten heartbeats after tiny lips pressed against her cheek and little feet dashed away.

High Scholar Lucius appeared at the gate as Andrixine swung up into her saddle. She followed Brother Klee to the gate and stopped a little behind him.

"At each chiming of the bells for services, we shall pray for you," Lucius said. He raised his hands, fingers spread as if he could catch the sunlight pouring across the valley. "Blessings of strength, wisdom and peace upon you, Bearers both."

Andrixine bowed her head for the prayer that followed. When she raised her head again, she caught the gleam of tears in the old man's eyes. He had never looked so frail before, yet so full of peace. She wondered what kind of burden it had been to him, to have Bearer and Spirit Sword hidden here under his charge.

"Peace to you, Sir. Thank you for everything. If all goes well, we will send for Alysyn before mid-summer," she said, and nudged Grennel to get him moving again.

"All will go well, Lady Andrixine."

"Ah, but she is not Andrixine," Brother Klee corrected, humor gleaming in his eyes. "She is he, and he is Drixus, my brother's grandson, and I am taking him to train with Malgreer, the king's chief warlord." He flung back his hood and stood in the stirrups, head tilted back as he sniffed the morning air. "Come, nephew. A long journey awaits us."

"Yes, Uncle." Andrixine nodded once more to Lucius and nudged Grennel to a trot. Brother Klee was already four lengths ahead and gaining distance with each second.

PART TWO
The King's Highway

Chapter Six

"WE'LL STOP FOR nooning," Brother Klee said three hours later, raising his voice to be heard above the pounding of their horses' hooves. They approached Maysford. "A swifter journey than you had coming, yes?"

"Between Alysyn and my own problems?" Andrixine nodded, grinning.

It was a glorious feeling of freedom to fly down the forest trail, knowing she moved closer to catching her mother's kidnappers. Then home. It would be a journey of weeks, but each step brought her closer to Faxinor and the truth. Revenge and her mother's rescue were uppermost in her mind, no matter how she tried to concentrate on her new duties.

After Maysford the road split, one arm going south through the Blue Shadows Forest and the other turning east, merging with the King's Highway. It led eventually to Cereston, the capital, where she would present herself to King Rafnar. More important, the King's Highway would take her to the road where the vision placed her mother and the kidnappers. There was no way possible they could have traveled so far in such a short time, so it was a vision of where they would be in the future. Perhaps if Yomnian blessed them, they would reach that point before the kidnappers did, before the wagon wheel broke off.

"Remember Drixus, you are a boy now. Perhaps it is all to the better that your voice was harmed. You sound like a boy caught between child and man."

"Is that good or bad?" She reined in as the man slowed his horse. Grennel tossed his head, snorting a few times as he adjusted to the new pace.

"Hindsight, *nephew*, is clearer, but not as beneficial. Look for the bad as well as the good in everything. Strive for the good, but expect the evil. That way, no matter what happens, you will not be surprised or disappointed."

"Brother—"

"Uncle," he corrected, waving an admonishing finger. "Yes, I know it is a sad way of looking at the world. You cannot afford to give anyone or anything a chance to steal your strength. Be always on your guard."

"Then this subterfuge of ours is a blessing?" She shook her head. Despite the slant of the conversation, she felt something good, almost cheerful stirring inside her. "Yomnian prepares me with everything that happens, then, good and bad?"

"Simplified, yes." He lifted his chin, gesturing at the village as it became visible through the trees. "Hungry?"

"Starving. My body is punishing me for passing by before."

"Next lesson. Care for your body as if you protected the king's heir and the Fire Jewels together. That is what you do, as Sword Bearer."

Fifteen minutes later, they rode into the town square of Maysford. The well was the focal point. Two taverns competed for business from opposite corners. Their banners proclaimed them the Lamb & Rose, and the Hawk & Lion. Shops sat on either side of the taverns, with the inn and its stables far down the street, near the village pond. The townspeople moved about slowly in the warmth, carrying bundles, leading horses and mules.

Dust rose up under their horses' feet, and the sun beat down warm and bright on her shoulders. Brother Klee led her to the Lamb & Rose, across the square from the smith. Dismounting, Andrixine glanced over her shoulder at the inn where her mother's party had stayed. She couldn't go there; someone might recognize her.

The tavern was relatively empty, the noon hour crowd still to come. Andrixine breathed a prayer of thanks for that. She trusted Brother Klee's judgment that her disguise was strong, but preferred to avoid tests so soon into the journey. He had lectured her earlier on her wish to avoid testing and trouble altogether.

"You asked why the first scholars built Snowy Mount so close to the Sendorland border, so close to danger," Brother Klee said as they rode through the forest hours earlier. "They knew that the best way to learn to trust Yomnian is to face danger. Not to rush into it, mind, but rather to *not* flee it. Do you understand the difference?"

Andrixine thought she did, but that still didn't help her feel any more comfortable with the first test of her disguise.

They took a table in a shadowy corner of the cool room smelling of wine, candles and a spicy stew almost ready for the nooning. Brother Klee ordered, letting Andrixine stay silent. The serving maid never even gave her a passing glance.

The bread was fresh and warm, the cheese sharp and the beer icy cold and well-watered. Andrixine sat back in the dim shadows of the corner table and closed her eyes. It felt good to sit and be quiet, to let others serve her and enjoy privacy from most staring eyes. Brother Klee handled everything from ordering their lunch to gossiping with the tavern man and the girl who brought their food. Andrixine suspected from the resemblance that the girl had to be the man's daughter or a close relative. They had the same midnight eyes and dark, curly hair, the same round faces and rosy complexions.

"Is there an armorer hereabouts?" Brother Klee asked when the girl came back to refill their mugs.

"Smith's the best, three day's journey any direction," she said with just enough pride Andrixine suspected some tie between the two. She looked closer and found a blue lover's knot braided into the tavern girl's hair over her left ear. She was promised to someone. Hopefully, the smith.

"Good. My nephew's sword needs a new grip before we reach the capital. He is to train with Malgreer," Klee added, his voice dropping as if he confided a secret. Through half-lidded eyes, Andrixine watched the girl look her over, the first real interest on her face.

"He's over-young for warrior braids, m'lord. Is he that good? And blue cord for holy service besides?"

Andrixine fought not to finger a braid bound with silver and blue cord. Had that been a foolish step, proclaiming her holy calling and rank? Brother Klee had given her the cords himself at her vowing; she had to trust him to know best.

"Drixus was called to service almost from the cradle. And yes, he's very good. The pride of our line." He chuckled and slapped Andrixine's shoulder affectionately.

"Yes, m'lord. If you like, I'll run across the way and warn Brick you'll need his services."

"Do that." He pressed a coin into her hand and settled back in his seat as the tavern girl stepped outside.

"I need a sword before I can have it repaired," Andrixine said under her breath.

"And you shall have one. Brick is renowned for his armor work. He's a friend, but I can't go openly to him without fabricating a story to explain our actions. When his sweetheart describes us, he'll know why I am here, and he will be ready."

"How many years did you spend in retreat, Uncle?" She sipped cold beer to hide her smile.

"More than a man's allotted span. They were years of peace and rest and a measure of forgetting." He paused to look into his mug. Wrinkles appeared around his eyes and mouth, reflections of sadness. "They were not wasted years," he continued after a few seconds of quiet. He looked up, a gentle smile wiping away the wrinkles. "Brick's father and grandfather were my friends. I taught them many old secrets of weapon design and craft, so someone would be ready for this moment. The only sword kept at Snowy Mount was the Spirit Sword. However, we cannot set out on your proving journey without proper provisions, can we, nephew?"

"You are my master, as well as my teacher and beloved uncle," she answered, lifting her mug in a shallow toast.

Fifteen minutes later, they stood in the back room of Brick's shop, inspecting an array of weapons in many different styles and nationalities. Andrixine lifted one sword after another, impressed by the variety and craftsmanship.

Brick watched her with bright, quick eyes, and she wondered if he saw through her disguise. There was an intensity to his gaze that unsettled her. He struck her as a little thin for a blacksmith, though his muscles strained his tunic and his calloused hand had swallowed hers when they were introduced. Andrixine knew she compared him to the smith at Faxinor, who was nearly a giant. Brick was tall, broad-shouldered, his thatch of hair unruly, the red faded to gold by the sun. She liked him, except for the piercing quality of his small blue eyes.

"I think this one," she said, keeping her voice low. She picked up a shorter sword, better for stabbing than slashing. The blade glowed from a fine polishing that made it a mirror. She would regret using the sword and dulling the bright metal.

"A good choice, young sir." Brick reached into the rack hanging from the ceiling. He brought down a scabbard of naturally colored leather with bright copper bindings and handed it to her. "Will you send the king's warriors to me, perhaps, to be outfitted when the war begins?"

"Brick has little modesty and lofty dreams. I admit, his handiwork gives him good reason for pride," Brother Klee said with a mocking growl. He clouted the young blacksmith on the shoulder and nodded. "Yes, a good choice, boy. Find yourself a crossbow. Not all the fighting we face will be close."

"Yes, Uncle." Andrixine sheathed the sword and hung it at her belt. It felt odd hanging there, competing with the memory of the Spirit Sword at her hip. She followed him down to the end of the room where crossbows and longbows hung from the wall. "He knows about the sword?" she whispered when she thought they were out of the cocky young man's hearing.

"He would rather slit his throat than betray me. He is rather counting on the business we will bring him." Brother Klee brought down a pretty little crossbow with blue-dyed strings and hawks carved into its golden wood. "Fancy, but well-made. Did you make this when you were laid up with that broken leg?" he said, raising his voice and turning to face their host.

"A happier sick time I never had." Brick shrugged, his face taking on a faint blush in the shadows. "I made some designs my father dreamed up but never tried. This will shoot further and faster than crossbows twice its size."

"How does it feel, nephew?" He handed it to her.

Andrixine obediently hefted it, sighted, raised and lowered her arm several times to get the feel of the weapon.

"Well balanced and light. I like it." She imagined shooting the villains who had taken her mother, and shuddered. She wondered why beauty combined so well with deadliness.

"Good, we will take that as well. Choose your bolts while I pick my own weapons." He strode away, leaving Andrixine to sort through the bin of arrows and bolts.

She chose four times as many as she thought necessary. There *would* be fighting, even with her father's soldiers to help, and a chance she couldn't stop and retrieve her missiles. Andrixine understood Brother Klee's references to being forewarned, forearmed and triply prepared.

When they rode from the village, Andrixine felt strangely dissatisfied. No one had looked twice at her. No one had challenged her possession of Grennel or her warrior braids. Perhaps it was the presence of Brother Klee even before he strapped on a sword. Dressed in his scholar's robe but armed with a silver-bound staff, wide shoulders thrown back and voice booming, he was an imposing presence. She didn't know whether to be glad of the safety his company created, or disappointed. She was supposed to be proving herself, was she not?

Then she looked at the sword bobbing softly at her hip, the new crossbow tied to her saddle, and knew she was being foolish. How could she have fought off anyone without weapons? Her ability to dodge, to hit vulnerable spots with fists and feet, would only stand her in good stead for a short time.

THEY REACHED THE site of the burned inn with dusk's shadows. Andrixine heard voices through the quiet of the forest, muted as if the bitter stink of burning still in the air muffled all sound and movement. Brother Klee raised his hand to signal a stop, and she complied. A prickle of warning raced up her back, silencing her before she could question him. Those were likely Faxinor soldiers up ahead. Or were they? Could the kidnappers have returned to find the man she killed?

Brother Klee closed his eyes a moment, face placid but for the hard, flat line of his mouth. Did the Spirit Sword show him what lay ahead in the violated clearing? She wanted to reach back and touch the cloth-wrapped sword, then shuddered at the blasphemy of demanding a vision. She was the servant of Yomnian's will. The sword was not given to her as a tool, but to lead her in service to Yomnian, King Rafnar and Reshor.

Brother Klee dismounted, and she followed immediately. Andrixine stroked Grennel's muzzle, signaling him to silence, and crept after her teacher through the shadows.

They were indeed soldiers stomping around the clearing, picking through the burned rubble of the inn, poking through the pile of ashes and stones and burned bones. Andrixine felt her mouth stretch into a grin, then stopped with a hand reaching out to touch Brother Klee's shoulder.

Those weren't Faxinor soldiers. She could tell by their ragged gait and stooped shoulders and a shuffle that was almost furtive. Their voices were all cracked, rough, spewing curses and coarse laughter as they examined the scene of tragedy. Kangan, Captain of the Guard for Faxinor, would never hire men who acted that way. Or if he did, he would soon drill it out of them.

Andrixine drew her sword without thinking as she finally made out the crest on the shoulder of one uniform: the rampant lion of Henchvery. These men had come from her Uncle Maxil.

"That's it, lads," the leader called, wiping his ash-smeared hands on the tails of his ragged coat. "Glad that filthy task is over. Let's hie it back to our last campsite. You couldn't pay me to stay here for the night."

"Lord Maxil will pay us enough, though, eh, Gurnen?" a rumpled excuse for a soldier called from the shadows, and spat for emphasis. The other men chuckled.

Brother Klee caught Andrixine's elbow and led her back the way they had come. She let him as her mind raced.

Her Uncle Maxil had somehow convinced her father to send his soldiers to escort them home, instead of Faxinor's. Why?

"We can't expect any help from my father's men unless we ride home," she said, after she and Brother Klee had mounted and returned up the path. "And worse—" She choked.

"There may be treachery inside your own castle walls," the holy man murmured. "The timing is too convenient."

"Could my own uncle have caused all this? Why?"

"You said yourself, he wants Faxinor. If you would not marry his son, then he must remove you. Your sister Lorien is next in line, yes? Would she accept his son?"

"Lori mooned after Feril, but not once he started trying to catch me in dark hallways." Andrixine shuddered, remembering times her hulking cousin had tried to steal kisses—and worse.

"Then all he need do is convince her that his heart is hers while she grieves and her status as heir is new and frightening."

"Father wouldn't permit it. He'd make Lori wait until the three months of mourning ended before they spoke the betrothal vows." Andrixine nodded, eyes narrowed as she stared unseeing at the trail ahead. "We have time to rescue my mother, then."

"Secrecy, nephew." The holy man spared her a wintry smile she could barely see in the darkness. "While your uncle believes you dead, he will not resort to harsher measures."

Chapter Seven

"FORGIVE ME." BROTHER Klee's words startled her as they dismounted in the empty inn courtyard at Worland's Forge the next evening. "For the sake of your disguise, you must tend to the horses." He shrugged as he lifted the bundles of their possessions off both saddles and slung them over his shoulder.

"That's all right, Uncle." Andrixine took hold of the reins of both horses. "For the sake of a bed and hot food cooked by another, I would willingly do dirtier work than this."

They had ridden late and slept only a few hours under the stars, then rode hard all that day to make up for the time lost at the burned inn. She ached in spots, and her muscles felt heavy, still not fully recovered. Though the weather was pleasant and warm, she welcomed having someone else do the cooking and a roof over her head.

"Be careful what you say, nephew. More rash promises than yours have been accepted as challenge." His eyes twinkled as he stepped inside the inn to arrange for their night's lodgings.

Andrixine nodded, understanding the warning on many levels. She smiled just the same.

The inn was a combination of tavern, inn, local stables, and from the smoke and tang of iron in the air, the blacksmith's hut. The courtyard was of packed dirt; roots and bits of stubborn tree trunks poked above ground in places. Cobblestone paving only appeared near the doorway. The odors coming from the stables were pleasant, clean horse. The aroma of dinner wafting on the breeze made her mouth water. She smelled spicy meat stew and bread, and Andrixine hoped she didn't imagine the warmed apple cider that sweetened the air. If the state of the stables was any indicator, the inn was clean and comfortable even if rough. That was all she cared about.

Brother Klee's sorrel gelding, Sand, was as finely-bred and well-mannered as Grennel. Both horses were a joy to look after. Andrixine took pains not to spend more time on one than the other, and finished by refilling their water buckets. Grennel snorted at her, swishing his tail in farewell. She laughed, reaching over the stall door to slap his flank before stepping outside. Pausing in the doorway, Andrixine raised her face to the darkening sky and laughed again, exulting in the faint ache of weary muscles and the good feel of hunger that made her glad to be alive.

"Hah! Listen to the frog," a cracked male voice called. Three gangly young men in rough-spun, patched clothes stepped around the corner of the stables.

Her first impulse was to explain the illness that had ruined her voice. Andrixine thought better of it, catching a nasty gleam in their eyes. They were like her brothers when they had mischief afoot, yet unlike them because she saw no humor in their faces. They were brothers or cousins, all blond with wide faces and the same heavy brows over tiny, close-set eyes. The speaker stood in the middle. He had the most intelligence in his face and carried a long stick carved into a semblance of a sword. The one to his left had a throwing stone, the tangle cords knotted and stained from much bad use and mending. The one on his right carried no weapon. The hunching of his wide shoulders and the dullness of his eyes suggested he relied on brute strength alone.

"Good evening to you," Andrixine said, deciding courtesy might slow them enough to allow her a strategic retreat.

"The voice is a frog, but the manners are a girl's. Must come from those braids." The leader guffawed like a donkey braying. "Did you get them from a horse's tail?"

"No, from a jackass," the left-hand one said, snorting in delight at his wit. The other two laughed loudly.

Andrixine winced. At home, such raucous laughter would have brought someone running, demanding to know what animal was being tortured.

"The fancy little lordling doesn't like us." The leader stepped closer, tossing his crude wooden sword from hand to hand. Andrixine wished Brother Klee hadn't taken their weapons with him. A real sword in her hand might have frightened them away before they decided to torment her.

After another look at the three blocking her way, she decided otherwise. They would have rushed her already if they thought she had a chance against them.

"I wish no arguments with anyone," she said. "My uncle and I are merely passing through."

"Your uncle?" The leader snorted and spat. "Didn't know they let little boy priests grow their hair so long." He reached out too quickly to be blocked and yanked hard on one braid.

Andrixine swallowed a yelp, refusing to give him any satisfaction. She caught his hand and dug in her nails until he let go. She spun away, releasing his arm at the last moment, enough to twist it painfully without doing any damage.

"So you can fight," he growled stepping back, rubbing his injured hand. He shifted the mock sword between his hands a few times, glancing at his companions. And leaped.

Andrixine stepped aside, bringing both hands together down on his neck. He bellowed and dropped the wooden sword. She snatched it up and leaped away as the one with the throwing stone flung his weapon at her. He didn't have time to wind up momentum. The stone clattered harmlessly against the stable wall.

The brute lunged at her. So perfectly timed was the attack sequence, she knew they had done this often. Likely to other unsuspecting visitors to the inn. Her disgust grew. Some bodily pain would be good for their souls.

She neatly sidestepped the brute and brought the sword down with a whistling slap against the back of his neck. He roared like a stuck bear and fell to his knees. A swing like that with a real sword would have cost him his head. Her breath came harder, surprising her. She hadn't been aware of any effort.

A faint whistling in the air alerted her and she ducked. The throwing stone sailed over her head, one string brushing her hair. If she hadn't ducked, it might have wrapped her throat, smashing her face and strangling her.

She let out a war cry that turned into a cracking roar. Three hard, fast, whistling swings with the stick. Three shouts of pain. She spun out of the way before any could touch her.

A blur in the corner of her eye made her leap. The throwing stone caught on her left foot, cracking against the side of her ankle and tangling. Two strings caught on a root pushing through the dirt of the courtyard.

A shout of triumph broke from the leader, and he leaped at her. Andrixine twisted out of his way, going to her knees. Her ankle twinged painfully. She swung up with the stick, catching him between his legs. His shout shattered, and agony cracked his face. He fell to his knees, choking.

"Enough!" a man bellowed.

The stone thrower ran. The brute growled and threw himself at Andrixine. She smashed him across his face with the stick sword, splitting lip and cheek. Blood spattered. Men appeared, captured the screaming, cursing youth and dragged him away.

Andrixine dropped back on her haunches, stick raised in defense.

Heir of Faxinor

Her heart thudded in her ears. Sweat blinded her.

"And who might you be?" the same voice asked as a shadow towered over her from behind.

Andrixine moved as far as her trapped ankle permitted and looked up at the widest, tallest, hairiest, reddest man she had ever seen in her life. His thick leather belt would have been enough for all her brothers, and enough left for slippers for Alysyn and Lorien. His baggy, faded clean clothes were dark blue, accenting the red of his hair. He scowled at her while she struggled for breath enough to answer. When he offered his hand, she hesitated.

"No fear, lad," he said, his expression softening. "I saw enough of the fight. It was most unfair—the fight usually is, with those three." A grin broke across his face as he lifted her to her feet. "This time, the imbalance was on your side."

"I don't wear these braids in vain, sir," she said stiffly, between slowing gasps.

"Indeed, you do not. Well done, boy." Brother Klee slipped through the ring of onlookers. His mouth was a flat line of worry, changing to a smile of approval a moment later.

"Your companion?" the big man asked when he saw the blue starburst pin indicating holy service on Brother Klee's robe.

"My great-nephew. He will train with Malgreer, if he survives the journey."

"Oh, he will. And now young sons of travelers will survive their passage through our village because of him. We've never been able to catch those three at their games, only suspected who to blame. Until now, thanks to your boy." The big man glanced at the inn. "Will you let me buy your dinners, sir?"

"I believe so. Do I address Hernon the Horseman?" Brother Klee said, gesturing for the man to lead the way.

"Have you come to buy?" Hernon's grin broadened as he moved to the inn. The others who had come to break off the fight were leaving, leading away the losers.

"Uncle!" Andrixine called, embarrassed that her call sounded like a wail. It was undignified after her recent victory.

"Drixus? Are you hurt?" Brother Klee hurried back to her side, concern on his face again.

"I'm tethered and I can't twist enough to reach." She gestured at her ankle, wrapped by the throwing stone, firmly tangled around the root by her exertions.

The resulting laughter from the two men made her face burn until she realized they laughed at themselves, not her. Andrixine held still as they worked to separate her from the strings, so the knife wouldn't damage her boot. It felt somewhat indecent to have two grown men kneeling at her feet. She had to remind herself she wore pants, not a skirt.

Brother Klee held her back a moment when Hernon set off across the inn yard to order their dinner. Andrixine felt a shiver of warning go up her back when her teacher narrowed his eyes as he studied her.

"Is something wrong?" she murmured.

"No. Merely...we've both learned an important lesson today, I think." Brother Klee smiled, breaking the somber set of his face. "You are more recovered from your illness than either of us expected."

"I didn't think so at the time," she said with a chuckle.

"Yes, you were. If your life had been in danger, the sword would have come into your hand." He nodded toward the inn, smiling a little more when she gaped. "The sword cares for its Bearer, Andrixine. Always remember that."

"THE BOY NEEDS to put some flesh on his bones, that's the answer," Hernon said after the trenchers had been cleared away and they finished dinner with nuts, apples and sweet, weak wine.

Andrixine conceded if they could eat this well every night, she would gain back all her lost flesh in a hurry. She caught herself before she looked down at the flattened front of her shirt, hanging loose to hide her tightly bound breasts.

"The problem is," the man continued, "fools like Redin and his cousins only see a skinny, pale boy. They see the warrior braids and the warning doesn't sink through their stone skulls. So they attack, thinking they'll have a jolly, bruising time and maybe come away with a few coppers extra in their pockets and your braids as a trophy."

"My nephew has been very ill. He nearly died," Brother Klee said, and paused. "I am sure our journey will put flesh on his bones and enough color on his face to ward off more foolish attacks. Not that I am altogether upset about earlier."

"You may not be, Uncle, but I wish you would leave my sword with me from now on when I tend the horses." Andrixine smiled to make her plaintive tone a joke. She decided she had not known many evenings this pleasant in a long time.

Hernon, thinking her a boy, had spoken openly his opinion of the times and the village ruffians, and his praise for her skill. If he had known she was female and nobly born, he would have been more circumspect in his language and not half as amusing. She smiled and sat up again to reach for her wine. New pressure on her ankle made her gasp. She felt the blood drain from her face in the wake of the thudding that pulsed through her leg.

"Nephew?" Brother Klee stood, reaching for her.

"My ankle. I must have twisted it worse than it seemed at the time." She felt unaccountably embarrassed.

The feeling didn't go away, because Hernon insisted on tugging off her boot and tending to her then and there. The innkeeper brought over an extra lantern and cloths for binding, in answer to Hernon's shout. From the speed and lack of questions, Andrixine guessed Hernon was a power in this village—and now it turned out he was a healer, too.

"Only bruised from the stone." He lifted her foot enough for her to see the purplish mark over the bone. "The binding of your boot helped. Sleep with your foot raised and the swelling will vanish by morning. The ache will continue a while, though."

"Again, we thank you." Brother Klee poured another glass of wine for each of them as Hernon sat down next to him again. "First the dinner, then the conversation and advice, and now tending the boy's injury. The bright spirits were guarding us this day, most certainly."

"Ah no, good Brother," the big man protested, laughing. "I thank *you*. If I had any hope of success, I would beg you and the boy to stay with us several days, in thanks. Those three ruffians won't bother innocent people for a long while, I think. We owe you both a debt."

"Believe me, friend, we would stay if we could. The boy and I have urgent work awaiting us. I am glad we met you, though, for who knows what the future will have awaiting us? We may have need of each other's help in the dim days ahead."

ANDRIXINE WOKE WITH a soft moan, her heart thudding in her ears. She bit the edge of the blanket to muffle more sound. What was wrong with her, to have such dreams?

On the other side of the dark room, Brother Klee lay still. She watched him while her breathing and heart slowed to a more normal pace. Good—he still slept.

"Visions, daughter?" he asked, breaking the renewed silence. He chuckled at her gasp, and the rush-filled mattress rustled as he sat up. "You forget, Andrixine, I am still linked to the sword so I may help and teach you."

"Did you see—?" She sat up and wrapped the blanket around herself, chilled despite going to bed fully dressed.

"No. But I sense questions troubling your spirit. Would it help to talk of them?"

"I am my father's heir." She flinched as the words spilled from her lips. "I am required to marry and produce an heir."

"You fear this would interfere with your duties as Bearer?"

"Bearers aren't allowed to marry—and I'm glad."

"Where did you learn that?" Laughter touched his voice, startling her.

"They can't—can they? We, I mean. It's like taking the highest holy vows and serving Yomnian."

"Everyone who puts Yomnian first in their thoughts and actions serves Him. And Sword Bearers do marry." He paused, the moment lasting so long the night quiet seemed to throb around them. "I was married for three very happy years before the war with Sendorland started."

"What happened? You don't have to tell me," she hurried to say, when a flash of sorrow cut through her like a cold knife. Did the Spirit Sword give her a taste of what he felt, just as he could sense her dreams with its aid?

"Yes, it seems I must." Brother Klee sighed, the sound ending in a soft rumbling of wistful laughter. "Her name was Nelora. I can still close my eyes and see her tiny, golden face and her eyes like ferns and her white-gold hair. I can still taste her kisses and feel her arms around me. Don't ever let anyone tell you that to please Yomnian you must give up loving and a lover, Andrixine. The marriage bed is as holy as the chapel where you made your vows."

"I understand," she whispered, knowing she could never understand until she felt the happiness echoing in his voice.

"I was on a solitary mission, an arrogant boy of twenty-five, still aching from the death of my own teacher. I met Nelora coming back from washing clothes at the river. She conquered me with one challenging look and one burst of laughter. She made me court her a full year. Love teaches you patience as the greatest pain never can." He chuckled a little louder.

"You married her and you were happy. And then the war started," Andrixine whispered, when the silence had grown a few heartbeats too long. She felt something in the air; a sense of sadness waiting to leap from the darkness, the happy memories turned into sharp pieces, like a shattered mirror.

"I left her in a village a day from the front lines because we had just learned a child was coming and I didn't want to be far when her time came. The villagers found out I was the Sword Bearer, despite our efforts at secrecy. When they found out she was pregnant, they immediately accused her of being unfaithful."

"What?" She flinched at the squeak of her voice.

"Some people think Sword Bearers are eternal virgins, I suppose. No matter." There was a rustling of cloth as he turned and swung his legs out of the bed and leaned back against the wall. "They imprisoned my Nelora and pronounced her a whore and adulteress and prepared to burn her alive. Fortunately, the innkeeper and his wife knew Nelora adored me as much as I did her, and they could also count. They knew I had fathered her child. They sent their sons to fetch me and risked their lives to help Nelora escape."

"Risked—" She choked on the word and the implications that sprung to her mind.

"I arrived in time to save them from the flames. Then we went hunting for Nelora. She was...ill for a very long time. Our son died at birth, and she lingered only a few months before she followed him," he said, his voice thinning but never breaking. "She still holds my heart, even eighty years later."

"I'm sorry. I didn't mean to awaken your pain."

"If we do not learn from others' pain, Andrixine, how will we avoid the same scars? There is hope in my pain, because I know Nelora and our son wait for me in Yomnian's halls. And yes." A chuckle touched his voice. "You must still marry and produce your heir. But be warned. Many will be scandalized at the sight of a pregnant Sword Bearer."

"Can you imagine me riding into battle with a belly as big as a barrel?" A cracking giggle escaped her.

"Yomnian save us from such horrors." His responding laughter sounded a little less pained.

"I wish I didn't have to marry ever."

"Why?"

"I saw them raping Cedes."

"Ah." Despite the darkness, Andrixine knew he smiled; sympathy and compassion and perhaps a little amusement. "Do you think your husband would force you? The Sword Bearer?"

"I don't want a husband who fears me. I want a husband who is warrior-minded, to support me and ride into battle with me." She stopped short, startled by the words. Where had such thoughts come from? "But I don't want to marry."

"Truly?"

"I dream of his—a man's arms around me, and such joy the whole world means nothing beyond his kisses. Then just before I see his face, I am Cedes and those men tear me apart in *their* pleasure."

"The pleasure of sharing and the pleasure of tormenting another. Which does Yomnian bless?"

"The first!" She flinched when her voice rose.

"How are your parents with each other?"

"Happy." Andrixine wondered why he asked such questions.

"The Bearer is served as she serves. Remember that."

"I try," she grumbled, and wished he wouldn't speak in echoes of holy writ and cryptic phrases so often.

"Go back to sleep, daughter, and pray for sweet dreams. We have hard riding to do tomorrow. There is a warrior band half a day ahead of us on the trail. We would do well to join them."

"Will they help us rescue my mother?"

"Time and more visions from the sword will tell." His shadowy form lay back down again. The rushes in the mattress rustled, and his blanket whispered as he drew it up to his shoulders.

Andrixine sat still a long while, staring into the darkness, waiting for her body to calm. Yes, her parents were happy. Her mother never shrank from her father's touch, but often invited it. Her own dreams of pleasure made her feel a new hunger—if only she could forget Cedes, naked and bleeding, voiceless in pain and terror.

Chapter Eight

"A TRAIL HOUSE. Larger and better kept than shelter houses, several steps below an inn." Brother Klee gestured at the dark shape emerging from the shadows of dusk the next evening.

"Another lesson?"

"Merely warning you not to expect more than a place on the floor. Or in the stable, if the house is crowded."

"The weather is pleasant. We could camp in the open, further down the trail." She didn't mind the idea; they had plenty of blankets and provisions.

"You should test your disguise in close quarters for more than a few hours." Brother Klee reached across the gap between their horses and grasped her wrist, emphasizing his words. "Until you gain true confidence in your ability to act a part, how will you have others believe it? You must learn to hold your own, to walk unprotected."

"If you think I can do it—"

"I know you can."

Grennel neighed, a mixture of question and challenge thrown into the darkening forest. Another horse answered near the black bulk of the trail house. Andrixine began to feel for her sword, then glanced up and found Brother Klee watching. He smiled faintly and shook his head, and she felt her face burning.

"There is a law of the open road you must learn, nephew. When night falls and men enter the trail house, disagreements are left outside. All travelers are equals, bound to give help and a full plate with grace."

"What if they're the men holding my mother?" she asked, lowering her voice, aware of the carrying quality of night air. "The road in my vision meets this one soon. What if they changed direction?"

"Then we will wait until morning and pray the night brings us a plan to rescue her," came the placid reply. "Did you think the warriors we seek are here?" He chuckled when she could only shake her head.

As they drew nearer the trail house, a flickering light appeared. A man stepped from the trees and darkness to meet them. Despite what Brother Klee had said, Andrixine suspected the man with the torch was relieved to see only two newcomers.

"Good evening to you," he called, raising the torch high to shed as much light as possible. He was a dark-skinned man, his hair and beard silvered. His red-bound warrior braids hung nearly to his elbows. Red, for the Oathbound. That was a good sign. He wore leathers and a bright blue shirt that shimmered like silk in the torchlight.

"And to you." Brother Klee gestured in blessing at the moment the man could recognize his robes as those of a holy scholar. "Is there room among you for the boy and myself?"

"Room in plenty, holy sir. It's been long since we had anyone to say evening prayers for us. Lord Jultar will give you a place by the fire if you would be pleased to join us."

"A pleasant welcome indeed." Brother Klee smiled, nodding.

Neither horse shied away as the man reached to hold the reins so they could dismount. Another figure stepped from the shadows as they approached the trail house. In the torchlight, he resolved into a young man, perhaps six or seven years older than Andrixine, wide of shoulder, tanned and muscled. From the cut and quality of his clothes, she suspected he was nobility. His dark hair had a touch of red when caught by the torchlight. He studied them curiously, his hand straying to rest on the hilt of his sword. She noted his warrior braids, barely past his shoulders, were bound with green apprentice cord and he hadn't earned the right to grow a beard. He had likely started warrior training in his late teens.

"This is Kalsan of Hestrin, Lord Jultar's apprentice. He will take you to our master for introductions, good sir." The man with the torch handed it over to Kalsan, who made a brief bow and beckoned for Brother Klee to precede him.

The man who met them introduced himself as Brenden, showed Andrixine where the well was behind the horse shelter, then went ahead to the trail house. Andrixine refused to hurry with her task, though she longed to hear the tale of this traveling group. Whether because of the Spirit Sword or her own sensitivity, she felt there was something different about them. Something strong and alert. There was a reason they were here on the road at this particular moment in time. She wished the Spirit Sword would grant her a vision beyond misty dreams of the faceless, silent man who kissed her and made her melt with conflicting emotions.

When she finished her chores and entered the squat trail house, she found it only half full. A bright fire burned in the central floor pit. Ten men lounged around it, resting on blankets and propped up by their saddles. From the looks of the kettle and the man ladling food into bowls, there was still plenty of stew left. It smelled wonderful, heavy with beef and spices. Her stomach growled loudly enough she feared someone had heard.

"Here, boy, don't stand there gaping," someone said with a rough laugh. A hand grasped her arm and tugged her inside. Andrixine didn't resist, sensing no danger in the laughter. Brenden guided her around the fire pit until she stood before the leader.

Jultar's silvery-white warrior braids hung past his elbows. The cords were Oathbound red and noble silver. His wide shoulders and straight posture belied the age clear in his hair and the wrinkles half-hidden by his silver and blond beard. A long scar along his right cheek added mystery to his piercing, clear gray eyes. His men, relaxed and laughing in his presence, showed Andrixine he commanded respect through admiration, not threat.

Jultar studied her a moment, then nodded and gestured at a spot to his right, on the other side of Kalsan. Brother Klee sat on his left, a bowl before him and a wooden cup in his hand.

"Be welcome, boy. Sit and eat," Jultar said with a smile.

"Thank you, sir." Andrixine remembered to bow instead of curtseying. Then she gaped as Jultar turned, letting the firelight hit the insignia on his shoulder, where his dull blue cloak fell away. He wore the golden hawk of the king's warlords, with the flame emblem behind it that meant *all* the men under his command were Oathbound. Andrixine looked quickly to Brother Klee as she sat, and the man nodded that he had seen it too.

Oathbound warriors in the king's service. The best of the best. What were the chances this meeting was a mere coincidence? Andrixine tried to quell the shiver of hope rising inside her.

Please, Yomnian, if I truly am your chosen servant... She refused to finish the prayer in her thoughts. Andrixine knew better than to try to make a bargain with Yomnian.

"The boy looks frail to boast such long braids, Brother. Is he adept?" someone called from the other side of the fire.

"Drixus has been ill, poisoned by an enemy of his family. We journey to take him now to Malgreer for his final training." Brother Klee turned to Jultar. "He has been challenged because of his apparent frailty and some have painful regrets for their boldness."

Kalsan settled down next to Andrixine and handed her a full bowl. She thanked him with a nod and closed her eyes for a hurried, silent blessing.

"I will keep that warning in mind, Brother Klee," the unseen man said with a chuckle.

"May I offer you our company?" Jultar offered after a moment. "We've been on a long hunt ourselves, and it will be good to travel with someone who knows the current state of things in the kingdom."

"There will be war, am I right?" Brother Klee said, his voice clear in the sudden silence of the room. Only the crackling of the fire and Kalsan's startled gasp beside her broke the waiting stillness around Andrixine.

"Why would you say that?" Jultar responded with the same calm in his voice.

"I was Oathbound before I took my vows and became a scholar. There are many signs which cannot be spoken but only seen by those who understand."

He was quiet a moment, staring into the fire, the light glinting on the starburst pin at his collar. The warriors watched him, nothing but careful interest on their faces. Andrixine schooled her features into neutral waiting, praying she wouldn't betray herself or Brother Klee with her expression.

"You have been through the mountains into Sendorland," he continued, "have you not? That is why you have been gone so long from our land. You have watched the people and listened to the whispers in the wind, and you can see and hear and taste the coming war." He turned enough to meet Andrixine's gaze. "We thank you for the offer and will go with you, but only as far as the Bantilli Trail south to Faxinor. We have a promise to keep to Lady Arriena Faxinor."

Chapter Nine

KALSAN STARED INTO the sun as it topped the trees. He fought not to blink until his eyes watered. When he closed his eyes, after-images burned bright gold. He grinned and rubbed at his eyes and opened them again. Childish games.

Next to him, the boy, Drixus rode quietly, listening to their elders talking. Kalsan rode behind Jultar and Drixus behind Brother Klee. The scholar was the boy's great-uncle, but Kalsan felt something wrong about the story. They were more master and apprentice in their dealings, though affection was obvious on both sides.

Maybe, Kalsan thought, he felt something odd in the boy because the uncle was odd. Who would ever have thought a holy man could see to the heart of their mission and guess what had taken the warrior band months of spying to learn? Brother Klee talked about past wars with Jultar as if he had been in them. Kalsan listened eagerly all the night before and now this morning, as the two men traded war stories like generals preparing for battle, examining and discarding old campaign strategies. Drixus listened so intently, Kalsan thought he could push the younger boy off his horse and he wouldn't notice until his bottom hit the pebbly forest road.

He liked Drixus. Kalsan watched the pale, thin boy for a few seconds. Something about his face and movements—had Drixus trained to be a holy scholar like his uncle and then changed to be a warrior? Sometimes holy folk had visions from Yomnian that led them to do strange things.

Kalsan wished he could have at least one vision, one bit of guidance. He had prayed hard last night, after the talk faded around the fire and they all curled up in their blankets to sleep. He envied Drixus, traveling with a man who could hear Yomnian's voice and understand holy writ when he read it.

Maybe he should give up being a warrior—only for a few years—and take retreat himself? Would that bring him closer to Yomnian's heart?

A moment of thought and Kalsan pushed that idea aside. He muffled a snort of laughter. What community of holy scholars would accept him? They would try, if only out of pity for his hunger, but he would never fit. No matter how much he wanted to learn to hear Yomnian's voice.

Looking at the boy next to him again, Kalsan decided Drixus couldn't be as skilled as the length of his warrior braids proclaimed unless he had been training as a warrior since he could pick up a sword. Kalsan vowed if Drixus asked him why his own braids were so short, he would pummel him, liking or no liking, frailty or no frailty.

They rode down the trail, and the sun climbed above the trees. Jultar and Brother Klee talked wars and strategies, Kalsan and Drixus listened, and the warriors behind them talked in soft tones.

His gaze kept drifting back to study Drixus. Something about the boy nibbled at his curiosity. The shape of his face—a trifle too smooth in the wrong places? Or was that just his youth? Would the advent of a beard in a few years get rid of that hint of sweetness, the curves of his mouth? Kalsan's face grew hot when he realized he had been staring at Drixus' mouth and eyes and letting images of various village girls fit the boy's features.

That unseen woman haunted his dreams every night, making the village girls somehow less appealing, even when they smiled and winked and flipped the hems of their skirts to give inviting glimpses of ankle and calf. Kalsan wondered if he would try to find his vision woman in every place he passed. Now he even tried to see her features on a young boy's face. Kalsan scolded himself to get such thoughts out of his head.

Drixus was fourteen at the most, Kalsan decided and turned his eyes to the trail and his ears to listening to his master. Fourteen, and poisoned by an enemy of his family. Nobility, by the silver in his braids. Not just a touch of the noble blood, but close enough to the inheritance to warrant enemies? His clothes were plain, though new. His saddle and horse were the betraying clue. Understated elegance in the saddle and a high-blooded horse, even if the color of the big, healthy stallion looked wrong.

Kalsan grinned, remembering the trouble he had that morning getting Fala out of her stall next to Grennel. She would be in season soon, and mares of her line had a tendency to choose their own mates. Kalsan understood Fala's restlessness. He hoped the village they stayed in that night would be large enough for dancing and music and pretty girls to shove the mystery woman from his thoughts.

But the mystery of young Drixus nibbled at his thoughts. Kalsan liked him well enough from the times they talked, and his manners and willingness to help with any chore. Maybe he was too willing. Maybe

Drixus was high enough nobility that this rough life on the road was little more than an adventure to him.

Kalsan wondered if Drixus was close enough to inheriting the ancestral estate that nasty relatives posed a problem, or even a threat. He paused a moment and sent up a prayer of thanks that he was the younger son of a younger son and would never inherit Hestrin. If that was Drixus' problem, he felt sorry for the boy.

Chapter Ten

"YOUR LESSONS CONTINUE, daughter," Brother Klee said under his breath.

Andrixine stared up at him, more startled at his term of address than the fact he had approached her from behind and she had not sensed him. Had she been that caught up in her grumbling, or was she that tired from their long day on the road? Jultar's warrior band set a demanding pace, as if to make up for time lost somewhere. She hadn't considered the day wearying until she got down from Grennel's back.

"We are quite alone," he said, a smile cracking the solemn mask of his face. Beyond them, the bustling tide in the inn's courtyard flowed without a pause to register their presence. "What were you thinking?"

"I am a spoiled child," she responded after a moment. It was no good hiding her thoughts from Brother Klee. "I want my lessons whenever I think of a question, and privacy to talk about anything." She shrugged and looked away. She couldn't decide if the twinkle in his eyes was comforting or not.

"You are comfortable with strangers, and your disguise is whole. You are accepted by seasoned warriors, who speak freely before you. Young Kalsan has a questing heart, and you always speak wisely in our discussions, grasping what he needs to know before most of the others. That alone shows the sword chose well when it chose you. These two days with Jultar's warriors have been an education for you, also."

"It's not the same." She turned, pivoting on the corner of the building where she leaned. "Forgive me—I sound like a whining child a third of my years."

"It is understandable." He caught her chin with two fingers and gently tipped her head up so their eyes met. "I am proud of you. Merely open your eyes and observe. Consider what you see and hear around you. And repeat your lessons in your mind."

A party of horsemen passed them, coming into the inn courtyard. She waited until a stable boy met the men and led their horses away.

"Easier said than done, Uncle," she said, shrugging and conjuring up a smile for him.

"That is the way of it in the beginning." He looked around as a voice shouted his name through the courtyard din. "Ah, supper is ready. Coming, nephew?" Brother Klee turned and headed toward the door of the inn. Andrixine followed.

Brother Klee was right, she conceded. Everything was a lesson to learn if she knew how to look at it properly.

Their journey had changed. Did it really hinder her that she couldn't ask all the questions that came to mind as they rode? At every village, Brother Klee always found the right person to ask questions, seeking the men who kidnapped her mother. There was no sign yet, but they would reach the place from her vision soon, and until then there was much to learn.

Lord Jultar recognized the experience and wisdom of Brother Klee and spent the days and evenings talking battles and strategy with him, asking about current feelings in the kingdom, the harvests, the rainfall this spring, on and on, until she thought the man knew everything there was to know about the land. Listening, she saw a pattern and could guess where the old warrior's questions led. Sometimes.

She liked Kalsan. He had a friendly smile and didn't challenge her. They shared the care of the horses, and he complimented her skill. He never lectured, as if she couldn't understand what seasoned warriors discussed. He asked what she thought when the evening discussions around the fire turned philosophical or theological. He even showed respect when she made a point that the older, seasoned warriors hadn't considered. He made her feel that maybe she wasn't as far from being a proper Sword Bearer as she believed.

The problem was that last night, after seeing Kalsan kissing a village girl, she saw his features in the misty dark mask of the man who haunted her dreams. Andrixine dreaded the thought of wearing a silly smile and mooning after Kalsan like that girl did when they rode away in the morning.

Better for her dreams to focus on rescuing her mother. Andrixine prayed every night for sword-granted visions. They came, they confirmed she and Brother Klee were on the right road, but they didn't help her feel any better. It was nearly a week now since they had taken to the road. When would they find the men who had taken her mother, or at least a hard, strong clue to their identities or whereabouts?

Andrixine decided she was disappointed they were staying in the inn tonight. Another night in a trail house would be delightful, cooking over a fire, listening to war tales, humming along when the few musicians in the group plucked songs from flute and harp. It made her nightly task of checking, cleaning and mending their gear almost pleasant. Being busy until she fell asleep kept her mind from roaming in dangerous directions.

Tonight there were stable boys to assist travelers in those tasks. Andrixine found herself with nothing to do after the evening meal. Brother Klee was again engrossed in discussions with Jultar in the warlord's room. There was no excuse she could make to have herself included, even if just to listen. If Brother Klee thought she would benefit from the discussions, he would have invited her.

She decided it would be good to explore the village for a little while. Night let the other members of their traveling party take advantage of the inn, the dancing square and the willing company of the village girls. Andrixine found herself alone to do whatever she wished. She certainly didn't want to watch Kalsan kiss another pretty girl.

She wandered down to the river, along the sandy pathway, listening to the gurgle of the water as it ran over the stones of the ford. The air was heavy with late flowers and leaves warmed by the sun all day. Would she be able to swim? No, the moon was too bright, too full, the trees and shadows too thin around the riverbanks to permit it.

She perched on a slab of rock overhanging the water and threw stones at the reflections of the stars. On nights like this back home, she could talk Lorien into swimming with her. They would put on old tunics and trousers and climb down the vines from her bedroom window in the dark, to wade in the pond in their mother's private garden. The water would be warm, holding the sun's heat in its shallows. Or if they escaped early enough in the evening, they would go to their special place in the forest where a bend in the river made a perfect swimming hole and where no one could ever come upon them unawares.

A tightness grew in her throat and pressure burned at the back of her eyes. Andrixine looked at the moon and found it blurring. Something warm trickled down her cheek and she wiped away the tear with surprise.

Perhaps she had been too busy to feel homesick until now. Perhaps the shock of everything that had happened to her was finally wearing away.

Voices. Andrixine moved off her perch, glad for the interruption. She caught movement among the trees further down the bank and her hand strayed to the knife at her belt. A moment later she realized the voices weren't threatening. No one who giggled that way could be a threat, except to sanity.

She stepped back into the shadowy shelter of the nearest tree and watched a young couple run hand in hand down to the water's edge. Both were average village youths, healthy, tanned from outdoor work, barefoot. Beyond that, Andrixine could see few details in the shadows and moonlight. The girl giggled again, setting Andrixine's teeth on edge. She watched them embrace, mouths fastened together as if they helped each other breathe.

She recalled the few times Feril had tried to catch her alone and kiss her. She hadn't liked it. He was always either drunk or trying to impress her with his strength.

Andrixine watched the couple at the water's edge. The girl stopped giggling. They sank to the ground, the girl in the boy's lap. In the night quiet, Andrixine thought she heard soft moans. She took a few steps closer, intrigued, then froze. They indulged in caresses, tugging at each other's clothes.

She was sure it was wrong for them to be so intimate—and wrong for her to watch—but she couldn't seem to turn away. Her breath caught in her throat.

"What would your uncle say?" Kalsan whispered, coming up behind her. He laughed, skipping backwards as she whirled on him, her knife half out of its sheath.

"My uncle—" Andrixine nearly blurted that she hated her Uncle Maxil, but she caught herself. She turned back to the couple by the river. She glimpsed movement, and her heart leaped into her throat as the boy leaned his sweetheart backwards until they lay entwined among the high grass. A vision of Cedes came to her, and she waited for the girl to scream. "He's—"

"Don't you know it's rude to spy on young lovers?" Kalsan took hold of her arm and started leading her away.

"But she—"

"She'd be calling for help by now if she didn't want him," Kalsan said, laughter thickening his voice. "Come on. Do you have a filthy mind and want to watch?" He jerked harder on her arm and quickened his pace.

"Is that really supposed to be..." She couldn't find the right word. "Pleasant?" she hazarded.

"Oh, indeed. You mean you've never..." His eyes sparkled, teasing and yet holding some disbelief.

"I've been too busy to learn about such things," she hurried to say, glad of the darkness of the trees to hide her blush. What about her dreams, she wondered.

"From the length of your braids, that's likely." Kalsan shook his head. "Such a sheltered life for one so skilled. Rather, as skilled as you're reputed to be."

"I can protect myself very well." She smiled at the badgering, sensing the teasing in his words. It was a relief.

"Oh, I don't doubt that," he responded so quickly Andrixine heard challenge in his voice.

"You do doubt me. You think my braids are decoration and nothing more."

"I didn't say that. But if you'd like to prove your skill with me—"

"I accept!" She held out her hand. Kalsan frowned, then closed his eyes and shook his head before accepting her hand.

"You may regret this, young Drixus," he said, no arrogance in his voice, but experience.

"Only if my uncle catches us."

They squared off in the courtyard before the stables. Kalsan went inside long enough to get wooden practice swords. Brenden agreed to act as judge. They backed away from each other ten paces and raised their swords high overhead to signal readiness. Several warriors from their group and a few people from the village gathered as onlookers. Almost everyone else was still dancing. Andrixine wondered for a moment why Kalsan hadn't been among them.

"Begin!" Brenden called, when it felt as if they stood with their arms raised for hours.

Both stepped forward, lowering the swords to shoulder height, eyeing each other, knees bent, balancing on their toes. Andrixine felt her mouth widen to an eager grin to match Kalsan's. This would be interesting, at least.

Instinct saved her shoulder from a nasty bruise. She caught the downward swing of his sword before she could think, spinning away and swinging her own weapon around to smash against his ribs. Kalsan caught it with an awkward sideways upward thrust and pushed her away. He laughed and backed up a few steps. Andrixine met his grin but saved her breath for the next lunge and parry.

She lowered her arms slightly, wondering if she could fool him into relaxing or attacking at the wrong moment. Kalsan stayed still, hands gripping the hilt tighter, his fingers turning white for a moment. Andrixine shifted one foot forward, then skipped back. Kalsan nodded, acknowledging her ploy. He swung wide, leaping back before the blade came near her. She held still, refusing to meet the attack and open herself.

With a shout, she spun on one foot and leaped forward, crouching low. Her sword smacked loudly against his thigh. She let herself fall forward onto her knees and then roll back to her feet again. As she turned, she slapped the back of his knees. A laugh escaped her as she caught the surprise on Kalsan's face. She grunted as his blade came down on her shoulder, glancing off when it didn't hit square.

Kalsan had the strength, the weight of body and leverage of muscle. She had the agility and speed. They were evenly matched. Hit for hit, point for point. Kalsan lost his breath trying to catch her. He seemed not to feel the blows she landed, but her shoulder protested further movement.

"What is going on here?" Brother Klee roared. He pushed his way through the crowd with Jultar right behind him.

"Practice, sir." Kalsan lowered his sword and stepped back. He smirked at Andrixine, daring her to attack.

"Practice?" The scholar sighed, his shoulders relaxing visibly. "Nephew, why can't I leave you alone for more than an hour without someone engaging you in a battle?"

"At least I had a choice this time." Andrixine handed her sword to Kalsan. "It's a pleasure to battle someone who will stop before blood is drawn." Her breathing was almost back to normal.

"Usually your opponent's," was the dry rejoinder. Brother Klee looked them both up and down, then turned to Jultar. "Now that the children have disrupted our talk for the evening, I think some wine would be in order." He gestured toward the inn doorway spilling golden light and music into the courtyard.

"Sound advice." The old warlord nodded. He winked at Andrixine and clapped Kalsan's shoulder before turning to follow.

"You're lucky they stopped you when they did," an onlooker said, raising his voice. "The boy almost had you. A little longer and he might have worn you down."

"I was just warming up," Kalsan retorted. He winked at Andrixine. "Help me put these away?" He balanced the practice swords across his shoulders and turned to go inside.

She followed him into the inn and upstairs. Along the way, similar remarks were thrown at them. She began to wonder just how good he was, that his companions found it amusing she had held up against him.

"Maybe you're falling ill," she suggested.

"Hardly." Kalsan pushed the door open to the room he and three others shared. He looked in, then tossed the swords onto the nearest bed. "It's still too warm to stay inside. Truth be told, I started to worry."

"Over what?" She followed him back down the hallway.

"You're good. You need a little flesh on your bones, build a little muscle, but you're in no danger from anyone overpowering you. Speed is as necessary as strength." He laughed as they headed down the stairs and thumped her on the back. Andrixine let out a yelp and caught at the banister, knocked off balance. "Sorry." He caught her around the waist and held her up until she planted her feet underneath herself.

"I'm sure you are." She forced a laugh. Her heart banged against her ribs and she found it strangely difficult to breathe until he let go of her.

"Ah, I'm falling in the world, no doubt about it. I can't even hold my own against a little boy." He looked around, then leaned closer, lowering his voice. "That's what happens when you get your braids trimmed."

"I wondered," she admitted.

"Not a fair fight at all," Kalsan said, shrugging. She could tell he still writhed inside at the memory, however much he tried to make light of it. "They had to come on me from behind and nearly knock my head off with a rock to do it. I'm still bruised from the blow—more than a week ago it was."

"Were there three?" Andrixine didn't know whether to feel sympathy or laugh. She knew what was coming in his little tale.

"I have no idea." Kalsan looked around as they walked out of the inn yard, heading back toward the river. "I was alone. Someone had been bothering the horses, and I went to quiet them. When I came out of the stables, someone smashed me with a rock. I woke up with my head splitting and one braid trimmed to half its length."

"No clue? Hernon didn't have any advice to help you track the culprits?"

"No, he—How did you know Hernon—Did you run into trouble in Worland's Forge?" Kalsan caught at her arm, stopping her short.

"A little. They thought me an easy target, since I'm just a thin, weak boy." She turned, trying to free herself and saw his face clearly in the moonlight—red from repressed laughter. "They were caught in the act and promptly punished."

"After you were finished with them, no doubt."

"No doubt."

"Drixus, promise me one thing."

"As far as I can."

"Should we encounter any troubles along our journey, fight at my side, will you? Between us—"

"You won't lose the rest of your braids," she interrupted. Kalsan stared a moment, his mouth falling open. Then he burst out laughing.

Chapter Eleven

TWO NIGHTS LATER brought them to another trail house. A band of five men were there already, roughly dressed, their horses badly used and put into the shelter without tending. Instead of greeting the newcomers as tradition demanded, they waited sullenly and silently at the door. No one drew a weapon, but Andrixine saw more than one man shift his stance so sword or knife became visible. Stiffening hairs prickled her neck as she dismounted behind Brother Klee, Jultar and Kalsan.

"Greetings, this fine evening," Jultar called to their leader, who stood with arms crossed a few steps before his men. "We ask the honor of sharing our provisions with you and exchanging news of the road."

"Of course. All are welcome." The man was of medium height, his hair dark and lank, beard unkempt, clothes the soiled remains of once fine fashion, his tone oily smooth. His eyes flicked over their band as they entered the clearing around the trail house. Annoyance touched his face.

Andrixine wondered if he had been sizing them up for an attack, despite trail house law. Maybe not right then, but later at night, after everyone had gone to sleep. She reminded herself to voice her suspicions to Brother Klee—if he had not already noticed the hints of danger.

Brenden and Rogan helped her and Kalsan with the horses, groaning about the length of their day in the saddle and how glad they would be to reach Cereston and stop journeying. She agreed with them but said little, her thoughts busy elsewhere. She was glad when they went indoors and left her and Kalsan to work in companionable silence.

A quick thrill mixed with disappointment touched her as she did a rough calculation of time and distance. Five days to reach Faxinor if nothing slowed them. Five days until she could see her father—admit she had failed—and work with him to find her mother. And only two days until Jultar's band left them to continue down the King's Highway to Cereston.

The joy of reaching home and sharing the burden with her father couldn't dull the pain and sense of failure at not having rescued her mother herself. Andrixine said another prayer for understanding, for increased faith and dedication to Yomnian. If this was a test, preparing her for harder service as the Sword Bearer, she couldn't quite repress a sense of resentment. Couldn't Yomnian have started with something a little less demanding and hard?

"It feels like rain tonight," Kalsan commented as she returned from the spring with another slopping bucket of water.

"Does that mean I shouldn't keep filling the troughs?" she returned, grinning. She dumped the bucket and, turning, got a better look at the wagon belonging to the five strangers. It looked...wrong, somehow.

"If it rains hard enough, we won't have to draw water for washing. We can all strip and dance through the raindrops and come out better all around by morning." Kalsan cocked his head to one side. "You don't like rain, Drixus?"

"Why do you say that?"

"You went pale."

"No, not rain..." She flushed as she caught up mentally with his conversation, then shook her head.

"Something about that wagon?"

"Nothing."

"No, it is something. Tell me." He caught hold of her by an arm and a braid when she would have turned and left. "We're friends, remember? Something bothers you."

"I would tell you—but not here. Listening ears could be dangerous, even in a trail house."

"After supper, then?" He held her until she nodded, then released her so they could continue their chores.

Andrixine worked hard, trying not to follow her thoughts too far. As she worked, her gaze returned to the dingy wagon with the mended left rear wheel. She noted where canopy posts had broken off, the decorative paint scraped away and the cushioned seats ripped out. Andrixine longed to get closer to the wagon, to crawl underneath and search for her father's signet burned into the wood. She didn't need that sign to identify it as her mother's stolen wagon, but others would before they believed her.

All during the meal and cleaning up afterwards, she couldn't get close to Brother Klee to voice her suspicions. Even more frustrating, at dinner she sat next to the man who, in her vision, had fondled Glynnys. Andrixine wanted to slash at his arm when he brushed against her while reaching for the stew pot. Any act of aggression, including an accusation of crime, violated the laws of the trail house. She knew the kidnappers would not hesitate to break those laws if it suited them. Her vows as Bearer of the Spirit Sword and the vows of Jultar's Oathbound warriors kept them from violating those laws. She silently seethed at the unfairness of it.

There were fewer men here than she had seen in her vision. The scarred man who had murdered Cedes was not with them. Was he perhaps somewhere else, maybe guarding her mother and Glynnys?

While the others settled down for the night, she slipped out of the shelter. No one followed. She made sure all members of both bands were inside before she left. Andrixine darted into the bushes around the clearing and watched the doorway. She counted to almost one hundred before the door opened again. Five drops of slowly approaching rain touched her face before Kalsan came out. She waited until he had closed the door, then stepped out of her hiding place and waved. He came silently, watching for spies.

"Now will you tell me? I thought you might fly through the ceiling at dinner." He settled down against the base of a sheltering tree. The rain made tiny tapping sounds on the leaves but wasn't strong enough to penetrate that thin shelter.

"Those men are kidnappers. The wagon belongs to a lady whose party they attacked nearly two weeks ago."

"Proof?" he asked after only a moment of thought. Andrixine breathed a sigh of relief—he didn't doubt her.

"Under the wagon, next to the front right wheel hub, in the exact center of the wagon bed and under the steps at the back are carved the signet of Lord Edrix Faxinor. Three crosses connected at their base. If you check the horses drawing the wagon, you'll find the same sign in the shoes."

"Faxinor? You mentioned Lady Faxinor before." Kalsan shook his head, his face growing troubled. "What is she to you?"

"She...nursed me through my illness at Snowy Mount."

"And that's why you and the Brother travel to Faxinor, to help find her?"

"Mostly." Andrixine wondered if she had really lied. She couldn't confess Lady Arriena was her mother; that would raise questions she couldn't answer.

"If only this were an inn and not a trail house," Kalsan whispered. He swore under his breath. "Jultar has faith in me, so I can witness."

"What are we going to do?"

"I'm not sure yet, little brother." He grinned, grasped Andrixine by her shoulder, shook her once. "We *will* find a way to help the lady."

They waited until past moonrise. Kalsan's prediction of a strong rain failed. The spattering of drops died after a few more minutes and the wisps of clouds melted away before the moon. Andrixine almost wished the clouds had been thicker, to hide their actions. More rain would have been an excuse for taking shelter in the stable if anyone discovered them. She stood watch at the entrance to the crude shelter, little more than a roof and boards haphazardly nailed between the support posts to keep the horses confined. Kalsan went inside. She heard the snorts and nickering of the horses as he checked them first. Then silence, before she heard him grunt as he slid under the wagon.

The gravel hissed as he moved across it, and she winced, imagining his discomfort. They couldn't risk torches; Kalsan had to trust the feel of the carvings under his fingers. The signets were large and deep, specifically to keep them from being carved out of the wood. Anyone who tried would find it necessary to replace portions of the wagon.

"Done," Kalsan whispered, reappearing behind her. He winked and gripped her shoulder. Together, they slipped across the clearing and into the trail house.

Brother Klee and Jultar were awake, talking in low tones before the fire. Two men from the other band sat in silence on their side of the fire. Andrixine was sure they kept watch on the warrior band. She picked her way through the sleepers to her bedroll in the corner. Behind her, she barely heard Kalsan talking to their leaders about their walk in the woods. She knew it was more to soothe the suspicions of the kidnappers than for their own elders. Andrixine envied his quick thinking.

Chapter Twelve

KALSAN'S SLEEP WAS broken into small pieces by odd dreams. He woke after each one to roll over and look for the strangers sleeping among the warrior band. Once, he woke with images of Drixus still before his eyes, racing after the kidnappers with a sword that blazed brighter than the sun. He checked for Drixus before he looked for the other men.

Why, he wondered, was he plagued with dreams like that and never granted a vision that would give him direction? He wanted Yomnian to send him a mission in life, something he could be proud of, something to dedicate his entire life to.

The first grayish light of false dawn peeked through the gaps in the wall and thatching when Kalsan woke from a misty dream of the sword maiden. She looked at him with Drixus' eyes. Kalsan took a deep, shuddering breath, enjoying the longing even as it frustrated him. Would he ever find her? And why did she have Drixus' eyes?

Then he remembered his restless night. In the dim gray light, the empty spaces on the floor were easy to see. His heart thumped loudly as he rolled over and untangled his blankets from his limbs. Kalsan looked to the corner where Drixus slept beyond the shelter of his uncle's broad back. The boy was still there. Kalsan crept through the warriors to Jultar's side. Several men twitched in their sleep but no one leaped after him or shouted an alarm. He wondered if there had been a drug in the food, to keep seasoned warriors asleep while the kidnappers fled. He supposed he ought to be glad they hadn't had their throats slit while they slept. He touched the floor where one of the kidnappers had slept, and the wood was still warm.

Jultar came awake the moment Kalsan touched his shoulder. His voice low and soft, watching the small, dark shadow of Drixus, Kalsan told the warlord what they had seen and done the night before. He finished by gesturing around the trail house.

"A chase!" Jultar called, pushing himself to his feet. The warriors rolled from their blankets, reaching for swords, mumbling but making no other sounds. Their steadiness and speed assured Kalsan that if there had been drugs in their food, the effects had been slept away.

Drixus went white when he heard the news. Kalsan worried the boy might be sick, then he saw the pained look Drixus shared with Brother Klee. He wasn't afraid, but angry. What lay between Lady Faxinor and him that the boy took her kidnapping so deeply?

"I should have done something last night," Drixus said as Kalsan joined him and his uncle.

"Because others violate the law is no justification to do the same. Especially us," Brother Klee said, grasping his nephew's shoulder. Drixus went a little paler. Kalsan couldn't understand the silent communication between the two. "It was well done, though," the holy man continued. "You noticed more than I, last night. We will have answers by noontime."

"And revenge?" Drixus asked, his voice a harsh croak.

"Justice, nephew. Justice."

The chase took less than half an hour. Kalsan was grateful for his restless sleep, though his head ached from weariness and his eyes were gritty. The kidnappers only had a small lead, made smaller by the pace of their damaged wagon, and Jultar's men were experienced trackers. The warriors mounted their horses and ate bread and cheese in the saddle, passing wine skins between their trotting horses as they rode.

Brenden and five others rode ahead when the trail branched, to circle around the fleeing kidnappers. Kalsan wished he could have gone with them. Then he looked at Drixus riding next to him, pale and tight-lipped with fury burning in his young eyes. He knew his place was next to his young friend—to control him, if necessary.

The trail through the forest soon grew wide enough for three mounted men to ride side by side without jostling each other. Jultar and Brother Klee led a few steps ahead of Kalsan, Drixus, and the last two warriors. Drixus stared at the trail, intent as if he alone could find the clues to lead them to their quarry. Kalsan felt sorry for the boy. He wished he knew the words to say to help him.

He spotted Brenden waiting at the end of a long, straight stretch of the trail, just where it began to curve. The man waved to them, then turned his horse and rode into the forest, nearly disappearing from sight. Jultar looked back over his shoulder, signaling them to slow. Kalsan grinned at the impatience that put a flush in Drixus' white cheeks, but the boy did obey.

The river ran near the trail, and there was a wide, clear space not far into the trees along the bank. The wagon and the kidnappers waited, their faces as sullen as the night before. The six men who had captured them sat their horses, swords and crossbows at the ready. Jultar rode through the loose ring of guards and dismounted. Brother Klee signaled

Drixus, and they stopped their horses at the edge of the trees to dismount. Kalsan followed, watching the captured men more than his friend.

"The noble warlord shows his true colors," the leader of the kidnappers called as they approached.

"Justice is my goal, friend," Jultar responded with a calm voice.

"Justice?" The man spat. "You used the sanctity of the trail house to spy on us and prepare to attack us once we were on the road again."

"Why are you so upset?" Brother Klee asked, his voice dropping to a calm that prickled the hair on Kalsan's neck. The leader blanched. "Were you planning to ambush us along the way, with your cart so conveniently hidden? Are you angry because your plan was found out?"

"We wished to speak with you this morning," Jultar continued, stepping closer, his hand on the hilt of his sword. "When we found you had left so early and with such quiet care, our suspicions were aroused. Can you blame us?"

"We are here. What is it you wish to say?" the man responded stiffly after a long silence.

"Boy." Jultar turned, beckoning for Drixus to come forward. "Kalsan has told me your accusation and what he found. Speak."

"I accuse these men of attacking the party of Lady Faxinor as she journeyed home from Snowy Mount. I accuse them of raping and murdering her servants and kidnapping her. My proof lies in the presence of her wagon and horses. All bear the signet of Lord Edrix Faxinor."

"Signet?" The bandit leader laughed but it was a choking, sickly sound. "What signet? Look at the wagon. See how dirty and broken down it is. How could it be a noble lady's wagon?"

"The dirt is recent. If we washed it, we would find good wood underneath." Kalsan stepped forward. "The signet is deeply cut into the wood underneath the wagon in three places. The mark is part of the horses' shoes."

The leader spun, lashing out with his fist so it filled Kalsan's vision. He ducked and swung at the man. But he was gone, rolling under the wagon to escape. Brenden and Marfil darted to the other side of the wagon before the ruffian could scramble to his feet. They caught and lifted him by his arms, suspending him off the ground between them. His men tried to break and run. Swords and drawn bows met them. Two pitched headfirst into the dirt, an arrow in the calf of one, a crossbow bolt in the thigh of the other.

"Running indicates guilt, wouldn't you say, Brother Klee?" Jultar wiped his hands against the sides of his shirt, turning in a leisurely fashion to the holy man.

"Indeed. Careful questioning would be in order." Brother Klee nodded. "I want to know the whereabouts of Lady Arriena and her maidservant, Glynnys."

"We never saw them," the leader rasped. He grunted, baring his teeth as the two men holding his arms shook him.

"Witnesses saw them in your company, fixing that wheel," Drixus said, pointing. "It was at the marker along the Soshan Trail, showing where the village of Hesteros the Sword Bearer used to be." He stepped closer to the man, nose wrinkling. Kalsan grinned, knowing the boy smelled the stink of fear. "Where are they?"

"I don't—" He stopped as Drixus whipped a knife from his belt and pressed it against his throat. He stared into the boy's eyes and went white as a corpse. "Morstontown. Waiting ransom."

"Morstontown is south of here, less than a day's ride," Jultar said, voice soft, smiling. "You just left them there? They won't expect you for several weeks, perhaps?" His smile faded as the bandit leader nodded, still staring at Drixus.

At Jultar's signal, the men released their captive. He fell to his knees with another grunt and a moan. Rubbing his shoulders, he struggled to sit up. New fear gripped him as Brother Klee approached, drawing his sword. Before the man could retreat, the tip of the blade rested at his throat.

"Friend, there is more information we need. What were your orders in the attack on the inn? Who hired you?" He kept his voice light, almost genial.

"No one," another man in the group shouted, angry pride in his voice. "We work for no man!"

"Why did you take the innkeeper and his wife with you, and then kill them and take back their share of the payment?" Brother Klee continued, the sword never wavering.

"Everybody died except the lady and her screaming maid," the leader mumbled, never taking his eyes off the sword.

"That's a lie." Drixus dug in the pouch at his belt. "I found the bodies of the innkeeper and his wife the next day along the road to Snowy Mount. Who would take dead bodies with them? They showed no sign of struggle, cut down by friends. I found this coin under their bodies." He held out a gold coin, and the bandit leader's eyes widened. "You were in too much of a hurry to count the coins, weren't you?"

"No innkeeper would have gold coins like that. Even the rich pay in coppers and silver tenths when traveling through country like this," Jultar observed. He joined Brother Klee before the kneeling bandit. The sword began to flick idly back and forth across the man's chest, moving aside his ragged shirt without cutting anything.

"We were paid by a scholarly man," the cowed bandit blurted. "Tall. Red hair. Long nose like a carrot. He had two bags of gold coins and gave us one when we agreed to do it. He told us when Lady Arriena was ransomed home and the deaths of the dark-haired maidens confirmed, we would get the other bag."

"Dark-haired?" Drixus' voice broke. "You had orders to kill *all* the maidens with dark hair?" Tears touched his eyes, startling Kalsan. "Were you told how many traveled with the lady?"

"Two maids, one blonde, the other dark. Two grooms—they were to die as well. A child with red hair. And the lady's dark-haired daughter. We were told to be careful of her, as she could handle a sword."

"Were you ordered to torture them as well?" the boy grated, his voice ready to break.

"Drixus, go to your horse," Brother Klee ordered, grasping the boy's shoulder when he would have shaken the fallen bandit. He met the boy's eyes, compassion and a stern light fighting down any protest. Nodding, Drixus stumbled out of the clearing. Kalsan followed.

The boy wrapped his arms around the pommel of Grennel's saddle, hiding his face against the warm leather. Through the trees, Kalsan heard the rumble of Brother Klee's and Jultar's voices. He touched the boy's shoulder and instantly faced a knife. Tears made Drixus' cheeks glisten in the morning light.

"Peace!" Kalsan stepped back, hands up. He tried to smile. Drixus stared for a few seconds, then blushed.

"Sorry," he muttered. He looked at the knife a long moment, then re-sheathed it.

"It's all right. You were there, weren't you? You saw the raid and you couldn't do anything about it."

"I had Alysyn to take care of—the lady's youngest daughter. She's only four. When I got back to the inn, everyone was gone. I had to make sure she was safe before I could do anything!"

"So, where is she now?"

"At Snowy Mount. I had to come look for Lady Arriena before I could be sure it was safe to send Alysyn home."

"You were going to rescue her all by yourself?" Kalsan whistled.

He grinned, liking the determination filling the boy, even if the plan was foolhardy.

"With Brother Klee's help, of course." Drixus sputtered a chuckle. He leaned back against his stallion and wiped at his eyes and cheeks. His breath caught in a gasp. "Kalsan, I know who is responsible. I suspected before, but now I know."

"Who is the man who hired them?" Brother Klee asked as he and Jultar joined them by the horses.

"His seneschal. I've been to his home often. I know the seneschal too well." He took a deep breath, trying to smile. "He tried to poison the heir. He failed, so his seneschal hired mercenaries to wipe out the traveling party. With the fire and the confusion in the middle of the night, it would look like an accident that the heir had been killed. Especially if she tried to protect her mother and sister."

"Who?" Kalsan asked.

"Maxil of Faxinor, Lord Edrix's younger brother. He wanted m— my lady, the heir to marry his son. He probably planned to kill her after birthing her heir, making Feril regent." Drixus trembled, though his voice was strangely calm.

"But he didn't know you would be at the inn, as a witness," Jultar said.

"No, he didn't. He never did know what to do with me." Drixus took a deep breath. "What do we do with them?"

"What else?" Brother Klee said, smiling softly. "I have a friend in Maskin's Forge, between here and Morstontown. One of the king's judges. He can hold our prisoners while we go on to Morstontown and rescue Lady Arriena."

"Truly?" Drixus whispered. His eyes glowed. For a moment, Kalsan thought the boy would throw his arms around Brother Klee and kiss him.

His stomach dropped, creating a hollow sensation in his middle as a new thought came to him.

What if—no, it couldn't be. Kalsan mentally slapped himself for such wild imagining. He hadn't had enough sleep, that was all. Just because Drixus moved with grace and looked delicate because of his long illness was no reason to think...

"Let's get going," Kalsan said, and stepped over to mount Fala. "I want to sleep in a real bed tonight."

The others laughed, including Drixus. His heart skipped a beat as the image of his dream maiden covered the boy's face.

What is wrong with me? Kalsan wondered. He forced himself to think of the name of the tavern girl in Morstontown who gave such sweet kisses. That was the cure for his strange thoughts.

Chapter Thirteen

"YOU LOOK LIKE someone just cut your braids," Brenden said as Kalsan returned to the small table they shared with Andrixine.

"Women," the young man muttered. He gave them a lopsided grin and slung himself into his chair.

Around them, the noise of a busy tavern late in the afternoon increased. Andrixine contemplated her friend for another moment, decided he would not speak his problem yet and looked around. Everyone wore their holiday best. Brightly colored vests and skirts, snowy shirts and embroidered knife sheaths.

"I know I haven't lost track of time, so it can't be a holy day," she said, jerking a thumb over her shoulder to indicate the happy, noisy crowd. Andrixine delighted in using the gesture. Her mother never permitted her brothers to use it at the table.

"Some sort of local festival, then," Brenden said. His grin widened, and he leaned closer to Kalsan. "So? What's with Lerissa? Did this one demand marriage?"

"Worse." Kalsan took a sip from the tankard the three shared and sat back. "What's taking our masters so long?"

"If it's festival, the outlying farmers are in town too. Which means inn rooms or even a stable corner are all at premium." He thumped the table. "Spill, lad!"

"Brenden, if he's having sweetheart trouble, maybe he doesn't want to talk about it," Andrixine said. She shrugged and tried to fight down a queasy feeling.

Kalsan, it seemed, had made sweethearts in nearly every village they passed through on their outward journey to Sendorland. Coming back along the same route, he had been visiting the girls and renewing acquaintances. Or trying to. There seemed to be some trouble, and from idle comments the others made, the trouble seemed to be all on Kalsan's side. Andrixine didn't like the feelings such talk gave her. Kalsan spent less time courting in each village they came to, and she had been oddly pleased. Now, it looked like he had been waiting for a specific maiden—and the maiden had betrayed him. Andrixine didn't understand her feelings, part sympathy, part disappointment, part nasty delight.

"It's two years since we passed through," the older man said, shaking his head and grinning. He took a long swallow from the tankard and set it down with a thump. "You didn't leave her with a baby, did you?"

"Bren, you know I wouldn't—I'm not like that. A few kisses in the dark, and that's where I stop. I may not be Oathbound like you, but I do know what's right and wrong."

"Sorry, lad," the older man said, his grin fading. "I do know you better than that." He waited until Kalsan nodded, accepting the apology. The twinkle returned to his eyes. "So, what is it?"

Kalsan's face flushed. "She's married."

"Poor Kalsan. A broken heart."

"No, it's something else," Andrixine said, listening to the sensitivity the sword taught her. She met Kalsan's gaze until her friend relaxed a little. He nodded.

"She was very...happy to see me. Hugged me, led me over to a dark corner to talk. I didn't see her marriage band until it slid from her sleeve." Kalsan took a deep breath. His voice shook a little, and Andrixine knew they were coming to the seat of the problem. "She wanted to go sparking. I saw the band and asked. She admitted she was married and three months gone with child—then went right on talking about meeting me."

"That bothers you." The strength of the relief she felt surprised her.

"She took vows." His voice dropped to a hissing whisper. "It's one thing to go sparking with a girl who isn't promised. It's another to help her break her vows. I won't."

"Some wouldn't hesitate," Brenden said.

"I'm not one of them." Kalsan took a deep breath and leaned back in his chair. "I might marry. I've had dreams..." He shook his head. "How can I ask my wife to stay faithful if I helped another man's wife break her vows?"

"You look like you're having a philosophical discussion," Brother Klee said, reaching their table.

"Have you been able to find rooms, Brother?" Brenden asked, standing.

"A rumor of rooms. The inn of the Hawk & Bells has several rooms, saved for merchants who won't arrive. The tavern keeper has given us a token to persuade the innkeeper, his brother-in-law, to give them to us. If someone else does not persuade him first. Come, we must be going."

Andrixine made sure she walked with Kalsan as they left the crowded tavern. He gave her a lopsided smile.

"Are you sure you're all right?" she asked as quietly as the noisy conditions allowed.

"Now I am. Maybe I just needed to talk it out." He clapped his hand on her shoulder. "You looked a little surprised."

"I've heard you were rather...free with your courting," she admitted.

"I wasn't so careful two years ago, but Master Jultar has taught me much since we last came through here. I might never be Oathbound, but that's no reason to act without honor, is it?"

Andrixine shook her head, smiling a little. They stepped outside and found their horses. She could spare little thought now for anything but maneuvering through the crowds.

The noise in the central square of Morstontown grew deafening, ringing and echoing off buildings and cobblestones. Andrixine wished she could press her hands over her ears, but she needed both on the reins to guide Grennel through the open spaces that appeared and disappeared in an unpredictable rhythm among the milling crowd. The stallion was steady, only twitching his ears in protest, but she couldn't be sure he would remain so. If revelers came too close to his hooves, perhaps lunged at him as they lost their footing, she had to be able to control him.

Jultar and Brother Klee led the way, almost out of sight around the roof of the town well. Brenden and two others rode in a knot ten feet from Andrixine and Kalsan. Their other companions were nearly to the far edge of the square.

"Once we cross the square, it will be better," Kalsan shouted, though he was so close their knees brushed. He rolled his eyes in mock agony. Andrixine laughed.

She glanced to her right, sensing a gap about to open and hoping to turn Grennel and get through before another barrier of sweetmeat and trinket vendors formed. A dark-bearded man in leathers pushed into the gap one step ahead of her. He smirked at her as she checked Grennel. Andrixine stared into his face.

A long scar ran from his temple, down to his jaw and along it. She knew that scar—twisted in a filthy grin as he got down on his knees to violate Cedes.

Andrixine reached for her sword even as the man frowned and stared at her. She urged Grennel closer, though a sweetmeat vendor clutched at her stirrup and begged her to look at the wares on his tray.

The rapist fled, pushing through the crowd. Mounted, Andrixine couldn't follow without trampling people.

"Drixus?" Kalsan leaned closer. "What is it?"

"It's one of them." She stood in her stirrups and tried to see over the milling crowd. In just two seconds of distraction, she had lost the man.

"What are you doing?" he blurted when she tried to wheel Grennel to move through a gap that didn't exist. Kalsan reached for her arm.

Andrixine had her knife out, slashing at him before she could think. She stared at his white face, the hard line of his mouth, the shock in his eyes. Her hand trembled. She pricked her thigh as she slid the knife into its sheath.

"Nephew?" Brother Klee somehow managed to get through the crowd without hurting anyone. Andrixine wondered if the sword could help her do that. "What is it?"

"The one who killed Cedes, he—" She lost the words and could only point helplessly through the crowd.

Slowly he nodded, staring into her eyes. The puzzled lines around eyes and forehead smoothed. She felt some reassurance—but why did they sit still when they should be chasing the man?

"Come. We're almost to the inn." He took the reins from her hands and quelled her protest with a stern look.

Andrixine shuddered at the thought of what she had almost done. Kalsan was her friend. The thought of hurting him made her feel sick. She hunched her shoulders and concentrated on Grennel's mane as Brother Klee led her through the crowds to the inn. She knew she should scan the crowds for the other men who might lead her to her mother's prison. They were so close! She closed her eyes, feeling hollow with strain when she spotted the banner marking the inn of the Hawk & Bells.

"Wine for the boy," Jultar ordered, standing at the doorway of the inn as she and Brother Klee rode up.

"I'm all right," she protested, embarrassment cutting through the emotions tumbling inside her.

"No, you are not." Brother Klee dismounted and handed Grennel's reins back to her. "You've had a shock."

"Shock, nothing!" Andrixine took the reins, tempted for a moment to turn the stallion and give chase. The scholar's stern look quelled that idea. Legs shaking, she dismounted.

"What was it?" Kalsan demanded as they moved into the inn's

main room.

In surprising contrast to the town square only one street away, the interior of the inn was dark, cool and relatively deserted. Andrixine supposed everyone was outside enjoying the festival.

Brother Klee pushed her down into the nearest chair, pulled out the chair opposite her and sat. He glanced over his shoulder at the few other occupants of the room. The people talked loudly, thumping tankards on their tables for service.

Brenden brought the wine. Jultar and Kalsan settled at the table with them, and the other members of the band left them alone. Andrixine found her hand shook a little when Brother Klee poured the first cup and handed it to her. She took a sip, then haltingly explained what she had seen. She met Kalsan's eyes as she told of seeing the men raping Cedes, how she had fought one man while the other murdered the girl and escaped. The shame in Kalsan's eyes startled her, but suddenly she felt better.

"I saw him," Kalsan said, giving them a tight smile. "It shouldn't be so hard finding a man that ugly, even among the crowds here."

"I suspect they brought Lady Arriena here just so they could vanish among the festivities and crowds," Brother Klee said. "Your priorities need refining, nephew."

"My priorities?" Her voice squeaked in indignation.

"Racing off after one man could lead you into ambush. What could you do on your own?"

"I'm not alone," Andrixine insisted. "I have—" She stopped short, feeling suddenly cold. She wished she had bitten her tongue off even if she hadn't mentioned the Spirit Sword. Looking at her cup, she concentrated on the pale pink wine to avoid the disappointment she imagined in Brother Klee's eyes.

"I would have been right behind you," Kalsan said. "Even the two of us might not have been enough if he had friends waiting around a corner." He clouted Andrixine on the shoulder, startling her. "You can't save every lady in distress by yourself."

"No, I can't," she whispered, remembering how she had hesitated, how her mistakes had let Cedes be killed, how she had been too late to protect her mother.

KALSAN THOUGHT HE understood how Drixus felt, having seen and then lost a man who could have led them straight to Lady Faxinor. He kept reliving that moment when he had grabbed the boy's arm and almost got his hand cut open. The fury he had seen in that young face chilled him. Kalsan sensed something behind the need for vengeance. Something personal and painful.

And what about those moments when he looked at the boy and saw the maiden from his dreams? Was he going mad?

The important thing, Kalsan reminded himself, was that he was Drixus' friend and liked the boy too much to let those odd moments come between them.

Night had fallen by the time their band had its supper, and the crowds filling the town wouldn't allow for searching. The inn's dining room was too noisy to allow discussion of strategy, and the one room all twelve shared was too stifling in the heat. Brother Klee and Jultar vanished somewhere to talk, and the other members of the band drifted off to the festivities. Kalsan wanted to go too, but he couldn't leave Drixus alone. The partial insights from that morning kept nibbling at Kalsan's thoughts. There was a puzzle he was close to solving. It galled him that he had all the pieces but could not fit them together.

What he had to do was find his young friend and try to help him. Just because he was losing his grasp on sanity was no reason to abandon a friend.

"We're not going anywhere for several days, and I doubt the kidnappers are either," Kalsan said, finding Drixus standing at the stable door, watching the busy inn courtyard.

"I hope not," was the sullen reply.

In the shadows, Kalsan could hardly see the boy's face. Drixus' voice struck him wrong. Despite being rough from adolescence, it had a hint of sweetness. It belonged to the gentle lines of the boy's face, the grace of his movements. Kalsan fought an urge to turn and run.

And what if Drixus *were* a maiden, dressed as a boy? Did that really change anything between them?

Kalsan pushed that thought down before he could even start to think of an answer.

"Let's take a walk. Cool off, stay away from the crowds." He gestured into the darkness toward the hints of moonlight on water. The festivities centered in town; no torches or tables or dancing rings lined the riverbank.

Drixus shrugged and nodded and let Kalsan lead the way. He said nothing, but Kalsan thought some sullen restlessness faded. They passed through a ragged line of bushes and trees between town and river. A tiny, steady spot of light far downriver showed where the mill stood, a massive, squat blot of darkness with a single lantern in its window.

Walking wasn't enough, Kalsan realized. What good would the night quiet do if his friend's thoughts kept going back to that moment in the crowd? He had to raise the boy's spirits.

He grinned when the idea came to him. It helped that he had toyed with it already, but he had hesitated because he didn't know what Drixus' reactions would be to the suggestion.

"Drixus, would you be oath-friends?" he asked, one hand already going to his knife.

"Oath-friends?" The boy's voice cracked. He smiled, face pale in the moonlight. "No one ever asked me before."

"My life for yours." Kalsan drew his knife and held out his hand, ready to draw the few drops of blood to seal the pledge binding their souls together in honor and Yomnian's service.

"No." Drixus' eyes looked like they would tear in a moment. "You can't pledge to me. There are secrets between us."

"Such as?" Kalsan could barely hear the boy's soft voice through the sudden thudding of his heart.

"I am not what I seem."

"Well, I already guessed Brother Klee is not your uncle."

"Subterfuge, to protect my life." A sheepish smile caught Drixus' lips for a moment. He—maybe she?—looked at the ground and twisted his fingers together.

Kalsan gasped as the pieces suddenly locked together. "You're the heir—Lady Arriena's daughter—you weren't killed. No wonder you nearly stabbed me!" He laughed, the sound echoing off the trees and the water. Both he and Drixus—what was her real name?—flinched at the sound.

"Please forgive me, Kalsan," she whispered.

"No, you should forgive me." He held out both hands, one palm up and the other with the knife blade ready to draw the blood for the oath. "Lady Faxinor, you are a warrior born and I would be proud to be your oath-friend."

Her head jerked up and her eyes widened, bright with tears even as an incredulous smile lit her face. Kalsan's heart skipped a few beats. He couldn't believe he had been so blind, not to see the lovely maiden behind the facade of the boy.

"Kalsan—"

"Could I know your name before we pledge?" he whispered, glancing around as if hiding a terrible secret. She laughed as he had hoped and wiped her eyes with the heel of one hand.

"Andrixine."

"Andrixine, heir of Faxinor, will you let this warrior pledge to be oath-friends with you?"

"I would like to be oath-friends with you, Kalsan of Hestrin. Very much. But another secret stands between us."

"Your betrothed husband won't like it?"

"I'm not betrothed. I would give half of Faxinor to avoid marriage." Her voice cracked and broke.

Kalsan flinched, remembering what she had told them of seeing her maid raped.

"I swear I don't care what secrets you carry. I don't want to know them until you are free to tell me. I will give my life to protect you from unwanted husbands. I'll swear that without an oath-friends vow," he added, lowering his voice.

She stared into his eyes as if she could see into his soul and read his resolve and the truth of his words. Her lips trembled, as if she wanted to speak words she feared to release. There was fear and longing in her eyes. Kalsan wanted to wrap his arms around her and let her cry until everything turned right again, like he used to hold his sisters. But she wasn't a village girl, free to kiss and flirt. She was a trained warrior, the heir of her father's estates. Even though he had noble blood, too, she was many steps above him.

"May Yomnian forgive me if we vow wrongly, but I need this," she whispered. "I will tell you the secret as soon as I can, and I pray you are not angry with me." She nodded and swallowed hard and held out her hand. "My life for yours, Kalsan of Hestrin."

"My life for yours, Andrixine Faxinor." He took his knife and gently ran it across the heel of his hand, nowhere near sensitive veins or where it would interfere with his grip on sword and bow. "Your battles and quests are mine, and mine are yours." He held out his hand, the thin line of blood gleaming dark.

Andrixine smiled, even as a tear finally dripped from one corner of her eye. "Kalsan, you may not like what you're getting into." Shaking her head, she held out her hand for him to make the cut instead of taking the knife to do it herself.

Kalsan swallowed hard, unnerved by the trust implied in that simple gesture. He made the cut and Andrixine repeated the oath. They clasped hands, holding their cuts together until the blood dried sticky between them. The moon seemed suddenly brighter, and the sounds of festivities faded, as if they had stepped into another country with the sealing of their oath.

When they released each other, Kalsan felt awkward. There was something about this moment, the quiet, the moonlight—it hinted at dreams he only half-remembered. They resumed their walk in silence. He glanced at Andrixine twice, and she seemed as unnerved as Kalsan felt. That, in return, made him grin.

"It's lovely out here," she said, her voice cracking. "Places like this make it hard—" She shrugged.

In the moonlight reflected on the water, her face was a little more visible. Softer, more rounded. Kalsan nearly laughed at himself, wondering why he had not seen the woman in her before.

"Hard?" he said, and cleared his throat. He had to fasten on her words to avoid the odd thoughts that pounced on him.

"Hard to believe war is waiting."

"The common people of Sendorland don't want to believe, either. The soldiers and merchants and nobles know."

"Always the nobles," Andrixine whispered. "Kalsan, how long would it take to wake Reshor if—"

"If what?" He tensed when she glanced over his shoulder.

"We're being followed," she whispered. "If the Sword Bearer appears," she continued in a louder voice, "how long do you think it will take to rouse the people?"

"The Sword Bearer?" Kalsan shook his head. He strained his ears to hear. How did she know someone followed? "I don't know if the Spirit Sword still exists." He loosened his knife in its sheath and wished he had worn a sword. "Who did Rakleer pass it to before he vanished? Or did Yomnian take back the Sword? No one knows, it's been so long."

"There's a—"

Four men pounced from the bushes to their right. Kalsan grabbed at Andrixine, jerking her out of the line of attack. He drew his knife and slashed at the closest man. She drew her own belt knife and pressed one foot against Kalsan's, so they could keep track of each other in the fight. They held their ground as the men dove in. Someone grabbed his arm, almost yanking him off balance. Kalsan turned, and suddenly there was someone between him and Andrixine. Fury gave him speed. He refused to have his oath broken so soon after making it.

Andrixine let out a yelp as one man blooded her. Kalsan spun, slashing. He saw the long swipe of blood and sliced shirt across her back. Then she turned, fending off another man. Kalsan stabbed the man who had wounded her.

Kalsan recognized the man Andrixine had tried to follow that afternoon. The ruffian grinned, raising his sword high and sidestepped out of Kalsan's reach.

"Andrix—" Kalsan felt a sudden flash of heat, like a fire had ignited. All the air vanished from the river clearing for half a second. Bright light illuminated them so their six shadows stood out in stark black relief.

"Beware," he finished, turning. He nearly dropped his knife when he saw the long, blazing sword raised high in Andrixine's hands. The same light flared in her eyes.

Andrixine leaped, the sword lighting the way before her. The scarred man dropped his sword and ran. Kalsan dove and scooped up the sword and leaped to his feet, slashing out and up at the next man who came after him. Behind him, he heard a man's choked scream, abruptly cut off.

Fire raced up his arm as the third man drew blood. Kalsan ducked and dropped to one knee and flung himself upward, putting all his weight into his sword. He caught the man just under the juncture of his ribs. The ruffian fell with his mouth wide open in surprise. Rancid breath gushed from his mouth, followed by a spout of blood. He went to his knees. Kalsan jerked his sword free, and the dead man fell sideways.

The fourth man darted past Kalsan, an unmanly shriek erupting from his mouth. Andrixine chased him, sword blazing. Kalsan's mouth fell open as he watched her leap over a rock to land directly in the man's path. The shrieking man brought up his sword, desperation clear on his sweaty face.

Kalsan didn't have a chance to watch. He flung himself on the first man, who slashed and lunged and kicked up dirt in desperation ploys.

"Hold him!" a man shouted. Torchlight spilled into the clearing. Running footsteps pounded in rhythm with Kalsan's heart.

He felt an instant of furious despair, thinking more ruffians had fallen on them. Then he recognized Jultar's voice. Brenden and Marfil appeared on either side, swords at ready. His opponent went pale in the torchlight.

"Do you surrender, or do we let the boy have you?" Brenden asked. The remaining man dropped his sword with a loud clang.

"Drixus?" Brother Klee called, entering the clearing at a pace that made his scholar's robes fly.

"Uncle," Andrixine nearly whispered, yet her voice was clear enough to be heard anywhere.

Kalsan turned to see her kneeling, holding the sword across her knees. The gleam and fire had vanished from the metal. She looked as pale as the prisoner. She stared, mouth working soundlessly for a few seconds.

"It came to me," she finally said.

"Of course. It protects its own," the holy man replied, a touch of laughter and exasperation breaking through the concern thickening his voice.

"Are you all right?" Kalsan asked and dropped to his knees next to her. He wanted to put an arm around her to support her. What if after all this she was the fainting type? That thought made him want to laugh for a moment.

"Yes." Her gaze shifted to Kalsan's arm. "You're hurt!"

"No more than you, nephew," the holy man said, kneeling at her other side.

Behind him, Brenden and Marfil dragged away the man, leaving Jultar and Brother Klee alone with the two. Alone, besides the dead bodies.

"That's a nasty slash, lad," Jultar said, stepping over behind Andrixine. He dropped to one knee and caught at the top and bottom halves of Andrixine's slashed shirt. "Let's get that off and—"

"No, Master!" Kalsan shouted, and leaped at the warlord, knocking him on his rump.

Jultar held on as he fell, mouth open in shock, the shirttail clutched in his hand. Andrixine yelped and twisted aside, revealing a bare, slim back and bloody strips of cloth falling away from around her chest. Brother Klee leaped to his feet, flinging off his outer cloak to wrap around her.

"She's a girl," Kalsan finished in a near-whisper, and put himself between his master and Andrixine, as if Jultar could see through Brother Klee's cloak.

Jultar nodded slowly, staring at Andrixine. "I can...see that." He swallowed hard. "Forgive me, lady, for insult to your modesty."

Kalsan felt a single burst of fury. What had his master seen? Then he realized the idiocy of the situation. He had struck Jultar, his master, who was like a father to him. The amazing thing was that Yomnian had not struck him dead for the sacrilege. An urge to laugh choked him.

"Who are you?" Jultar asked.

"Who do you think she is?" Brother Klee returned.

"I know that sword." He gestured at the sword lying neglected in the dirt.

"From where, Master?" Kalsan asked. He gladly focused his

attention on the sword to push the other considerations from his mind. Stooping, he reached for the sword to pick it up.

"Kalsan—" Jultar stopped, his mouth comically hanging open, one hand out as if to stop him.

"Master?" Kalsan froze in the act of handing him the sword. Seeing the uncharacteristic fear in the warlord's face, he handed it to Brother Klee.

"Didn't I teach you properly?" Jultar whispered. His gaze stayed on the sword. "Didn't I teach you to know the Spirit Sword if you should ever see it?"

"The Spirit Sword?" Kalsan clenched his fists, feeling a ghost of fire in his flesh. "Why didn't it burn me?"

"You are my oath-friend," Andrixine whispered. She tried to smile.

"Ah. That explains something." Brother Klee nodded to Kalsan, who had the sudden sense the holy man approved. He rested the blade in the crook of his arm, against his sleeve.

"Then you are the Sword Bearer," Jultar said. "Klee is short for Rakleer?"

"Rakleer, yes, but I am not the Bearer." Brother Klee turned to Andrixine.

"That's the other secret?" Kalsan blurted. Pride washed over him, glad that he had vowed to her before knowing. She had to know that he was a true friend, not a glory-seeker. He had vowed to *her*, not to the sword.

Andrixine nodded, bestowing a tight smile on him, and wrapped the cloak a little tighter around her shoulders.

"Lady, who are you?" Jultar asked. He dropped to one knee before her and held up both hands, palms pressed together. "Let me pledge myself to the Bearer and the Spirit Sword."

"Please, Lord Jultar..." She cast a pleading look at Brother Klee. It wrung at Kalsan's heart. Woman grown she might be and chosen by the Spirit Sword, but she was still unsettled by all this.

"Can't we do this later?" Kalsan interrupted. "She's bleeding." He had to concentrate on his duties as her oath-friend.

"Indeed she is," Brother Klee said. "Since she is the Bearer, the sword shall care for its own."

"WE DON'T HAVE time for more conventional healing," Brother Klee said, raising the sword.

Andrixine closed her eyes, nodded, and gripped the posts of the bed. They were alone in the room their band had taken for the night. Brother Klee had washed her wound, a long, shallow, burning cut across the small of her back. Now, she stretched out on her stomach and waited for the drastic healing he promised.

Through her closed eyelids, she still saw light blaze from the sword. Heat tongues licked at and stung her seeping wound. Andrixine bit her lips against crying out.

"Endure a moment more, daughter," Brother Klee whispered. He laid the flat of the sword along the wound.

Ice touched her savaged flesh and raced up her spine and down, spiraling through her guts. Andrixine gasped, and her breath caught in her lungs.

"Finished." Brother Klee draped a blanket over her and turned to slide the Spirit Sword back into its scabbard.

Andrixine sat up, trembling, and tugged off the ruined shirt. She gathered the blanket around herself and reached for the fresh breast-bands draped over the headboard.

"What do we do now?" she asked as she wound the bands into place.

"We rescue your mother, of course." Brother Klee brought her a clean shirt. "Jultar is telling his men. It is best they know the truth."

"Yes, I suppose so." She struggled to put the shirt on under the blanket. Standing, she let the blanket fall and finished lacing her shirt closed. "All right," she said, and walked over to the single window in the long, stuffy room. It commanded a view of the river.

The warriors shuffled into the room, all eyes on her. Andrixine didn't know whether to laugh or cry over the change. Only two hours before they had been teasing her, yanking on a braid or nudging her aside or towering over her—treating her as a little brother, with affectionate roughness.

"It is sheathed and hidden again," she said, when she noticed a few sets of eyes searching the shadows.

"Sword Bearer," Jultar said, "may we ask your name?"

"Warlord Jultar of Rayeen," Brother Klee said, moving up to join them, "I present Lady Andrixine Faxinor."

"The heir." He frowned, comprehension bright in his eyes. "And your own kinsman tried to kill you."

"This subterfuge is to protect her life," Brother Klee said, his voice still calm but with an underlying ring of command. "Until her murdering uncle is apprehended, we cannot let anyone know Andrixine Faxinor lives."

"My life for hers," Jultar hurried to say. "It will be the highest honor of my life to serve the Sword Bearer."

"And mine," Kalsan added in a strained voice, pushing his way to the front.

"We are all here to swear to you," the warlord said. "Will you take our oath?"

"Brother Klee?" she pleaded, unsure what to say.

"Warriors, do you truly wish to serve the Sword Bearer?" the scholar asked. A low rumble of assent filled the room. "Lady Arriena is a prisoner. Show your dedication with action, and then we will speak of easy things like oaths."

KALSAN STAYED IN Fala's stall and scratched his saddled mare's nose, listening as Brother Klee and Jultar questioned the prisoner. The stable was amazingly quiet for all the ruckus and jollity filling the town. With five stalls between him and the one where they held the bound and bruised prisoner, Kalsan could hear every word.

His disappointment ached worse than his bandaged arm when the man spilled the information readily. Kalsan wanted an excuse to batter the man. He thought over what Andrixine had told them of the attack at the inn. There wasn't enough pain to pay for what those men had done.

Kalsan glared as Jultar and Brother Klee led the prisoner past the stall. Jultar saw Kalsan and nodded for him to follow.

"It is not far," Brother Klee announced to the waiting, mounted warriors.

Andrixine sat her stallion at the doorway to the stables, her eagerness shining brighter than the torches several warriors carried. She nudged Grennel closer to the bound man, and he cringed away from her.

"Where?" she asked, her voice harsh with strain.

"At the eastern edge of town," Jultar answered. He swung up into the saddle of his horse and drew his sword, pointing. "An old grain storage bin, made into a wayhouse. We will have to dismount and come upon it in quiet, but they only have two men there with Lady Arriena and her maid." He smiled, baring his teeth at the prisoner. "They are waiting for their companions to come back with the ransom money."

"They'll have an uncomfortably long wait, won't they?" Brenden drawled.

Andrixine laughed with the others. Kalsan thought her voice pure music, but for the bitter delight that turned it harsh.

It was a ride of only ten minutes, and they dismounted when the lights of the wayhouse were pinpricks among the trees ahead. Jultar led the way, with Brenden and Marfil behind him. Kalsan walked behind them with Andrixine between him and Brother Klee. Walking next to her, Kalsan felt her restlessness vibrating through the air. He was glad of it, distracting him from trying to see her features in the moonlight. Why, with this important rescue ahead of them, did his thoughts keep catching on the fact that she was a maiden? He kept telling himself that it didn't matter; their oath and her position as Sword Bearer was all that mattered.

Why didn't he believe himself?

"They're both inside," Brenden whispered, passing along news from the warriors who had gone ahead. "We're to storm the door and windows, and Marfil and Doyan will come down from the roof."

"Do you think they'll try to harm my mother?" Andrixine asked, resting one hand on the hilt of her ordinary sword.

"They won't know what happened, my lady," the man answered with a grin, his teeth gleaming in the moonlight.

"Oh, please, Brenden..." She sighed, then a mischievous smile tweaked at her lips. "I prefer being called Drixus."

"That might not be permitted," Brother Klee said as they turned to approach the wayhouse through the trees. "King Rafnar will send an honor guard from the Sword Sisters for you. They won't permit such familiarity."

"Appearances and protocol." Andrixine made the words sound like curses. Despite his discomfort, Kalsan grinned. "Commander Jeshra never put up with such idiocy. Why should I?"

They reached the dark bulk of the wayhouse, and their band divided to their assigned tasks, moving to the door, the windows, or climbing to the thatched roof. They worked in teams, one to break down the barrier and the other to dash or swing or tumble through, weapons ready. They were perhaps too many men to send against two ruffians, but nothing could be left to chance. What if someone moved a moment too slow and their enemies had a chance to hurt the prisoners?

Kalsan, Brother Klee and Andrixine would be the last to enter. While the others overwhelmed the kidnappers, they were to find and release Lady Faxinor and Glynnys.

Jultar raised his hand, barely visible in the spatters of moonlight breaking through the trees. Kalsan glanced at Andrixine, her face a pale slash in the darkness. He wanted to put his arm around her, to give comfort.

Wood creaked, groaned and snapped under only a few blows.

Light spilled out into the darkness as shutters shattered under blows from hard arms and swords and axes.

Two men shouted—Jultar's warriors attacked in silence. No women cried out, and Kalsan worried about that. What if their prisoner had given them the wrong information? What if they attacked the wrong place and there were no prisoners waiting to be rescued?

What if the ladies had been killed?

Andrixine pushed past him. Kalsan had to run to catch up,

They burst into the wayhouse, blinking against the smoky glow from the tumbledown fireplace. Jultar stood over one man, held flat against the ground by Marfil and Doyan. The other man cowered in a corner, arms covering his head, trembling while three warriors stood over him.

"My lady," Brenden called. He gestured at the men. "Do you recognize them?"

Andrixine only took a few seconds to look at each man. She nodded, then strode across the room to a sagging door, held closed with a board wedged against the latch. Kalsan looked around the room, guessing its size. The second room had to be little more than a closet.

She kicked the board away. The door stuck at the bottom corner. Andrixine tugged hard, making the wood scream. Kalsan smiled at her determination and strength.

A single candle lit the tiny room where two women sat on a narrow cot, hands folded in their laps, staring at the sword-carrying figure before them. Kalsan stepped up behind Andrixine, wanting to help, not sure how.

"Mother?" she said, her voice breaking.

Silence. Brother Klee brought a lantern. By the fitful light, the women's condition became clear. Their clothes were filthy, torn in places; hollows in their pale cheeks showed their captors had not cared about feeding them. Their blonde hair hung flat and greasy, though someone had made an effort to keep it neatly dressed.

The taller woman had a poise that labeled her Lady Arriena Faxinor. Kalsan saw her eyes begin to blaze like Andrixine's. She lifted her chin, a tight smile tugging at her lips. The other woman clutched at her torn skirts and cowered back against the wall. Lady Arriena stood and held out her arms.

Andrixine flung herself into the room to wrap her arms tight around her mother. Lady Arriena's legs buckled, and her daughter held her up. Silence filled the wayhouse, letting the woman's sobs ring clear into the darkness beyond.

"It's all right, Mother. You're safe now." Andrixine raised her head to look at the maid unfolding herself from the corner. "It's all right, Glynnys. They won't hurt you again."

Brother Klee stepped up to the door and held out a hand to the maid. She let him lead her from the room while Andrixine stayed with her mother. She guided her back to sit on the cot and knelt next to it, holding her shaking body.

"Alysyn? Where is she?" Lady Arriena whispered through her slowing sobs. She wiped tears from her face, trying to smile. Color began to seep back into her cheeks. "They told me both of you were dead, but if you're here—I couldn't believe them. I *wouldn't* believe them. I kept praying and—Alysyn?"

"Safe at Snowy Mount." She glanced over her shoulder at Kalsan waiting at the door. Andrixine grinned at him. "Alysyn is safe, but I don't know about Snowy Mount."

"Oh, Andrixine!" A slightly hysterical chuckle escaped her mother. "They were so sure you were dead. I saw your uncle's seneschal pay them gold and I thought he was ransoming me—but he only asked if you were dead and went away."

"I know, Mother. We found the other men. Uncle Maxil hired them. But that's all over now. Come." She stood, holding out her hand to help her mother rise. "We'll take you from here and let you wash and change clothes and eat, and then we'll go home."

"Go home," Lady Arriena echoed. She smiled a little more steadily now and let her daughter help her stand. "Oh, your poor father. What has he been thinking?"

"He'll be all right soon," Andrixine assured her. She put her arm around her mother's waist to steady her as they walked through the door.

"My lady?" Kalsan held out his arm to offer support. He felt proud when Lady Arriena bestowed a smile on him and let him twine his arm through hers.

"Andrixine," the woman said, stopping short as they reached the stronger light. "What did you do to your hair?"

Kalsan burst out laughing at the crooked grin and blush that crossed Andrixine's face. She stuck her tongue out at him, then began to chuckle, tears in her eyes.

BROTHER KLEE WOKE the innkeeper and a maidservant to get food and hot water, soap and clean clothes for Lady Arriena and Glynnys. They put the women in the single room their entire band had been prepared to share. Brother Klee brought out his satchel full of healing herbs and dosed both women and told them to sleep. There were only a few hours left until dawn. With no other rooms to be had, the warrior band would find places to rest in the stable or in the soft grass along the river. They were used to far worse conditions.

Before she went to stay with her mother, Andrixine met with the warriors in the stable. Jultar had told her it was an honor to serve the Sword Bearer and their glad duty. Such words made her uncomfortable. She had to thank them, let them know how much it meant to her.

"If we have served you well, we only ask to be allowed to give our oaths to you," the warlord said when Andrixine stumbled through her thanks.

He stood between her and his men, in the main aisle of the stable lit by a single lantern. Kalsan stood at Andrixine's right, Brother Klee on her left—it seemed to be their chosen places now. The warriors stood at attention, eyes gleaming, proud smiles on their faces, alert and strong despite the hour and their lack of sleep.

"There are no other warriors I would rather have with me when Sendorland attacks," Andrixine said.

Jultar went to one knee before her. He unsheathed his sword and placed it in her hands and clasped his palms together over the blade. One wrong move from either of them and he might lose a hand. Andrixine held still, knowing what would happen now and hating it. Jultar recited his lineage, emphasizing members of his ancestry who had also served Sword Bearers.

"I swear my strength and the knowledge of my years to the service of the Sword Bearer. To her safety and her aid, to her honor. To the freedom of our land and to the honor of the king. May I die with the light of the Spirit Sword in my eyes," he finished, finally removing his hands from the blade.

"Lord Jultar of Rayeen...I thank you." She raised the sword so its tip didn't touch the ground. Brother Klee had advised her to follow her heart instead of ritual. "I know if I had asked, you would have given all without the pledge. I value your experience because I am over-young. Perhaps Yomnian guided us together for you to fill what is lacking in me." The words failed on her tongue. Andrixine felt the gazes of everyone fastened on her.

She lifted the sword, turning it around, balancing it on her sleeve. With the hilt facing away from her, she handed the sword back to Jultar.

"I swear my life for yours. If I could, not a single life would be spent in vain." Her throat ached.

"Well said," the old warrior murmured, taking back his blade.

"I claim next place," Kalsan said, stepping from her side. "We swore blood oath, but I must swear to the sword and its Bearer as well. It's different," he added, voice lower.

Andrixine let him put the hilt of his sword into her hands. It was indeed different. Somehow, the second oath put a distance between them. The vow of oath-friend had been between them alone, and special. They had shed blood defending each other.

She fought the hot pressure in her eyes that signaled tears. Had she lost something precious, in being revealed as Bearer of the Spirit Sword?

PART THREE
Faxinor

Chapter Fourteen

"DO YOU RECALL how we wrung the confession from the men who kidnapped your mother?" Brother Klee asked.

They rode south on the Bantilli Trail toward Faxinor Castle, the morning still dewy and full of gray shadows before full dawn. Glynnys had been left with a cousin who lived in Morstontown. The man was mortified to realize she had been so close, a prisoner, and offered to send word to the families of Lily and Cedes, to tell them the sad news of their deaths. Andrixine felt some weight leave her shoulders at having that bitter duty finally resolved.

Lady Arriena rode a horse bought in Morstontown. The recovered wagon wasn't fit to ride, and the trip would be faster if she rode. When Andrixine didn't ride beside her mother, Kalsan took her place to aid Lady Arriena. He claimed it was his duty as her oath-friend.

Now, Andrixine rode next to Brother Klee and Jultar to confer with them. By early afternoon tomorrow, they would reach Faxinor Castle, and they had to make plans. Jultar had appointed himself her war chief. Andrixine was glad to let him handle plans and strategy, but she still needed to be part of it.

"Yes. With force and threat of death," she said after only a moment to think over the question. "Nothing truly spoken, but the actions interpreted clearly enough."

"Threats. Force. Pain," Jultar said. "Not always effective. Some choose death over telling what they know."

"There is a more accurate means than threats," Brother Klee said. "Some confess to crimes they never committed, to escape pain."

"Trickery."

"Besides trickery. The Spirit Sword has the power to discern truth from lie. You must pray and command the sword to seek out falsehood. Touch the sword to the one you question. Its light will reveal whether he speaks truth or lie."

"This is for my uncle, then?"

"We need a confession he will not contest later. Even without experience, you can discern truth from lie by the color of the light. Blue so pale it is silver-white is honesty. Red near black is deception. And one other thing, Andrixine." The holy man paused and pressed his lips together until a white rim formed around his mouth. She knew he didn't like what he had to say next, but duty pressed him.

"It regards my uncle?" she ventured.

"Very much. There is always a danger of influencing the sword to see from your perspective. Merely influence," he emphasized, raising a hand to forestall her question. "You cannot *force* the Spirit Sword to do your bidding, but you can influence it with the intensity of your emotions. Regarding your uncle, what you feel for him must be tightly controlled when you handle the Spirit Sword. You must pray with an honest desire for truth and justice in your heart."

"It will be hard."

ANDRIXINE RODE UP to the ironbound gates of her home swathed in a cloak and hood. They had been blessed the last few hours and miles. The day started sunny but turned before noon to rain, miserable and cold, making everyone in their band anonymous under their cloaks. Andrixine had longed to see the golden-gray stone of Faxinor Castle glow in the afternoon sun. The rain made even the tallest towers look heavy and earth-bound and menacing.

Jultar parlayed with the gatekeeper, Abner, whose father had put Andrixine on her first pony. She had grown up with Abner, playmates until his increasing responsibilities took him away. He was a dusty brown, awkwardly thin and tall young man, so diligent sometimes he didn't see what was directly before him. She didn't fret when he left the gate closed and went into the castle to receive his orders from the seneschal. His care for her family pleased her.

Was he a little more curt than usual? Had there been too many unwanted visitors lately? Did Abner correctly interpret the mood inside the castle? Andrixine wondered over questions and possibilities until her head ached and he returned.

He opened the man-door to one side of the gate and stepped out, bowing to them in formal greeting. He spoke the words of full welcome and hospitality and begged them pardon the somberness of the household because crisis had touched the family. Andrixine knew how to cure that particular malady. She fought a grin of anticipation as Abner's underlings opened the gates wide. In moments, they were inside the castle, heading for the stables.

"Lord Jultar," Abner said, approaching the warlord as he dismounted, "Lord Edrix wishes to speak with you. He wishes to make an alliance with you. Will you come?"

"Of course." The warlord turned slightly to meet Andrixine's eyes. It was hard, when she had to keep her hood down to avoid being recognized by her own servants. She and her mother would try to stay hidden until they knew the climate of the castle.

Andrixine nodded, signaling she trusted him. Her mind raced. An alliance? She suddenly understood—her father wanted the war band's help. Perhaps to stage a rescue? He couldn't insult Jultar's rank by asking to hire him, so he asked for an alliance instead.

She had to tend Grennel herself. The servants would recognize the stallion, even with his coat dyed and his mane clipped. Kalsan stayed with her, and they tended the horses as they had always done. Brother Klee took Lady Arriena, swathed in her cloak, into the castle and asked for a private room. He explained that the band escorted a lady, who was ill from the rigors of the trail, to the capital. The subterfuge would keep her hidden until they knew if Faxinor Castle was safe from treachery.

It took some effort not to run ahead of the servant who led them to their assigned rooms. Andrixine knew the part of the castle reserved for visitors, merchants and travelers. She and her siblings had played there often, exploring, pretending to be lords and ladies in a different castle. The wide halls paved with golden white flagstones, walls paneled with sweet-smelling, red-gold wood, and tapestries over doorways against drafts—coming home made her feel giddy, with a cold core that warned her to walk carefully.

To her amusement, the servant assigned her and Kalsan the same room. Andrixine pressed a finger to her lips to silence her oath-friend's protest, and fought laughter. She waited, leaning against the door until the man's steps faded down the hall.

"My honor won't be sullied," she whispered, delighted with the frown still making his face a thundercloud.

"But Andrixine—" He sputtered to a stop, fists digging into his hips, visibly off-balance and hating it.

"I'm going to my mother in another moment. What could you do in such a short time?"

"You'd be surprised how quickly a man moves when he's tempted," Kalsan growled.

Andrixine felt her face warm. "You thought I was a boy only a few days ago."

"A very pretty boy." An embarrassed grin brightened his features. He stayed on the other side of the room.

"Thank you, Kalsan." She tried to smile. "Even when I was at my best, no one ever told me I was pretty."

"They don't know you like I do." He shrugged, his grin turning lopsided. "Well, like I *thought* I knew you."

She couldn't think of what to say. Mentally slapping herself, she knew she had to act or she would spend the rest of the day standing there, trapped in his crystalline gray gaze.

Andrixine opened the door and slipped down the long hallway to her mother's room. Kalsan followed. He stayed outside, guarding the door when she went in to wait with her mother. Brother Klee was not with her, choosing to stay unseen until the family had been reunited. Lord Edrix and Lady Arriena had long counted the holy scholars and Renunciates of Snowy Mount as their friends, and it was possible that Maxil of Faxinor knew the holy scholar on sight. If either Lord Edrix or his brother saw Brother Klee too soon, everything might be endangered.

Lady Arriena smiled, glowing with eagerness for the reunion. She took her daughter's hand when Andrixine sat next to her. Lady Faxinor had recovered in mind and spirit from her trials. Her body would soon follow. Andrixine was proud of her mother.

"My lady?" Jultar said after a single knock. He entered the room and pretended to ignore Andrixine, who stood and moved aside. "Lord Edrix, this is the lady asking shelter. Her needs must be attended before my warriors are free to help you." He smiled broadly as Lord Edrix Faxinor stepped into the room.

"Whatever Faxinor Castle can do to help," Lord Edrix began—then stopped short, his mouth falling open as he stared.

Jultar escaped in the breathless moment, forcing Andrixine back inside the room when she would have left to give her parents some privacy.

"Arriena!" Lord Edrix gasped and reached for his wife. He snatched her up from the couch and spun her three times around before setting her on her feet. Andrixine backed into a corner and studied her boots as her parents kissed.

Lady Arriena tangled her fingers in his dark curls, holding him close as they kissed long and fiercely. Her toes barely touched the ground as her husband held her tightly. Between kisses, he gasped her name and stroked her hair. Tears gleamed in his dark brown eyes. His long, sun-browned face was flushed.

"My love," he whispered, as their kisses slowed. He kept her close against him as they sank down on the couch. To Andrixine's delight, he lifted his wife onto his lap.

Why had she never seen before how *much* in love her parents still were? Andrixine tried to look away, to give them some privacy, but a newly discovered hunger kept pushing her to steal glances. Would she ever know such love?

Her face flamed when her thoughts strayed to Kalsan. Had he been teasing or just trying to make her feel good, or had he spoken his heart when he said she was pretty? Andrixine knew desire wasn't the same as the passion and devotion her parents felt, but it was a start—wasn't it?

"Sweetling, how—no," Lord Edrix interrupted himself with a laugh. "I know how you got here. But how were you rescued?"

"Visions and miracles," Lady Arriena said, laughter and tears mixed in her voice. She drew back from her husband's embrace. "What do you know of our adventures?"

"Adventures!" He choked a moment. "Maxil's soldiers brought word the inn had been burned, four bodies in the stable and another in the inn. The ransom demand came just three days ago—and boasting they had killed everyone else, so we had best obey." A growl of sorrow and hurt filled his rich voice.

"No, Edrix. Look." She held out a hand to Andrixine.

Feeling awkward and suddenly missing her long hair, Andrixine moved out of the corner. As if her mother's hand held a rope that tugged her, she stepped up to the couch.

Lord Edrix stared, disbelief and hope warring on his face. His lips twitched as he tried to smile. Lady Arriena slid from his lap and nudged him to stand. He did, slowly, as if unaware of his body. He raised his hand, lightly tracing the fall of one braid and the line of her missing hair. Then the first gleam of tears appeared at the corners of his eyes.

"Father?" she whispered.

"Andrixine..." He tried to say more. His lips moved, but no sound came out. Lord Edrix gave up trying and enfolded her in a rib-creaking embrace. She felt his tears soak into the cloth of her shoulder.

"I'm sorry," she whispered, her voice breaking.

"For what, silly child?" He moved her away so he could look at her again, his hands gripping her shoulders so tightly they ached; she knew she would have finger-shaped bruises.

His voice was rough as he chose laughter over tears. He kissed her forehead, her cheeks. The smell of him, leather and sweat and the herbs her mother kept in his clothes chest, was a surer sign of homecoming than anything.

"How?" was all he could say.

"You trained her well," Lady Arriena said. "She hid Alysyn and then came to rescue us. Her sword kept her alive and your training kept her safe."

"Alysyn!" Lord Edrix shook his head. "How could I forget Alysyn? Where is she?"

"At Snowy Mount, Father. When all is well here, I'll send for her." Andrixine chuckled. "Mother refuses to let me go for her just yet. She thinks I'll get into trouble."

"Arrogant child," he growled. Grinning, he settled back onto the couch and took hold of his wife's hand again. "You rescued your mother—how?"

"There's too much to tell you, Father. And," she admitted reluctantly, voice dropping, "danger in our castle. Is Uncle Maxil here?"

"Of course. He insisted on being here to..." He shook his head, frowning. "I don't like your phrasing."

"I'll tell him," Lady Arriena said. "Why don't you go get your sister and brothers? We'll have a grand conference in your father's study."

"Yes, Mother." Andrixine felt some relief at having that task taken from her hands. She knew her father loved his brother, no matter how poisonous he could be.

One more hug for her parents and she stepped outside into the hall. Kalsan waited alone for her.

"Are you all right?" he murmured. "Is your mother all right?"

"She's fine, now that she has all of us to worry about again." Andrixine nodded, feeling a smile return, along with a loosening of tight muscles in her gut and shoulders. She had to believe everything would be all right.

"Where do we look?" Kalsan asked when she explained her errand and they started down the hall.

"Lorien will be in the gardens, even in the rain. She's the perfect lady, you know. She sews beautifully and tends flowers and plays four instruments and dances like a flower fairy. You'd like her."

"For about half an hour," he said with a chuckle. He glanced with interest at the tapestries and paintings decorating the hallways used only by the family.

"Oh?" Andrixine fought a sudden lightness in her chest. "Don't you like accomplished noble ladies?"

"My sisters are accomplished noble ladies. Why do you think I apprenticed myself to Jultar and haven't been home in nearly five years?"

"Bored?"

"We're much of a kind, oath-friend." He sketched a salute to her.

Andrixine couldn't quite understand her reaction to his words. Delighted or worried? The rest of their journey down familiar hallways that felt foreign was silent.

The door to her mother's private garden hung open, meaning Lorien had escaped outside to her flowers. Andrixine tried to put herself into her sister's mind. What did Lorien feel, thinking her sisters dead and her mother held for ransom?

The rose arbors made good shelters in the rain with their thick lattice tops and interwoven leaves. Andrixine headed for the first, ignoring the soft spattering of cool rain. Kalsan followed, her shadow. She was glad he was there. He felt more familiar, more "home" than the garden where she had played with her brothers and sisters.

Lorien hadn't taken shelter in the first arbor, or the second. Andrixine found her sister curled up on a stone bench in the third, a shawl wrapped around her, long golden curls lying loose down her back and her chin resting on her knees. Lorien had all their mother's golden, sculptured beauty. Already, many heir sons had offered for her, to strengthen alliances between their family lines and Faxinor. Lorien had been flattered. Andrixine wondered how her sister felt now as the heir, the one to choose instead of being chosen.

"Lori?" she said, pausing in the opening of the arbor. This one was large enough for eight to stand inside and a dry shelter in the soft rain.

"Hullo." Her sister raised her head and studied them. Andrixine found it amusing Lorien spent more time on Kalsan. "Do I know you?"

"I should hope so." She stepped closer, very aware that Kalsan stayed outside, letting the misty droplets slowly soak his clothes. She silently called him coward and wished they could have traded places.

Dawning comprehension touched Lorien's face, mixed with confusion. Andrixine held out a hand to her. Lorien tried to turn away but Andrixine moved along with her, forcing the girl to look at her.

"You're frightening me," Lorien said, visibly summoning her courage. "Go away."

"Why?"

"Because I'm the heir!" She slid off the bench and pushed herself to stand on shaking legs.

"That sounds like Uncle Maxil has been lecturing you on how important you are. Why do you listen to him?"

Lorien shook her head and tried to back away. She yipped like a trampled puppy when Andrixine caught her by the wrists.

"Lori, look at me! You know who I am," she said, her voice harsh with intensity. "Remember when we shared my room and you dropped your doll out the window? I climbed the ivy to get it. I promised I wouldn't let anybody make fun of you, the first time you came to the great hall for dinner, remember? When a snake frightened your pony, who caught him before you were thrown?"

"But—you're dead!" Lorien whispered, tears filling her eyes.

"No body, you goose." Andrixine wanted to laugh but didn't dare with her sister in a state of shock.

"Uncle Maxil said—"

"Uncle Maxil has hated me since I slapped Feril for trying to kiss me." Andrixine bit her lip against blurting all the truth about their uncle. "He would be very glad to see me dead, so you would be the heir and marry Feril."

"Not likely!" Lorien freed one hand and wiped at the tears on her cheeks. Then she gasped. "Andrixine, you *are* alive!"

"That's what I've been trying to tell you." She laughed to keep from crying as her sister enveloped her in a trembling, tight embrace.

"Oh, Andrixine—Mother's being held for ransom!" she moaned, her voice muffled against her sister's shoulder.

"No, she isn't. She and Father are in his study right now. I'm supposed to bring everyone for a meeting."

"A meeting?" Lorien pushed herself to arm's length to look at her sister. "Are we in trouble?"

"Maybe." She released her and led her outside. "Lori, this is my oath-friend, Kalsan."

Her sister nodded to Kalsan, blushing slightly. Andrixine felt something tighten in her chest when Kalsan bowed. Why did he have to grin at her sister like that?

"Let's go," she said, and led her sister through the rain at a smart pace.

"Where's Alysyn?" Lorien asked in the hurrying quiet.

"At Snowy Mount. I thought that the safest place to leave her until I could find how things stood here."

"How things stood?" Lorien stopped short. "Did you think I'd fight you for the inheritance?"

"No. But someone tried to murder me. I had to be sure I was safe, and you, before he knew he failed." She yanked on her sister's arm to get her moving. Kalsan pushed on Lorien's shoulder to help.

"Andrixine...you've changed," she whispered, a little breathless as they hurried on.

"If I hadn't, I wouldn't have survived. Things have happened, Lori..."

KALSAN STAYED BY the door, studying the tips of his boots, feeling like an intruder. It didn't help that Brother Klee also witnessed Lorien's tearful reunion with her mother in Lord Edrix's study.

He risked looking up to find Andrixine. She was too quiet. He found her standing next to her father, grinning, tears in her eyes, safe in the curve of her father's arm. Lord Edrix looked rightly proud of his tall, thin daughter.

"I don't want to let go of you," Lady Arriena said, cupping Lorien's face in her hands and smiling down at her daughter. "Will you go get your brothers? I don't want to send for servants yet, and I know you can do it quietly."

"Of course, Mother." Lorien wiped at the tears gleaming on her face as her mother released her. She sketched curtseys to the others and hurried for the door. A muffled giggle escaped her, and she pressed both hands over her mouth, eyes gleaming with mischief and laughter.

"I think this is all a little too much," Lady Arriena said with a breathy chuckle. She nodded thanks when Lord Edrix and Andrixine hurried forward to offer their arms. They led her to a long, low couch under the casement that looked out over rolling, emerald wet fields. Andrixine sat at her parents' feet.

The laughter faded from her eyes, though she still smiled. Kalsan wondered, how hard was this for her? He wanted to sit with her, offer an arm for comfort, a shoulder to lean on. But her parents were here, and she was heir of Faxinor, and every hour made him more aware of the barriers that would destroy their comfortable companionship.

"Your mother has told me everything," Lord Edrix said. He held his wife close, an arm around her waist, and rested his free hand on his daughter's head.

"How much is 'everything,' Father?" Andrixine nearly whispered.

"The inn, the fire, going to Snowy Mount, why you had to cut your hair, the rescue."

"Ah." She nodded and didn't look happy.

Kalsan understood. The Spirit Sword. Lady Arriena had chosen not to tell her husband. Why? Why was Andrixine so loathe to tell her father? Kalsan knew he would have bellowed the news to the entire countryside if he had been chosen.

Which was probably why the sword hadn't chosen him.

"We have some complications, Father," she began, after glancing at Brother Klee. Kalsan couldn't read the silent communication between them.

"She told me about the seneschal and the kidnappers' confessions," Lord Edrix said, his smile dying. "I don't want to believe such accusations against my brother, but...He has always held himself above the law, entitled to rewrite it to suit himself."

"When your father and I married," Lady Arriena said, "your uncle tried to have your father disowned."

"Why?" Kalsan blurted.

"My mother is from Sendorland," Andrixine said with a shrug. "Some nobles said she would pollute the bloodline and her children would be disloyal to Reshor."

"I think that's been proven a lie," he muttered.

"Proof *is* the hardest part," Lord Edrix said. "My brother is ruthless enough to disavow his seneschal and say the man plotted alone. We must make Maxil confess and root out his supporters, or none of my children will be safe."

"We can take that confession." Brother Klee crossed from his chair to stand before Lord Edrix, his wife and daughter.

"I should have known you'd show up to help us again, old friend," he said with a smile.

"When you and your lady married, our visionaries spoke of Yomnian's hand on your future. Andrixine is the result of your obedience and trust. We must do all we can to protect her. You should know, my friend, before I took my vows I was Rakleer." He smiled tightly as Lord Edrix reacted to the name. "The Spirit Sword is here. With it, we will draw a confession no one will ever be able to contest."

"He's a ruthless man." Lord Edrix shook his head. "He was furious when Andrixine refused Feril. When we heard Andrixine and Alysyn were dead, Feril began to court Lorien."

"That must have been interesting," Andrixine muttered.

"Lorien has grown up a great deal since you vanished, my dear." He tousled his daughter's short hair. "She told Feril in no uncertain terms to stay away."

"Andrixine, isn't there something else you should tell your father?" Lady Arriena prodded gently.

"More?" Lord Edrix grinned, but uneasiness crinkled his eyes. "What other surprises do you have for me?"

"Andrixine is more than your heir now, Edrix." She gestured for their daughter to stand. "I've thought much since her warriors rescued me. Finding a suitable husband—"

"Her warriors? But they are Lord Jultar's men."

"We are sworn to her service," Kalsan offered from his corner. Andrixine gave him a lopsided smile of thanks, but he doubted his words had helped matters.

"Sworn to her?" Lord Edrix repeated. "But why? And what about a husband? I thought we agreed we would give Andrixine plenty of time to choose."

"We don't have time, Father." Andrixine stood, and her eyes took on that weary somberness that made Kalsan's heart ache. "Mother is right. I must marry and produce an heir quickly. We will be at war with Sendorland within a year; two, if we're lucky."

"But what does this have to do with you?"

"Brother Klee is the *former* Sword Bearer." Andrixine straightened her shoulders. "Father, I'm the new Bearer of the Spirit Sword."

Kalsan knew from the tightness in her voice, Andrixine wanted to cry. He wanted to hold her, feel her tears soaking his shirt. There was nothing he could do to help.

"FATHER?" DEREK, SIXTEEN years old, followed Lorien into their father's study. "You wanted to see us?"

Behind him came Martyn, Erik and Pollux, fourteen, twelve and nine years old. Andrixine was used to seeing their dark mops of hair flying as they ran and played through life, their long Faxinor faces alight with mischief. The four somber boys, images of their father, were a drastic change she disliked.

"No, I did," Lady Arriena said, stepping through the door from their private apartments.

"Mamma!" Pollux shrieked, breaking the stunned silence. He nearly flew across the room and leaped into his mother's arms.

The other three boys followed close on his heels. Lady Arriena laughed, tears in her eyes, as the boys nearly pummeled her with their eager embraces. Her hair was mussed, her face wet with kisses and her gown smeared with whatever had stained the boys' hands. Andrixine knew her mother would cherish the stains forever. She stayed in the corner, hiding in the shadows until the first shock faded.

"They've been too quiet," Lorien said, joining Andrixine in the corner. She grinned at her sister, abandoning her superior, eighteen-year-old's poise. "Even Nurse was grumbling over how biddable they've been."

"They're worse than starving puppies in the kitchen," Andrixine said with a chuckle. "I think Mother enjoys it."

"You owe me a long story, you know."

"I know."

After a few more exclamations and rambunctious hugs from Pollux and Erik, the reunion calmed enough that Lady Arriena could sit beside her husband on the couch again. The boys draped themselves all around her, leaning against her knee, perched on the couch arm next to her, hanging over the back of the couch. Pollux insinuated himself between his parents, giggling and grinning when his brothers realized his triumph.

"Yes, I was kidnapped. It wasn't a lie somebody sent to hurt you and your father," Lady Arriena said, when the boys quieted enough to let her speak. "I was rescued. Would you like to see who found me and brought me home?"

"Lord Jultar?" Derek guessed.

"He was part of it, yes," Andrixine said, as she stepped from the shadows.

All four boys stared, the room suddenly so silent she could hear them breathe. She fought to keep her face solemn, though she wanted to burst out laughing. Derek stood and took a few steps toward her. She recognized his protective stance, putting himself between danger and those he loved.

"I've cut my hair," Andrixine said. She stepped closer and held out her arms. "I'd tell you to go see Grennel, but he's been disguised, too."

"Andrixine?" Martyn's voice cracked.

"Rixy's dead," Pollux shrilled, shaking his head. He hid his face in his mother's lap.

"No I'm not, Polly-dolly." Andrixine laughed when her little brother jerked his head up and glared at her. He hated that nickname.

"You look like a boy," Erik said, standing but not leaving his position at the arm of the couch.

"That's the idea, goose. How am I supposed to survive a trip through hostile territory if everyone thinks I'm a soft, helpless girl?"

"Helpless?" Derek began to chuckle. "You're the last one I'd dare call helpless." He took a few steps closer, opening his arms. The three younger boys followed suit, chattering and exclaiming, grabbing hold of her hands, embracing her, tugging on her braids to make sure it really was her. Their parents made no attempt to hush them. Soon, the happy volume in the small room had grown enough to make Andrixine wince.

Brother Klee and Kalsan excused themselves when the boys managed to tug her over to the couch, demanding her story and quieting enough that she could actually speak. The two men had to report to Jultar, or so Brother Klee said. Andrixine felt a moment of panic—she suddenly felt lost among her own family.

She settled down on the floor in front of the couch, leaning back against it, legs folded under herself. Her father's hand rested on her head. Lorien curled up next to him, with Derek and Martyn kneeling before her, Pollux back between their parents and Erik next to her, leaning against their mother.

Andrixine started her tale with waking at the inn and hearing something in the forest. She skimmed what happened to Cedes, Lily and the grooms, yet felt the tension grow in her father's hand resting on her head. Lorien gasped a few times, and she pictured her sister clasping both hands over her mouth. The boys drank in every word of the chaos and blood as if it were some great adventure.

When she described her dreams of the Spirit Sword, no one reacted. When she told of her first sight of the sword her father choked, as if he smothered a sob.

"Brother Klee is Rakleer," she said.

"Rakleer? The Sword Bearer? And he's here with us?" Derek looked as if he would leap to his feet at any moment and race out to talk with the ancient warrior.

"Brother Klee is the *former* Sword Bearer," Lord Edrix corrected, his voice cracking. "The sword called your sister."

"Andrixine?" Delight washed over Martyn's face. He reached for her hand. "Please? Let me ride with you to war?"

"Me!" Pollux squeaked, falling over himself as he tried to reach her with one leap. He fell almost into her lap.

Andrixine choked on a laugh that threatened to turn into a sob as she helped him right himself. The other two boys remained quiet, but she could see the desire, the pleading in their faces.

"Let me finish my story, will you?"

She described her journey with Brother Klee, meeting Jultar's party, how they had been spying. When her brothers asked about the warriors' adventures, she was glad to tell them to ask the warriors themselves. It would get their minds off her for a little while.

A knock on the door came as she finished reciting their mother's rescue. Andrixine wondered if someone had been listening outside. If Kalsan or Brother Klee, that was all to the good, nothing discovered. If a household servant or her despised uncle, then danger.

Derek got up to answer the door, admitting Brother Klee and Jultar. The holy man carried the sword, still hidden in cloth. Her brothers stared. Andrixine stood and held out her hand for the sword, to give them what they wanted. Perhaps then she could swear them to silence.

She unwrapped it, and Martyn leaped forward to catch the cloth before it touched the ground. A soft glow surrounded the sword. The room's light was dim enough to make the soft nimbus visible. Gently in the awed silence, she slid the scabbard off the blade and raised it, pointing toward the ceiling. She whispered a prayer of petition and humility as Brother Klee had taught her. The glow grew.

The former Sword Bearer broke the quiet of the moment, stepping forward to take the cloth from Martyn's hand. At his nod, Andrixine slipped the blade back into its scabbard. The two older boys sighed as the bright blade vanished from view.

"Your sister and I need to talk with these lords," Lord Edrix said, looking around the circle of his children. "I must warn you to keep her presence and the sword a secret."

"But why?" Pollux asked.

"Because someone has tried to murder her, and we have not caught him yet. If he thinks she is dead, then she is safe. Do you understand?"

"I can protect Andrixine," the youngest boy protested. He stepped up to his sister and grasped her arm. His gaze begged her to believe him and to let him stay.

"You have an important job," she said, gathering her brothers and sister closer with a gesture. "I need you to be my eyes and ears, while I stay hidden. You'll be my first spies."

"To serve the Sword Bearer is a warrior's greatest honor," Jultar said, lips twitching as he fought not to smile.

Martyn's eyes grew wide and bright. He traded glances with his brothers, then spun on his heel and hurried out. Lorien and the others followed.

"Good lads, all of them. And the girl," Jultar added. "How may I and my men serve you, Lord Faxinor?"

"You already have. Now I understand why you hesitated when I asked your help." Lord Edrix gestured for the men to take seats. Andrixine settled down next to her mother.

"Another task awaits us."

"Yes, and I have more evidence against my brother." He sighed and took hold of his wife's hand. "Maxil suggested that particular trail through the forest to bring my wife and daughters home. He investigated the inns and decided when to send the soldiers to meet them. I trusted him with the ones most precious to me. I knew he wanted power. I didn't think he would stoop to murder."

"He fooled us all." Andrixine wished she could ease her father's pain.

"You never trusted him, no matter how kindly he spoke." Lord Edrix took a deep breath, visibly shaking off his sorrow. "Gentlemen, will you help me find justice?"

"WHY CAN'T SHE just appoint her sister or one of the boys to take her place as the heir?" Kalsan asked, as he threw himself into the window seat in Jultar's quarters.

"It isn't that simple," Jultar said, smiling slightly as he watched Kalsan. "Unless she is proven unworthy as heir, the Council of Lords won't permit that. Holy writ warns of the punishment on those who harm the firstborn. Harm can mean taking the birthright—or letting that heir disavow the birthright."

"I'm glad I'm far and away from such problems!"

"Yes, I imagine you are. Though I think you'd handle the responsibilities well. Between us, my men and I have mended your flaws." He leaned back in his chair and put his feet up on the table, chuckling when Kalsan glared affectionately at him. "Lad, you honor your oath, worrying for her."

"We can't prove her unworthy as heir, can we?"

"If she is unworthy, the sword would disavow her."

"Disavow how? Kill her?" The younger man shuddered.

"I don't understand why you want to release her from her duties. Her father can carry the estate and his duties for at least two more decades, perhaps more. She should be able to fulfill her duties as heir and Bearer without any conflicts."

"She has to marry and produce an heir. Andrixine—" Kalsan leaped from the window seat and began pacing. "She doesn't want to marry anyone. She hates displaying herself to possible suitors, like a mare looking for a stallion."

"Her words or yours?" his master asked, chuckling.

"Hers!" Kalsan clenched his fists, hating the twisting sensation in his guts as he imagined Andrixine married for duty, no affection between her and her husband. It was as much a crime as if those ruffians *had* raped her.

Kalsan realized Jultar had been speaking to him, but he hadn't heard a word.

"Sir?" he stammered, turning to face his master.

"I said, such considerations aren't in our hands. Her parents will choose the best husband for her."

"Don't we have a responsibility?" Kalsan retorted. In a quiet portion of his mind, he was amazed at his temerity. In the last few days he had disagreed with his master and struck him. "We're sworn to protect her. Don't we have the responsibility to guard her happiness? Don't we have the right to..." He ran out of words.

"Yes," Jultar said, his voice so soft Kalsan almost couldn't hear it over the thudding of his own heart. "We do have the right to concern ourselves with the Sword Bearer's welfare. What sort of husband would suit her best?"

"A man who can protect her, who understands battle."

"In other words, not a fancy-dressed farmer who prefers writing poems about battles over fighting them."

"Not exactly like that," Kalsan protested. He suspected Jultar mocked him.

"A man who will put her comfort, her wishes first. Nobly born, but several steps from the line of descent. A man trained for warfare." The warlord nodded, an odd sparkle in his eyes.

"Someone she can talk to, someone she trusts."

"That narrows the list. I'll have to ask her parents who of her acquaintance fits those requirements." Jultar stood.

"You're going now?" Kalsan moved a few steps toward the door, as if he would block the older man's path.

"Of course. The Sword Bearer must present herself to the king soon. When matters are settled here at Faxinor, we will take her to the capital. I think it would be best if Andrixine married before we leave."

"It's not that simple," he grumbled. His head swam with images of Andrixine enduring a hurried wedding, and a stranger riding with the war band—next to her, where Kalsan rode now.

"No, lad, I think it will turn out to be remarkably simple." Jultar chuckled, shaking his head as he opened the door and stepped out into the hall. Kalsan followed a few moments later. It was nearly time to close the trap on Maxil of Faxinor.

Lorien met him in the hallway just outside the great hall. Kalsan barely noticed her blush when he bowed to her; all his thoughts focused on Andrixine. The younger girl let him escort her into the hall. She introduced him to several visiting nobles, friends who had come to support the family in their time of crisis. Kalsan forgot their names seconds after hearing them. He helped Lorien step up to the dais holding the head table and turned to find his place. He was to watch Feril, Andrixine's cousin. After hearing him described a dozen times on the journey to Faxinor, Kalsan thought he could find the hulking young man by his sound and smell alone.

"A word of warning, friend," a smooth baritone voice said from behind him.

Kalsan turned and nearly burst out laughing. Square face. Wispy brown moustache and beard. Short-cropped hair. Stooped shoulders. A choking cloud of cedar scent enveloping a hulking body overdressed in bright festival clothes. Andrixine had described her overbearing cousin perfectly, with the accuracy born of loathing.

"Yes?" Kalsan hope he smothered his grin in time. From the unchanged seriousness of Feril's expression, he must have succeeded.

"Lady Lorien considers my suit, so kindly do not interfere."

"Forgive me, I was only being courteous. As a guest in this house, I offer no suit." If he was to keep Feril from making trouble, it would be smart to be friendly and stay close. "I am Kalsan of Hestrin." He held out his hand, knowing he would probably dislike Feril's touch.

"Feril of Henchvery." His grin displayed teeth starting to go brown. His hand was as slimy as Andrixine had said.

A flash of anger hit Kalsan at the mere thought of that hand touching Andrixine.

Feril nodded toward Lorien, seated at the high table and chatting with Derek. "Lovely, isn't she?"

"You're a lucky man, friend." Kalsan let Feril lead him to a table in the front ranks.

"I was luckier when her sister considered my suit. Lorien will be a good wife. She'll be a fair tumble, but Andrixine..." There was genuine regret in Feril's chunky face.

Could he have had actual feelings for Andrixine? Kalsan felt nauseated at the thought.

"She would have put up a good fight on our wedding night," Feril continued, his mouth a wet leer. "I was looking forward to taming her, as much as commanding Faxinor."

"Taming her?" He gripped the bench as he sat to keep from reaching for that fat neck.

"She fancied herself a warrior. She trained with Sword Sisters—and you know how that kind hate men. I would have had to break her like a horse. She'd have liked it, too," he added, his voice dropping to a hungry rumble. "Ah, but she's dead, and Lorien is too much a lady to be any fun."

Kalsan hoped Feril fought long and hard when it came time to make him a prisoner.

Chapter Fifteen

ANDRIXINE WATCHED AS Lady Arriena finished fixing her hair. It was almost time for dinner, and this evening would prove to be more memorable than any since Derek had brought a sack of puppies to the table. Did her mother find calm by focusing on little things, taking her mind off the coming dinner?

"How do I look?" Lady Arriena said, turning from the mirror at her low dressing table. She smiled at her daughter, turning her head so the tiny crystals in her earrings swung and tinkled.

"Wonderful. Beautiful." Andrixine felt a tiny knot of tension loosen in her chest. Her mother had visibly improved tenfold since reaching home.

It was good her mother looked so radiant and strong and happy now. Appearances were half the battle facing them this evening. If Lady Arriena looked worn or unhappy, it would be a sign Maxil had beaten them, even if only momentarily.

The cream-colored, flowing gown with rose flounces and sleeve linings and collar suited Lady Arriena, enhancing her golden and rose coloring. Andrixine knew her mother was fit to appear in the king's court.

In contrast, Andrixine wore black pants, white shirt and black vest. It would enhance the cream-brown of the scabbard, making her seem like a vision from a troubling dream—hopefully her uncle's nightmare.

"Well, I believe we are ready." Lady Arriena stood and held out her hand to her daughter.

They went downstairs arm in arm, supporting each other. Andrixine felt the slight trembling in her mother's arm, and that comforted her, somehow. If her mother was nervous even slightly, then it was permitted for her to be edgy, too.

They stopped on the other side of the heavy tapestry that served as door and draft-block into the hall. Through the thick wool full of battle scenes and hunts in bright colors, Andrixine heard the clatter of dishes and the scrape of benches as servants finished putting food on the tables and the guests took their places. She smiled, imagining her uncle's puzzled frown when he was told to sit somewhere new tonight.

Until today, the seat to Lord Edrix's left was Lorien's, as heir. The seat to his right belonged to Lady Arriena, but Lord Edrix had permitted his brother to sit next to him at meals. Tonight both seats were empty, with Lorien two seats down on the left, Derek two seats down on the right—and Maxil at another table entirely. The sudden, unexplained change had to gall the man. Andrixine liked considering it.

Her sworn warriors were among the guests, strategically placed to ward off trouble if anyone chose to side with Maxil.

The scraping, rattling and rumbling of voices quieted in the hall as Lord Edrix stood to invoke the evening blessing. Lady Arriena released her daughter's arm and put one hand on the tapestry to push it aside.

"Bless me, that I may serve fully and well," Andrixine whispered, resting both hands on the hilt and scabbard of the Spirit Sword. She felt stronger touching it.

"We have been in mourning," Lord Edrix said, his voice clear and ringing through the heavy tapestry. "The absence of my lady wife has been hard, but our sadness fades. Hope, as the sages have said, is the greatest elixir of all."

"Brother." The smooth, deep voice of Maxil of Faxinor broke in. "Do not raise our hopes, only to have them dashed."

"Dashed?" Lord Edrix laughed, the sound sharp and bright.

"You have the ransom money ready. The men who kidnapped Arriena will contact you soon. But can they be trusted?"

"No, they can't," Lady Arriena whispered. She shared a bitter smile with her daughter.

"It doesn't matter," Lord Edrix said. "We have proof Yomnian does indeed work among us." His voice grew louder as he stepped off the dais and approached the tapestry.

Lady Arriena pushed it aside and gave her hand to her husband. A unified gasp rose from the guests as they recognized her. Andrixine pressed one hand over her mouth and bit it to stifle a laugh of triumph. Her uncle's face paled, mouth dropping open, eyes glazing in what could only be confusion.

With all attention focused on her mother, Andrixine could enter. She slipped past the tapestry and stayed against the wall in the shadows cast by the torches in their sconces. Every eye focused on the returned Lady Faxinor, most faces smiling as Lord Edrix explained how Jultar's warriors had rescued his wife.

"With my lady's return comes news that nothing was as reported," Lord Edrix continued.

"Brother, you raise our hopes too much," Maxil interrupted. His voice cracked. His face assumed its usual slight smile that always seemed to hold a trace of mockery.

"Do I?" Lord Edrix said.

Andrixine stiffened, chin rising in response to the strength in her father's voice.

"There is no real proof of my daughters' deaths."

"The bones, brother. The men found five skulls among the ashes. The two grooms, the maid, Andrixine and Alysyn."

"I have my doubts." The platform creaked as Lord Edrix stepped forward. "Your men didn't report to me. Why?"

"To spare you." Maxil gave his brother a shallow bow, his wine-colored festival tunic shimmering with his movement.

"I should thank you for that courtesy. I *should*. But I have other news. Five burned bodies. The two grooms, yes. The maid Lily, yes. Another maid, Cedes, who joined my lady at Snowy Mount. Ah, you never heard of that addition, did you?" He paused, tilting his head to one side as he studied his brother's face. Maxil stood a little taller. "And the fifth, a bandit killed by Andrixine. Curious—no one found my daughters' bodies."

"The report is a lie. I demand to question the one who brought it!"

"Here," Andrixine called, stepping into the light. "I brought the report, Uncle." She smiled at the gasps and murmurs that moved through the hall at her appearance.

"My dear Andrixine," Maxil gasped. His legs shook so he had to lean against the table. His narrowly handsome face paled.

Andrixine tugged on her belt to bring the sword into view. "Would you sit? We have much to say, and our meal grows cold."

Maxil closed his gaping mouth and sat heavily. Beside him, Feril stared, his mouth open, a glow filling his face that made Andrixine's stomach twist. Could it be her cousin had mourned her? Did he still want her, after she blacked his eye last fall?

Andrixine fought an urge to flee, until she saw how Kalsan glowered at Feril. She wanted to laugh, and hug Kalsan in thanks.

"There will be a festival," Lord Edrix began, his smile widening. "To celebrate the return and rescue of my dear ones. But of higher importance is the sword Andrixine wears."

Andrixine stepped up onto the dais. She bowed to her parents, Lady Arriena now seated in her proper place. Lorien and Derek dragged Andrixine's chair forward and set it facing the guests. She stood before it, clasping the scabbard in both hands.

"A great honor has been given to Faxinor," Lord Edrix continued.

"Our firstborn, our daughter, Andrixine Faxinor has been chosen as Bearer of the Spirit Sword. There will be war with Sendorland perhaps in a year, and Andrixine will lead all our armies."

"You can't leave until you marry me!" Feril roared. He struggled up from his place at the table, nearly kicking Kalsan as he pulled his fat leg over the bench.

"The Sword Bearer's husband must be a warrior worthy to fight at her side," Jultar boomed from the back of the room. "You are no warrior. You are no fit husband for her." He strode down the aisle between the tables to stop before the dais, facing the astonished guests, one hand resting on his sword.

"Who gives you the right to make that decision?" Feril stomped around the end of the table to face Jultar.

"Lord Jultar of Rayeen, Oathbound warlord to King Rafnar, has sworn fealty and is my war chief," Andrixine said.

"Father promised you would marry me. This old man doesn't have the right—"

"Kalsan, silence this fool!" Jultar gave a negligent wave of his hand.

Kalsan leaped like a pouncing hawk, wrapping one arm around Feril's stocky chest and yanking him off balance. He bared his teeth in a fierce grin. Feril struggled, bleating. Kalsan flung him to the ground. He slid until he fetched up against the wall, when he finally chose to fall silent.

Turning to bow to Andrixine, Kalsan met her gaze. The fire that burned in his gaze, his grin, made her feel giddy.

Silence resumed in the great hall. Andrixine swore she heard the breathing of each person, the beating of every heart in the room. She waited until everyone focused on her, then she slid the sword from its scabbard. Against the black of her clothes, the bright blade's light was like the moon on a cloudless night.

"Let us do what is right and honorable," Lord Edrix said. "Let us, her own people, swear loyalty to the Spirit Sword and the Bearer."

He moved over to stand before Andrixine. She sat, the naked blade resting across her knees. Then her father knelt before her and laid his hand on top of hers. Andrixine hated the sight of him kneeling before her, but this had to be done.

He swore fealty and all his honor to serve the Sword Bearer, the Spirit Sword and Yomnian who had sent them. Lord Edrix went further than required, swearing the most dire of punishments should anyone break their oath while under his command.

"Who will be next to swear?" Lord Edrix called. He surveyed the people before him, ending with his brother.

As if someone moved his arms and legs like a marionette, Maxil stumbled up the two steps to stand before Andrixine. Sweat beaded on his forehead and dripped down his long nose as he reached out with infinite slowness to rest his hands over Andrixine's on the hilt.

"Let justice be first in my heart and mind," Andrixine whispered, her voice harsh, penetrating the quiet of the room.

Maxil gaped. Sweat flowed until his pointed beard glistened and his shoulders shook.

"What do you fear, Uncle?" she said.

"Nothing." His voice came out a dry rasp. A smile jerked at his lips and he finished reaching for her hand.

Andrixine moved her hand aside so his palm touched the hilt of the sword. The silvery blue light flared, turning crimson with black streaks. Maxil tried to pull away. His hand stayed fast against the sword.

"Maxil of Faxinor," she said in a steady voice. "You are accused of plotting the murder of the heir of Faxinor. First by poison, then by the hands of bandits." She gestured at the angry twisting of colors around the blade. "The sword testifies you knelt to swear falsely. It testifies to the hatred in your heart. As Sword Bearer, I command you to speak truth."

"No—I—" Maxil twisted, straining to free his hand. Sweat rolled into his eyes, down his face, leaving dark, spreading spots on his rich clothes. He gasped and collapsed into himself. "They lied to me," he moaned. "They said they killed both girls."

"They did, but we had a new maid with us, with hair as dark as mine. I saw them rape her. Did you give orders that we should be tortured before we were killed?"

"Yes," he whispered, a sob shaking him.

Andrixine bit her lip against asking for his reasons. It said much about her uncle's hatred for her, that he wouldn't allow her a clean, quick death.

"Who poisoned me, and how was it done?"

She waited while he swayed, whimpering so softly only she could hear. Finally, Maxil raised his head. Paralyzing terror leached the color from his eyes.

"Aldis. In a box of sweets."

"Aldis?" She lost her breath a moment. Of her two cousins, she actually loved poor, lack-witted Aldis. He had always seemed so harmless, so childlike. The feeling of betrayal hurt. "Did he know what he was doing?"

"No," he whispered. "He wanted to give you a present because he thought you were angry with him. We knew you would never suspect him."

"We? Feril and you?" She looked for her cousin, who wore unfeigned horror on his face. Andrixine spared a moment to be grateful Aldis was dining with her younger brothers and wasn't present to see his father humiliated. His adored Maxil, who oddly enough doted on his damaged son.

"No. He wanted to own you. He would have warned you, the idiot!" The light flared pale blue to testify to the truth.

"There! You see?" Feril bleated from his spot on the floor. "I adore you, Andrixine. I want to spend the rest of my life in the light you cast."

"That's what he told *me* this morning!" Lorien said with a giggle. "Can't you think of any lies, Feril?"

"I would never hurt you," he whined, sweat beading his face as it turned bright red. Several people chuckled.

"No. You just wanted to break her like a horse," Kalsan said. "What were the words you used? Something about taming her, breaking her on your wedding night?" He took a step closer, and Feril cringed away from him.

"Feril of Henchvery, unless you wish to be considered a threat to the Sword Bearer, never speak of marriage to me, is that clear?" Andrixine said in a deathly quiet voice. Her odious cousin went pale and nodded. She turned her attention back to his father, the real source of her troubles.

"Maxil of Faxinor, as heir of Faxinor I cut you from the family name and bloodline. For your treason against your lord and his heir, you are condemned. Your confession before so many people cannot be denied. Know that the Spirit Sword cannot lie. Not even to please its Bearer," she added, dropping to a whisper.

Maxil collapsed as the sword released him. He lay still, not a fold of cloth moving. Andrixine signaled for two of Jultar's band, who were waiting. They caught him under his arms and in that position of shame they carried the pale, voiceless man from the great hall.

Silence. She didn't want to look and see fear on the faces before her. The light surrounding the blade faded to its normal silvery, soft glow. The hilt felt cool in her hand, soothing. Andrixine wished she could run from the hall and hide in her room, but she had a duty to perform.

"Those who have committed no crime have no reason to fear," Brother Klee said in the silence, startling and relieving her.

She watched him approach the dais. The holy man had never appeared so mysterious and yet such a source of strength and shelter before. When he reached her, Brother Klee rested his hand on her shoulder and looked out over the silent people.

"Let all who are not divided in their hearts and loyalties," he continued, "come now and swear oath to the Sword Bearer. Yomnian calls us all to protect our land."

"LORD JULTAR SAYS you worry about Andrixine's marriage," Brother Klee said, coming upon Kalsan in the stables.

The younger man had gone there the moment the interminable meal had ended. Several of Lorien's suitors had come to offer condolences to the family, and in what Kalsan thought extremely bad taste, two had switched their suits to Andrixine—during the swearing ceremony, of all the inappropriate times. The fact that the sword hadn't flared and burned them for their gall irritated Kalsan to no end.

What sickened him more was hearing his neighbors talk at dinner. He felt more comfortable with Fala and Grennel than in the castle. Everyone was delighted and thankful Lady Arriena had been returned, and stunned to learn Andrixine had not been killed. Half the people Kalsan heard cared more about who would dare to marry Andrixine with such odd adventures behind her, rather than the implications of the Spirit Sword waking.

It was small comfort that Grennel permitted Kalsan to groom him when he had finished brushing Fala's coat to a high gloss—and plaited her forelock besides. Kalsan tried not to think how ironic it was that the finicky stallion accepted him, when the lady who owned him moved further from his level and higher above his reach with every passing day.

"I'm her oath-friend," Kalsan said, putting down the brushes. He didn't want to look at the man, but he was leery of the slightest rudeness. After all, Brother Klee had once been the mystical warrior, Rakleer.

"Is that the only reason?"

"You should hear them talk, as if everything she endured has made her—" He wished he hadn't put the brushes down because he wanted to throw or pound something. "It's like she carries some horrid disease."

"I assume you don't agree?" A chuckle hung at the back of his voice. "Andrixine must marry before she leaves to meet with the king, to guard against the slightest scandal. She will have an honor guard from the Sword Sisters, of course. We have sent to the chapter house for that. Her need for an heir before she goes to war demands she marry quickly."

"How soon?" Kalsan asked, his mouth dry.

"By full moon."

"That's not fair! Where will she find a suitable husband in only two weeks?"

"There are eight noble sons, second- or third-born, within half a day's ride. Four are here now. They have all expressed interest in Andrixine."

"They're not right for her!" He began pacing within the confines of the aisle outside Grennel's stall. "None of them can handle a sword well enough to save their own lives, let alone protect her."

"Andrixine needs no protection. Her husband will be there to support her, to guard her honor and act as intermediary." Brother Klee paused, tilting his head to one side to study the younger man. Kalsan hated how everyone seemed to study him that way lately, as if they saw something that fascinated them.

"They can't even decide what to have for dinner, let alone help her lead armies and navigate court."

"You know a great deal about their flaws."

"After seeing her maid raped and considering the available husbands, it's no wonder she loathes the thought of marriage."

"Does she?"

"Yes!" Kalsan halted, turning to stare. Something in the man's voice sent a chill up his back.

"Lord Jultar says you have listed the proper qualities in the man who can marry Andrixine. Who here fits?" He waited, but Kalsan could only stare at him, something choking him silent. "A warrior who likes Andrixine, whom she likes, who understands her position, and who carries noble blood so her children will be acceptable to the nobles. There are several men in Jultar's company who fit those criteria," the holy man continued, again with that infuriating little smile.

"They're all too old," he muttered.

"Now age is a factor? Who does that leave?"

"Me!" He caught his breath, suddenly light-headed and too warm—yet he felt incredibly better. "And I don't care what anyone says against me."

"Do you truly want this, or does your sense of honor push you against your will?"

"Brother Klee—" Kalsan's face grew hot, yet he felt like laughing and weeping. "What am I going to do?" How could he feel such hope and despair at the same moment?

"We are to meet with Andrixine and her parents shortly to discuss this little requirement." Brother Klee chuckled when Kalsan choked over his choice of words. "Come with me. I'm sure her parents will agree that you are the most suitable choice."

"They don't know me."

"I know you, Kalsan of Hestrin. Jultar of Rayeen will stand for you. Andrixine counts you among her closest friends. And consider this." He waited, as if he could hear Kalsan's heart thudding in his ears and wanted it to calm a little. "You and Andrixine are oath-friends. You have bound your souls together before Yomnian. Like a man and woman betrothed."

"Don't joke about something like that!" Kalsan blurted. Then, unaccountably, the merriment in Brother Klee's eyes brought answering laughter up from deep inside him. Kalsan's legs trembled, but he felt remarkably better. When the holy man gestured, he could do nothing but follow.

ANDRIXINE PLACED THE Spirit Sword in the rack next to her bed, then closed her eyes and sank down onto the cushioned trunk at the foot of her bed. The pleasant familiarity of her room filled her with peace and security. She could navigate her room with her eyes closed, going from bed to window seat to wardrobe to bathing nook and dressing table without tripping or running into anything. Her room was three times the size of inn rooms she had stayed in, the carpets thicker and more pleasant than the rough, splintering rushes, the candles scented. No more rancid fat-burning lamps.

Still, despite the pleasure of being home and secure in familiar, luxurious surroundings, something felt wrong.

A knock on the door broke her from her thoughts. Andrixine took a deep breath and went to answer, knowing it was the summons she had been dreading. A serving woman curtseyed and kept her head bowed when she spoke.

"M'Lady, your father asks you come speak with him and your mother," she said.

"Thank you. I will be with them in a moment." She closed the door and muffled a sigh. So, the silly rumors and changed behavior had started already. Andrixine put on slippers instead of returning to her boots, opened the door and walked the long, winding hallway to her parents' suite.

Lord Edrix and Lady Arriena sat on a couch, facing the door. Brother Klee and Jultar stood on either side of the couch. Kalsan leaned against the wall by the window. They appeared to be engaged in pleasant conversation, but some sense of warning stopped Andrixine on the threshold. Kalsan avoided looking at her. What was wrong with him?

"Andrixine." Her father smiled and gestured for her to sit between him and her mother. She settled gingerly on the edge of the couch and saw Brother Klee and Jultar exchange a questioning look and shake their heads.

"Have you considered your next step?" Lady Arriena asked, taking one of her daughter's hands.

"We have to go to the king." She looked to Jultar, who nodded. "Lord Jultar has his report to make, and he must notify the king immediately that a new Sword Bearer has risen."

"You have your duties here to attend to, first," Lord Edrix said, his voice soft. The apology in his eyes confirmed her sense of impending trouble.

"Must I take a husband?" Andrixine bit her lip as she realized she whined.

"Now, more than ever." He tousled her hair, smiling sadly. "You said yourself, perhaps a year until war finds us. Brother Klee and Lord Jultar have been giving us advice."

"Who have you chosen for me?"

"You have the final say. We don't want to force you, only to help you make a reasonable, responsible choice—"

"In a few day's time," she interrupted. "Father, can't I step aside, give the title to Lori or one of the boys?"

"We already discussed that," Jultar said. "Several people proposed that option, but it would not be permitted either by the Council of Lords or the sword."

"You require a man who accepts you as a warrior, who understands your duties as Bearer and heir, who can support you in battle, who is a kindred soul, who is pledged to your honor and is of noble blood—we must consider your heir, of course," Brother Klee finished.

"Who fits that list of requirements?" she nearly whispered. Andrixine felt her lips curving in a smile. She had often imagined second and third sons making such a list, weighing the advantages against the disadvantages of marrying her.

"Me," Kalsan said, stepping forward.

"How can you do this to him?" she blurted, her voice breaking as she stood. She wanted to race from the room, but everyone watched her, and there was no escape. "He is my oath-friend! How can you force him—"

"It's the only answer," Kalsan said, reaching out a hand as if to grasp hers. "In a way, we're already betrothed through our vows as oath-friends."

"A fine way I'd serve you as oath-friend, if I forced you to marry me!" She wanted to hit him.

Yet, something inside her spread wings to soar, singing in wordless delight. Ruthlessly, she squelched it even as she longed to drown in the glorious dream.

"Nobody is forcing me." He scowled, and that was far better than the unreadable look that was like fear or pleading, yet neither.

"Enough!" Lord Jultar said, and the laughter in his voice shocked Andrixine more than the aching certainty that she had hurt Kalsan, somehow.

"Kalsan of Hestrin, do you willingly ask Andrixine Faxinor to consider you as her husband?" Brother Klee said, stepping up next to Lord Jultar.

"Yes. Of course." Kalsan scowled at the floor.

"Andrixine, do you object to Kalsan as your husband?" Lady Arriena asked, her soft voice startling after the rougher voices.

"Mother—"

"Is there someone else you would rather have us consider?" her father asked. "We approve of Kalsan. Brother Klee and Lord Jultar both speak highly of him."

"No, Father. You know there is no one else." Now she found it hard to look at anyone. "But Kalsan shouldn't be forced to do this because of his oath. He should have the right—"

"It's my choice." The very quietness of Kalsan's voice silenced the thundering of her heart more effectively than a shout. "I've been searching and praying for months now, asking Yomnian to give me some great duty to serve Him. I wanted a calling. This *is* my calling. To serve at your side and watch over you. It's the greatest honor of a warrior's life to give his oath to the Sword Bearer. Yet this is a higher honor, to bind my life into yours as your husband." A strangled laugh escaped him. "If you really are my oath-friend, don't deny me this!"

Everything went still inside her as she raised her head and looked into Kalsan's eyes. He truly believed what he said. There was no anger, no fear, no grudging sacrifice. If anything, he feared her rejection.

The quiet anger ceased nibbling at her as she realized the truth of what Brother Klee had said. Kalsan was the husband for her. The sort of man she needed to marry. He would never hurt her, never demand his husbandly rights.

She blushed a little as she realized she had feared that.

In short, he was the perfect match. He *wanted* the burden of being the Sword Bearer's husband. He saw it as a grand mission from Yomnian. How could she deny him the greatest destiny he could imagine? What sort of friend would she be?

It was the perfect solution for both of them.

And yet...

"Yes, thank you, Kalsan. You honor me. I will...gladly...marry you." Andrixine tried to smile, but the events of the long day wrapped around her and turned her limbs to heavy weights.

"That wasn't as hard as we anticipated," Jultar muttered. He burst out laughing when Andrixine and Kalsan both glared at him, then exchanged exasperated glances of mutual suffering. To their chagrin, Lady Arriena and Lord Edrix and Brother Klee joined in the laughter a moment later.

"THOSE TWO WERE made for each other," Lord Edrix said, after Kalsan had bade them good-night and Andrixine left moments later.

"They remind me of us," his wife said.

"Oh no, love, we weren't that blind, were we?" He laughed.

"Indeed, you were," Brother Klee said as he settled down into a chair facing them. "I remember. I was tempted to bang your heads together until you saw sense."

"Now don't leave me out," Jultar said. "You three have a story, and I want to hear it. Matchmakers must stick together."

"Matchmakers, indeed," Lord Edrix muttered, giving Brother Klee a considering look. "If my daughter and Kalsan are as happy together as we are, I don't mind tricking them into doing what's good for them. They're rather miserable right now."

"They each think the other is making some terrible sacrifice and feeling terribly guilty about it," Lady Arriena said with a chuckle. "Much like you, love."

"Ah, but you were already my wife when I made the offer."

"No more hints!" Jultar roared. "Tell me the tale!"

"Hmm, where to begin?" She settled more securely into the circle of Edrix's arm around her.

"Lord Edrix was an ambassador to King Iren of Sendorland, twenty-three years ago," Brother Klee said. "Lady Arriena was cousin—is still cousin—to Lord Mordon Traxslan, then-Prince Drahas' most trusted adviser. The nobles in Sendorland believe their women exist only to make politically astute marriages for their families, provide suitable heirs, and keep their husbands happy. Lady Arriena was a scandal. She wanted to be a scholar and hated the thought of marriage."

"Much like our daughter, I'm afraid," Edrix muttered. His wife wrinkled up her nose at him and lightly slapped his hand.

"Lord Mordon decided to punish her and use her to trap Lord Edrix. The plan was to fabricate a scandal, to force Lord Edrix to betray his country to save his honor."

"I was the perfect tool," Lady Arriena said. "I was silly enough to believe Mordon had finally relented and was letting me pursue my studies. He wanted me to attach myself to Edrix and ask him and his party all sorts of questions in the name of bettering understanding between our countries. They learned many things about Sendorland my horrid cousin didn't want them to know and thought that I was too dim-witted to know."

"We had quite a few theological discussions," Lord Edrix said, taking up the tale, "comparing the restrictive image of Yomnian in Sendorland with the loving parent we worship in Reshor. We fell in love, but we were distracted by discovering a plot to kill the king. We had to run for our lives."

"To escape Mordon, they pretended to be young lovers, fleeing relatives who wouldn't let them marry." Brother Klee took over. "That happens often in Sendorland. They had quite a bit of help along the way."

"Ah, so your High Scholar performed the marriage ceremony when you gave them shelter?" Jultar guessed. He grinned, delighted in the happy ending.

"Not quite." The holy man chuckled. "They were too busy to ever discuss their feelings. When a harvesting party from Snowy Mount found them, they were nearly dead from exhaustion and exposure and didn't know they had reached Reshor and safety. We heard the story of them being fleeing lovers, and decided that the only sensible thing was to marry them immediately. Neither one can tell you a thing about their marriage ceremony because they were both barely awake for it."

"It was rather disconcerting to wake up and find myself next to Edrix that first morning. And rather nice," Lady Arriena added, blushing even as she laughed. "He was the soul of honor, promising he would explain everything to the High Scholar and have me released from my vows with no smear on my good name. That made me furious, and I was too exhausted to understand why."

"They gave each other the silent treatment for several days, before they started to talk." Brother Klee chuckled. "I was delighted when you two stopped being angry with each other and started realizing you wanted to stay married."

"And too honorable to trap our beloved in an unwanted marriage," Lord Edrix said with a chuckle. "I hope we aren't wrong, my friends. I hope we haven't made those two miserable for the rest of their lives."

Chapter Sixteen

IN THE MORNING, Andrixine had a multitude of tasks to occupy her thoughts and time. She sent Alysyn's nurse and four of her father's soldiers to Snowy Mount to bring her home. She chose Derek to serve as her page. Brother Klee and Jultar both promised to take her brother aside and teach him what he needed to know to serve in court and on the battlefield.

Four Oathbound warriors left for Cereston to give the king a preliminary report from Jultar. Andrixine suspected Jultar had written more about her in his report than the preparations for war in Sendorland. She found she anticipated meeting the king and the rigors of court, in contrast to her upcoming marriage.

And yet, her dreams had been full of Kalsan—once she finally fell asleep. Not unpleasant, but unsettling. She remembered only snatches of her dreams, but knew they were of Kalsan. Kissing village girls. Being teased about his many casual sweethearts by the other warriors. He was the faceless man who kissed her and created feelings in her she had never known.

When she came to the hall for breakfast, Kalsan was there before her. He looked up, startled when her father called greeting to her. Andrixine could barely force herself to nod and say good morning to him. She hurried past him to the high table and knew she had seen relief on his face.

She threw herself into her day's work to fill her mind with thoughts of anything else but her coming marriage.

Mid-afternoon, she helped her father draw up the charges against her uncle for the king's judgment. As victim of the man's schemes as well as heir to the lord who recommended punishment, Andrixine had to be part of the process. She found no satisfaction in recounting the events of the last few weeks or remembering the months spent convalescing far from home.

Feril had lodged a formal protest the moment he heard Andrixine had accepted Kalsan's suit. She could almost laugh as she read the badly written complaint detailing his far superior claim to take his place as her husband. Even with dozens of witnesses to her order that Feril never speak of marriage to her, he still had the gall to claim his "right" to marry her. Didn't the fat, greasy idiot realize that his father had no power to promise him anything—least of all a bride who didn't want him?

The other suitors had left. No one had the gall or bad taste to resume courting Lorien. That was a relief to more than just Lorien. Andrixine imagined her sister was rather sickened by the whole process, when she had looked forward to her days of courtship only last fall. She felt sorry for Lorien, but better that her sister learn some of the harsher realities of life now, before she left the shelter of her ancestral home.

"What of Aldis?" she asked, when she signed the parchment denying Feril's suit and sprinkled sand over the ink to dry it.

"He'll stay here with us, for the time being," Lord Edrix said. He leaned back in his chair, letting himself slouch with that unpleasant task done. "If you feel uncomfortable—"

"I don't blame Aldis," she hurried to say. "He was a tool. What surprises me is that Uncle Maxil loves him more than Feril."

"Aldis looks like his mother, Gersta. There was much love between Gersta and my brother."

"Two of a kind." She flinched at the bitterness in her voice. Two of Gersta of Henchvery's three older brothers had died mysteriously, but the third had outlived her, and his son had many guards. He probably felt threatened because his sister gave her sons the Henchvery family name, not their father's. Seven Faxinor children stood between Feril and his uncle's estate, and only one cousin stood between him and lordship of Henchvery. Perhaps Gersta had been poisoned in her turn, damaging Aldis before birth? The entire family sickened Andrixine.

"It looks that way now." Lord Edrix sighed. "I like to think Maxil wasn't so hard until he came under her influence."

"Father, she's been dead fourteen years. That's a long time for bad influence to last."

"Yes. You're right. We should send Feril away as soon as possible. He'll probably try to ruin your wedding."

Andrixine wanted to laugh at the idea. What could her obnoxious cousin do to compete with her own unsettled feelings?

"I put Pollux in charge of Aldis—they get along the best. He says Aldis is miserable. He keeps apologizing for what Uncle Maxil did. As if he could have stopped him."

"Remember this, Andrixine," her father said, reaching across the table to cover her hands with his. "In the days to come, you will pass judgment on your enemies. Be merciful. Many of the soldiers whom you will defeat and take prisoner in the years ahead won't understand the reasons for wars they fight."

"I don't understand either!" she burst out, a bitter chuckle making her voice ragged.

"Then be kind. Always remember many innocents are hurt, whether you reach for justice or revenge."

"Yes, Father." She closed her eyes, feeling tired and centuries old under the weight of her responsibilities.

KALSAN STOOD BEFORE the assembled household, guests and friends, retainers, landholders and Faxinor soldiers that evening and wished he had cut out his tongue days before. He was sure he had done the worst possible thing as Andrixine's oath-friend by proposing himself as her husband.

She was as lovely as he had imagined, standing next to him as her father and mother and Brother Klee read the holy writ to ratify their betrothal. Her warrior braids had vanished, tucked up into a crown of flowers, white and blue and gold. Her figure was slim and graceful as a young willow, accented by the clinging folds of her pale blue dress.

Pale was the proper word. Her skin was too pale, as if she had not slept or eaten properly for days. Her hand was cool and utterly still in his clasp. Her eyes didn't sparkle as he had hoped his bride's eyes would on the day they signed their marriage contract. The few times he could see her eyes.

Andrixine avoided looking at him. Kalsan couldn't read enough expression in her somber face to guess her feelings. Terror? Relief? Resignation? Resentment? The expected bridal nervousness? Was she angry with him and keeping her silence because she knew she had no other choice?

As Brother Klee read the commands to husband and wife to prepare them for their vows in ten days, Kalsan couldn't keep his mind on the words. He wanted to talk with her, ask her how she felt, plead his case. Yet when would they have a private moment together until they were actually married? He knew she would avoid him, as she had all day today. Their wedding night would be too late. He had to settle their questions before the ceremony. His uncertainty was as irritating as the stubble of the beard he was now allowed to grow.

Jultar, Lord Edrix, Brother Klee and the remainder of the warriors had awakened Kalsan early that morning for another ceremony. For some reason he couldn't fathom, they agreed he was ready for Oathbound red cord for his warrior braids, and a position in the band of

Oathbound warriors. The honor didn't thrill Kalsan half as much as he had imagined. What had he done or said that made his master think he was spiritually mature enough for the honor and duty?

Kalsan wished for the days when his longing for a beard and freedom from shaving was his only problem.

He looked at Andrixine now, listened to her make her vows with a calm, quiet voice and wished he had the nerve to break into the betrothal ceremony and insist she come away with him to talk before they made their vows. But he couldn't seem to get the words up his throat. He could barely speak when it came time to make his vows. He clearly heard Brenden and Marfil snickering softly somewhere in the great hall behind him.

What was he going to do?

Shouts and squeals and the sounds of something heavy slammed repeatedly into the flagstones in the hallway broke through the quiet as the ceremony ended. Kalsan turned, releasing Andrixine's hand, and clasped the hilt of his sword. His first thought was to protect her; his second, relief at the interruption. He was only two steps behind Jultar and Lord Edrix as half the people in the room moved to investigate the disturbance.

Feril shoved his younger brother hard against the wall, causing the blubbering, trembling red-haired boy to slam against it and fall to his knees. By Aldis' bruised, bleeding face, he had endured a dozen collisions already. Red-faced, muttering obscenities, Feril stomped up to the boy, who curled into a fetal ball, and drew back his leg to kick.

"Don't you dare!" Andrixine thundered. She flew through the gathering crowd and grabbed his upraised fist, twisted him halfway off his feet, and shoved hard. Feril landed face-first against the wall, almost in the same spot where Aldis' tears and blood and snot smeared the stones. "Listen to me, everyone! Aldis is under my protection. Is that clear?" She knelt and wrapped her arms around the sobbing boy.

"Your protection?" Feril shrieked, spattering blood from his split lip. "That little idiot helped my father escape!"

It took nearly two hours to calm Aldis enough to get his side of the story. By that time, Kalsan and Jultar led search parties to comb the estate and found no trace of Maxil. They did find two horses missing, and the cook complained that four loaves of bread had vanished from the kitchen.

Kalsan's anger and dismay cooled a little when he returned to report to Lord Edrix and Andrixine and saw Pollux sobbing in a corner, refusing comfort from Lorien and his mother. He remembered that the little boy had been put in charge of his older, dim-witted cousin. Pollux was likely crushed by the knowledge that he had failed, somehow.

No one had thought to refuse Aldis when he wanted to visit his father in his temporary prison. The guard hadn't even thought to stay close enough to listen to their conversation. Aldis did everything his father told him, from convincing Pollux to play Hide 'n Seek so he could steal the keys to his prison room in the stables, to sneaking out to the stables to saddle the horses when everyone else was too busy to notice. Aldis stayed behind because his father promised he would come soon and make everything all right with Andrixine.

Kalsan could imagine what Maxil meant by "all right."

Feril had refused to attend the betrothal ceremony, mostly because no one would take his side in protesting Andrixine's marriage to Kalsan. He went to the stables to berate his father, and found the guard unconscious where his prisoner had left him. He found Aldis close by, innocently playing marbles and telling himself what a good boy he had been, helping his father.

Maxil knew what he was doing, choosing the right time of day to flee. With all the traffic in and around the estate in the last few hours, there was no way to find his trail.

"We have to go after him," Kalsan said in the silence after he and Jultar made their reports. "What if he had people waiting to help him, in case something did go wrong? What if he goes to the king and tells him you're an imposter?"

"One look at the Spirit Sword will prove that lie," Jultar said.

"Yes, but first the king must draw close enough to *see* the sword," Brother Klee said from the side of the room, where he had listened and watched in silence.

"Then we should send out several parties like arrows, all aimed at each place where this traitor could go," a new voice announced from the doorway. Female, it rasped with years and rang with humor and strength.

Kalsan turned to see a tall, silver-haired woman dressed in leathers, wearing a worn, purple cloak with the linked sword and leaf emblem of the Sword Sisters. Her warrior braids had Sword Sister purple and the gold cord of the royal line. Her lean, weathered, hawk-nosed face brightened with a smile as she crossed the room and dropped to one knee before Andrixine.

"I'm here to serve, lass." She drew her sword and proffered the hilt to Andrixine.

"Commander Jeshra—" Andrixine began.

"No, you command me, now." She winked, her smile widening. "I knew you were blessed with rare talent and a thousand pities you couldn't join us, but Yomnian knows best. Half the chapter house waits in the courtyard, ready for your command."

Andrixine slowly rested her hand on the hilt offered her. She sat up straighter. Her gaze swept the faces of everyone gathered in the room. A tiny smile caught up one corner of her mouth as a muffled gulp and sob announced Pollux's presence in the doorway behind Kalsan.

"We ride," she announced quietly. "We have already lost time trying to learn the tale. I will ride to Henchvery, to try to overtake him there. Lord Jultar, will you and the Oathbound ride to Cereston?"

"Command me," the warlord rumbled.

"Kangan?"

The captain of Faxinor's soldiers stepped forward, one hand on the hilt of his sword.

"We are going north and east. If my uncle fled south or west instead, where would he go?"

"I know two sure places," the man said, nodding his dark head, his obsidian eyes glinting at the challenge.

"I trust your choices."

"Can I go too?" Pollux asked, his voice breaking with new sobs. "Please? Let me help?"

"Pollux..." Andrixine sighed, rose and crossed to her brother. She knelt and gathered him into her arms as he burst into tears again. "It's not your fault," she said, in answer to words mumbled against her shoulder.

"No, it's not," Kalsan said, and knelt next to her. "Andrixine told you to watch Aldis, to make sure no one was cruel to him. She didn't tell you to keep him from doing something wrong, did she?"

"No," the boy gulped, raising his head and looking at Kalsan with a flicker of hope in his eyes. He knuckled away his tears and looked at his sister.

"Kalsan's right. You did exactly as you were told. I'm to blame, because I didn't tell you to keep Aldis away from Uncle Maxil."

"There, you see?" Lady Arriena said, stepping out of the doorway where she had watched. "I told you your sister wouldn't be angry."

"Let me help?" the boy pleaded.

Andrixine cast Kalsan a helpless look. He almost laughed, yet he understood. How could she refuse to let her brother come on what would be a grueling ride, without destroying his fragile confidence?

Then he had an idea.

"You have to stay and protect Aldis while Andrixine is away," he said. "Make sure Feril isn't cruel to him. That's a very big job, but I think you can do it."

"Feril's big," Pollux said, eyes wide, but he seemed to have left his tears behind. Perhaps the idea of standing up to his nasty cousin had a great deal of appeal.

"Go to my room and get my practice sword from the chest at the foot of my bed," Andrixine said, releasing him. "You can use that if Feril is mean to Aldis."

"Really?" A grin brightened the little boy's face. When his sister nodded, he dashed across the room to Aldis and grabbed hold of the bigger boy's hand. "Come on, Aldis. I have to go get my sword so I can protect you!"

Feril glowered as chuckles rippled around the room. Kalsan barely noticed, delighted with the look of understanding and gratitude Andrixine gave him. Then the moment passed as they settled down to the business of finding Maxil of Faxinor before he could cause more damage.

Chapter Seventeen

"HE'S RATHER CHARMING," Commander Jeshra said, breaking the night quiet of the plain where the Sword Sisters had camped for a few hours of sleep.

"Who?" Andrixine said, though she knew.

She had caught the appraising glances her teacher had given Kalsan before their search parties rode out. Despite everything else they needed to consider, planning strategy and trying to think three steps ahead of her uncle, she should have known Jeshra would bring up Kalsan eventually.

"That young warrior of yours. Those long, somber looks he gives you when you aren't looking at him make my old heart skip a few beats. I remember when my own sweetheart mooned after me."

"Kalsan isn't my sweetheart."

"He was ten years my senior and a tough old soldier, but he was tongue-tied and clumsy every time we looked into each other's eyes. Come to think of it, so was I." She chuckled. "Your warrior is rather good looking, too. That's a bonus. Why, lass, you're blushing!"

"Jeshra, please don't torment me. Don't make me want—" Andrixine caught her breath, refusing to let bitter words spill out. She feared they would sound like the nattering of a love-struck adolescent. She couldn't take the thought of her admired teacher laughing at her.

"Make you want to feel desirable?" Jeshra said softly. She grinned with a mist in her eyes. "I remember wanting a man to kiss me and hold me. You're afraid he won't touch you because he's being forced to marry you? Oh, lass, it can't be that bad." She slid over on the log they used as a seat before the fire and put an arm around Andrixine's shoulders. "You want him to want you, don't you?" She had the grace to sigh instead of laugh when Andrixine blushed hotter and nodded.

"Kalsan said it was the greatest honor to serve the Sword Bearer, but that doesn't make it *right* for us to marry."

"He's marrying his duty and not you, is that it?" A groan that was half laughter escaped her. "You wonder if he sees the girl with stars in her eyes, or if he sees the Spirit Sword?"

"That's exactly it." Somehow, spoken, her doubts didn't sound quite so petty as she had imagined. "Am I being selfish?"

"Not at all. You're too noble for your own good." Jeshra shook her for emphasis.

That earned a smothered giggle; the Sword Sister commander had a habit of shaking all her subordinates and trainees like that at one time or another, partially in affection, partially in comfort, partially in amused frustration.

"You said he swore the oath-friend vow before he knew you were the Bearer, yes? You're still friends, aren't you?" She waited until Andrixine nodded. "Well, be glad in what you do have. Let time and proximity do its work. You'd be amazed how a few months of morning breath and grubby field living will drive away the glamour to reveal the real person. If he doesn't learn to see and appreciate the woman you are beneath all your duties and titles, then he's a fool. And somehow I don't think you or the Spirit Sword would suffer a fool in your presence."

"You think so?" Andrixine whispered.

"I know so. And if that doesn't work, I'll thrash him until he gets some sense into that handsome head of his."

Chuckles followed, quickly hushed. Dawn was only a few hours away, and the other Sword Sisters needed their sleep.

THE NEXT DAY they struck gold. They met up with Maxil's seneschal and four Henchvery soldiers, ostensibly coming to Faxinor to report to their master. The surprise of all five was genuine, meaning Andrixine's uncle had not met up with them or reached his home. Commander Jeshra put them under arrest and they headed east, to take their prisoners to Cereston and the king.

When they reached the Bantilli Trail they were a day north of Faxinor and two days from Andrixine's wedding. She hoped her teacher had forgotten, but that hope was dashed when Jeshra sent Andrixine home with an escort of four Sword Sisters and an order to wear skirts and cosmetics and perfume whenever possible. Andrixine laughed, despite her frustration. There were literally hundreds of friends and allies coming to the wedding. She couldn't embarrass her parents by running away; she had to follow through on her duty and responsibilities.

When the five rode into the castle courtyard late in the afternoon, she learned Jultar's band had returned from Cereston that morning and had found no sign of her uncle at the capital. All hope of arrest now lay with Kangan.

Kalsan's brother, two sisters and their families had arrived along with Jultar's band. His parents were serving as ambassadors to Eretia, across the ocean, and wouldn't know of the marriage for weeks. Kalsan had taken his family on a day-long tour of Faxinor with all four of Andrixine's brothers. Knowing how her brothers loved to ramble and explore, they would not be back until nightfall. That suited Andrixine perfectly. She needed to be alone to think and settle her thoughts and feelings, and the last thing she needed was to run into Kalsan unexpectedly somewhere. Especially since what she had to settle concerned him.

They were to be married the next evening, after all.

To her chagrin, Jultar had assigned his warriors in rotating shifts to be her bodyguards. Maxil could have found a place to hide on the vast Faxinor estates. If he had a chance to attack Andrixine, he would. So Marfil was her guard until she grew tired of wandering the inner gardens and decided to try to sleep. Dusk was turning to night, the air just touched with a refreshing chill, and bright stars in a cloudless sky promised a glorious day for the wedding festivities. It would be glorious, if she could get enough sleep to let her appreciate it.

Andrixine thought of the dress her mother had made her try on for fitting, just after dinner. The multiple layers of gossamer white, shot with threads of silver and gold, made the most lovely yet simple dress she could have ever wanted. Her spirits had lifted a little and she dared hope Kalsan would look at her and realize she was a woman, too. She let herself dream of a delighted smile on his face and eagerness in their first kiss.

She managed to smile at Marfil when he took up position before her door, and bade him good night. Andrixine hoped she could sleep and her dreams would be pleasant ones.

She closed and shot the bolt on her door and looked at her bed, her body aching to curl up in the cool sheets and drift into sleep. Her thoughts turned to the suite of rooms which had been prepared for her and Kalsan while she was away, hunting. Her mother had made her inspect them after trying on her wedding dress. Andrixine had looked at the big, curtained bed and felt like a rabbit caught in a serpent's stare. In less than a day, she and Kalsan would be escorted to that suite of rooms to begin their married life. She knew it would be impossible to sleep tomorrow night, lying next to Kalsan, wondering what he thought, what he felt, when he would start to regret this step he had taken.

"Andrixine?"

Kalsan's whisper wrung a gasp from her. Andrixine looked

around her darkened room, hand pressed over her heart. Was he at the door? How could his voice come so clearly through the wood? Why hadn't Marfil knocked?

"Sorry," he said, stepping out of the shadowed bathing nook. "I've been waiting for hours."

"What are you doing here?" she said, managing to keep her voice to a whisper.

"We need to talk." Kalsan lifted his hands as if he would reach for her, then let them drop to his side.

"Now? In my bedroom?" She gestured at the door.

"I know about Marfil. That's why I snuck in here before you came back. He wouldn't let a man talk to his sweetheart if he was going to die in the morning."

"We're not sweethearts." Her face warmed at the bitterness in her voice, and she turned away so he couldn't see.

"No, we're not." Kalsan seemed to choke for a moment. "But we'll be married at sunset tomorrow. I'm not stepping up to the altar until we clear a few things between us."

"You don't have to."

"I do."

"Kalsan, I know you were coerced, and I'm sorry. If we had more time..." Andrixine blinked hard to fight the tears burning wet at the backs of her eyes.

"Coerced?" A sharp bark of laughter escaped him, quickly muffled behind his hand. "Andrixine, do you trust me?"

"Yes."

"With your life?"

"Of course." She looked at him now. Kalsan had never been so pale, so solemn before. She couldn't blame that all on the moonlight shining straight into her window.

"Then why won't you believe I *want* to marry you? Don't you know it would kill me to see you marry someone else?"

She wanted to sit to fight the sudden dizziness, but the entire castle had vanished around her. All she could see was Kalsan's face, the earnestness in his eyes.

"If it's so distasteful to you, to marry me—"

"No!" Andrixine flinched, then realized her voice had barely been loud enough to reach to her door. What if Marfil heard? Would he storm the room and attack Kalsan before he recognized him? The idea of Kalsan hurt by her foolishness calmed her. Danger made her think clearly—it was the demands of being a lady that put her off balance and turned her muddle-headed.

Kalsan smiled, his face gleaming, and Andrixine knew he understood all she meant in that single word. Suddenly, she could breathe again.

"Close your eyes." He took a step closer.

"What?"

"Do you trust me? Then close your eyes."

For just a moment, she hesitated. What was he doing?

Then she decided, for now and always, she trusted him. He was her oath-friend. What kind of marriage would they have if she didn't trust him now? She closed her eyes and stood perfectly still, waiting, wondering what he intended.

He put his hands on her shoulders, startling a squeak from her. His breath touched her face. Andrixine felt that familiar, melting warmth from her dreams become reality now. She liked being this close to him, the slightly musky odor of him, linen shirt and woolen trousers and clean sweat.

"I've been thinking about this for days," Kalsan whispered, his breath brushing her lips.

Andrixine froze as Kalsan pressed his lips against hers.

A fragment from her dreams flitted across her mind. *The pressure of a man's arms around her. His lips against hers. The melting warmth flooding her body.*

She wanted that feeling to be *real*, not a dream. Andrixine raised her arms, gingerly resting her hands against his waist.

Kalsan slid his arms around her, drawing her close against him and continued the kiss. She hadn't expected that, or how her knees tried to fold as his body warmth flooded through her.

At first, his lips were soft and still against hers. She had to force herself to breathe, afraid to move. Then his lips parted, gently moving against her mouth. Andrixine let her head tilt back, responding to the increased pressure of his mouth.

When she flinched, he paused. Kalsan didn't move away, but waited. Her heart thudded in her ears. She tightened her fingers in the folds of his shirt, knowing there had to be more, *wanting* more. When he laughed, the sound was muffled and tickled inside her head. She forgot to breathe. She felt his pulse throbbing rapid and hard against her lips. She tried to mimic him, and that only increased the warm melting feeling.

"Who taught you to kiss?" Kalsan drew back all too soon. He guided her head to rest on his shoulder and wrapped his arms tighter around her. She liked that.

"Taught?" The question made no sense. Then she laughed, breathless, muffled against his shoulder. "You just did."

"Promise me, Andrixine. You'll never kiss anyone but me."

"But, Kalsan—"

"Promise me?" He tipped her head back and sealed her lips with another kiss before she could respond. "Andrixine, please?"

"You're—" She struggled to regain a sense of balance, and her breath. "Kalsan, you're the first. You're going to be my husband. I promise, no one will ever kiss me but you."

"Your husband. My wife." He stroked a long strand of hair out of her face, tucking it behind her ear. "We'll be married tomorrow. We have to settle some things, first."

"You said that already." She bit her lip against an urge to tell him to stop talking and kiss her again.

"I wish you weren't the heir, or the Sword Bearer. I would have asked to marry you without those problems."

"Problems?" She wanted to laugh, but wasn't sure why.

"Is there any chance...Andrixine, I won't touch you unless you're willing. I swear that, on the blood of our oath-friend vows." He released her, stepping back so there was nearly a handspan of air between them and only his hands on her shoulders. The sudden coolness made her shiver. "Andrixine, if you truly don't want to marry me, I'll leave."

"Leave?" She clutched at his arms.

"Of course, the way you kiss..." He grinned, mischief in his eyes. "You make it hard for a man to be honorable, my lady."

Andrixine took a deep breath. "What makes you think I don't want to marry you?"

"Those mournful looks you give me—the few times you do look at me. That's a starting place."

"I thought you were being coerced!" She flinched when her voice rose. Still, no response from her guard in the hall.

"Does that mean you do want to marry me?"

"Kiss me again?"

He gave a strangled sound, half-laugh and half-groan, and gathered her into his arms. Andrixine wrapped her arms tighter around him, to hold on and never let go.

"Marry me," he whispered between slow, soft kisses.

"Yes."

"Forever, Andrixine. Past death, into Yomnian's halls."

"Forever."

"Tonight." Kalsan suddenly drew back, so she nearly stumbled, tugged off balance. His eyes blazed. "Why not? Why do we need to wait?"

"But—the ceremony is only tomorrow evening."

"Our lives aren't our own." He led her to the window.

"What?"

"You are the Sword Bearer. I am your guard, your liaison. Everything we do will be noted and made a part of history."

"Oh." A gasp escaped her when he pressed on her shoulders and she found herself sitting on the edge of the sill.

"We have to make our own happiness, create a world no one can ever intrude into." Kalsan sat next to her and swung his legs over the side so they dangled over her mother's garden.

"But, Kalsan—"

"Tomorrow's ceremony is for history. Tonight is for us."

"Kalsan—"

"We can go to Brother Klee, and he can take our vows."

"What are we doing on the window sill?"

"What will Marfil think if we walk past him and he didn't see me enter your room?" Kalsan grinned and gestured at the thick network of climbing vines below them. "I remember you talking with Lorien, about climbing these vines and..." He shrugged.

She could only laugh.

THE CLEARING LAY in a protective ring of brambles and tall pines, at a bend in the river that fed the Faxinor estates. Kalsan sat with Andrixine wrapped warmly in the curve of his arm, leaning against the trunk of the tallest pine tree. The ground was soft with moss and fallen needles and thick mats of grass. They came to this clearing after finding Brother Klee and making their vows. It was a special place all through Andrixine's childhood, reserved just for the children, where they could stage mock battles and adventures in far-off lands. He had laughed and enjoyed this glimpse of her life, when she told him about some of her childhood adventures and dreams here. They sat and talked and watched the moon travel across the sky. Sometimes they spoke of the coming war, sometimes their plans for when the war ended.

They even spoke of children, which surprised Kalsan. He had thought that would be a tender subject with Andrixine, since the only reason they were marrying at all was because of her need for an heir. She had blushed when she admitted she wouldn't mind having a child now, with him as the father. Kalsan had kissed her until they were both breathless.

Andrixine dozed off moments ago in one of those silences that felt as clear and sweet as the night sky above them. Kalsan liked watching her sleep, her head resting on his shoulder, mouth slightly open, leaning so trustfully into his support. He liked the idea that he would see her like this quite often now.

"Please, Yomnian, let it be many years together," he whispered. He tipped his head down to kiss her forehead. Andrixine woke with a tiny start.

Her eyes got wide. He held perfectly still, afraid to frighten her. Then, to his delight, she smiled and snuggled back closer against him.

"Sorry," she whispered.

"For what?"

"Falling asleep on you like that."

"I doubt we can arrange to fall asleep at the same time." That made her laugh. "I like watching you sleep, Andrixine."

"I make less trouble when I'm asleep." That made him laugh in turn.

"I could swear Brother Klee was expecting us. You think the sword warned him?" He sighed when she nodded. Kalsan told himself to get used to such things from now on. "He was mightily pleased with us. I think he approves."

"I know." She smiled a little wider.

"Maybe..." The thought that had been pressing on him while Andrixine slept grew clearer. "Maybe Yomnian approves, too. Maybe the way we feel right now, being so happy—you are happy, aren't you?" Kalsan held his breath, afraid she would hesitate or say something kind, not what was in her heart.

"Kiss me and let me show you how happy I am."

"I don't dare. Your kisses will make me a drunkard." That made her smile and blush. Kalsan vowed to always keep that sparkle in her eyes, the hint of laughter in her voice.

"What were you saying before?"

"Hmm?" He had to backtrack his thoughts. It was hard to think, with Andrixine pressed close against him and the scent of her filling his head. "Oh—Yomnian. I was thinking...maybe this is what happens when we do what's right. When we obey, Yomnian gives us our heart's desire, too."

"Heart's desire? Kalsan, I can't think of anyone I want more as my husband, but am I really what you want?"

"You are the only wife for me. If we didn't have that ridiculous ceremony to endure tomorrow and we didn't have to go to Cereston, I'd beg you to run away with me right now. It would be a grand life, wouldn't it, going wherever Yomnian sends us, using our skills to protect the weak and defenseless?"

"That's what we're doing already."

"Hmm, true, but with the entire world watching." He wanted to kiss her again, but Kalsan looked into her eyes and knew he wouldn't be able to stop. His bottom was growing numb from the bumpy ground under the tree. This wasn't the most comfortable place for their first night of marriage. Fine for sitting and talking for a few hours, but nothing more.

"We have to go back, don't we?" she whispered, and groaned when he nodded.

"Thinking about tomorrow, waiting to be alone with you again, will be pure torture." He pressed a quick kiss hard against her lips and wisely withdrew his arm. "You will think about me, won't you?"

"How can I stop thinking about you?"

"Our marriage began tonight, Andrixine. Don't ever forget that. Much as I want to make love to you—" He lost his train of thought a moment when she blushed and looked away. She didn't show any fear, and that realization stole his breath. "Much as I want that, what we have right now is far more important."

Andrixine nodded, her eyes half-hooded and thoughtful. Slowly, moving as if her joints were as stiff as his, she got to her feet. She waited, a question in her gaze as he stood. Kalsan held out his arm, inviting her back close against him. Her eyes sparkled as she tucked herself in under his arm and they fell into step together. Was that what she wanted, but didn't dare ask? It surprised him that she was so innocent in so many simple things. Then again, she would not be the Andrixine he admired and desired if she was like any other girl.

"Whore," Feril growled, appearing from the shadows to block their path.

Kalsan felt battle-ready tension shove aside the sweet, relaxed softness of Andrixine's body in the curve of his arm. He hated that change, even as his own trained reflexes kicked in.

"You're mine. Father promised you to me. And I catch you sneaking around with this mercenary." Feril gestured disdainfully at Kalsan with a long, gleaming sword.

Two dark shapes emerged from the shadows into the moonlight, revealing themselves as ruffians of the type who had kidnapped Lady

Arriena. If there was any doubt of Feril being his father's son, it was erased now.

"You belong to me. Faxinor belongs to me. You're just as much a filthy Sendorland slut as your mother!"

Andrixine leaped and slapped Feril hard, making his head rock back on his shoulders. He stared for two heartbeats, his face white but for the blood-red handprint across his flabby cheek. His eyes were wide and bordered on filling with tears, like a nasty little boy who never expected a spanking.

Kalsan fought not to snicker. A tiny snort escaped anyway.

"You!" Feril staggered backwards, red fury wiping away the mark on his face. He raised his sword.

Andrixine gasped as a bright light burst into being, centered around her hand, and coalesced into the Spirit Sword.

Kalsan stepped forward, knowing the Spirit Sword would not appear unless her life was in danger. He drew his knife. She leaped to stand beside him, her left foot pressed against his right foot, as they had done during the ambush at the river. The blade burned in the shadowed clearing, providing more than enough light to fight by.

"Hold him!" Feril shrieked in a cracking voice. Five seconds had passed since Andrixine slapped him.

Waving his sword, he flung himself at Andrixine. She dodged him easily.

The other men lunged at Kalsan in tandem. He swung and leaped back, furious they had separated him from Andrixine so easily. He drove forward, praying they wouldn't realize how predictably they moved. They braced themselves before every swing, every lunge, giving him perfect warning to counter their attacks. They had swords, he had only a knife, and yet he knew the battle was with him. It had to be with him. His duty demanded he stand as Andrixine's shield. He had been preparing all his life for moments just like this, and he refused to fail.

Nothing could make him fail, with the taste of Andrixine's kisses still sweet in his mouth.

From the corner of his eye, he saw Feril advance on Andrixine, his mouth wide open in a hungry smile, his eyes bright. He heard the man snarl, the tone vicious, triumphant, taunting.

One man leaped in too close. Kalsan slashed down with his knife at the sword arm. The man screamed and dodged back, dropping his weapon. Kalsan snatched it up and lunged after him. The other man leaped to intercept, and their blades clashed.

Kalsan spared half his attention to defend himself and tried to follow Andrixine's battle. The cousins were a startling contrast: a heavy, lumbering body advancing on a slim, graceful form that danced away with sparkling ease.

The man attacking him, dark and thick like his master and smelling of sweat and ale, got too close. Kalsan slashed, aiming for his shoulder. The man ducked in at the wrong moment. He let out a squawk like a stuck pig and stumbled backwards amid a gush of crimson from his throat.

An answering roar blared from Feril's throat. The second ruffian stared, terrified. In that momentary reprieve, Kalsan saw Feril lunge at Andrixine, sword clutched in both hands, aiming for her belly. The Spirit Sword moved, trailing her arm like the tail of a comet. The sword blocked his swing with an upward arch. Feril's sword went flying. The Spirit Sword swung up and twisted in mid-air for half a heartbeat before plunging down, to plant itself deep in his chest. Andrixine pulled the sword free, her face pale, and stepped back as her hateful cousin crumpled to his knees.

Kalsan turned back to his opponent. The remaining man had vanished. Somewhere among the trees, a man shouted and weapons clashed. So, there was a soldier on patrol out there.

The Spirit Sword blazed bright. Blue flames writhed the length of the blade, erasing Feril's blood as Andrixine took a step toward Kalsan. She looked once at her dead cousin and shuddered.

"Kalsan?" she whispered. There was something pitiable in her voice.

He ran to her and wrapped her tight in his arms. Kalsan whispered her name over and over. Her flesh felt cold through her clothes, and she shivered.

Dark quiet returned to the clearing as the glow of the Spirit Sword faded. Andrixine clutched at him, and he prayed he never had to let her go.

"It's all right," he whispered.

"Kalsan, I didn't want—"

"The sword chose you. The sword guides you." He turned her and led her toward the stream with an idea of trying to wash the blood off their hands, maybe their clothes. Anything to wipe away the memory of what had happened. She moved as if she didn't know what her body did. "It protects you."

"Yes." The single word was a cracked, gasping admission, full of pain. "But Feril was my cousin."

"Would you rather he had raped you, or killed you?"

"Or killed you?" she whispered. Some of the stricken look faded from her eyes.

Kalsan lost his breath a moment, realizing how much the danger to him affected her. What had he done to deserve that?

She said nothing while they knelt on a slab of rock, still warm from the afternoon sun, and washed the spots of blood from their hands.

"I never really hated him until now." She settled down on the rock and dripped water on the larger bloodstains on her shirt. She sounded closer to her normal voice again. "He said he would rape me and make you watch, and then he'd kill us. I held the Spirit Sword in my hand, burning—he didn't even see it. Didn't care. He just wanted to kill." She looked at the sword, which lay quiescent on the rock next to them, then pressed against him, resting her head on his shoulder.

Kalsan held her, trying to share the warmth of his body to ease the shock she had to feel. No matter that Feril had been trying to kill her, he was her own flesh and blood. He remembered the first time he had killed, forced to it in self-defense. He stumbled into the forest and vomited, and then scrubbed his sword until he threatened its edge. Jultar had found him and sat with him, saying nothing, keeping him company until he regained his inner balance.

That wouldn't work with Andrixine. She would think and brood until she blamed herself for everything. He had to do something. Say something. He knew Brother Klee would arrive soon, having felt the Spirit Sword move to protect Andrixine. They were married, but silly as it was, he didn't want anyone to find them sitting here, wrapped around each other.

"I dreamed about you even before we met," he offered.

"What?" She raised her head from his shoulder, blinking owlishly.

"I had dreams of a maiden with long, dark hair touched with flame and the loveliest, thin face. No one else attracted me since that first dream. And then I found out you were a maiden, and it was like Yomnian gave His approval. Perhaps He was warning me you waited for me, so I should be careful." He chuckled, but she didn't join him. "Andrixine?"

"I dreamed of you, too." She shook her head. "Even when I was still sick over what I saw them do to Cedes, I had dreams of a man—my husband. I felt nothing but joy. He had no face and yet when I think of those dreams, he has your face."

"I'm flattered, my lady."

"You should be." Her teasing tone fell flat.

"Andrixine—"

"Fighting Feril, all I could think of was the danger to you. The thought of losing you hurts. Kalsan, please—"

"Not even death can keep me from you. I swear it. You are my holy mission, my duty and my reward. I will always be with you."

"You had better, or I will hunt you down no matter where you go."

Now she managed to smile, though crookedly. Now he could get her to leave the clearing.

Jultar, Brother Klee and Lord Edrix headed the search party that found them halfway back to the castle. They had already met up with the soldier just bringing his prisoner in. Kalsan wanted to laugh at their astonishment, but feared the sound would be harsh and unnaturally loud.

It took only moments to exchange stories, how they had defended themselves and how Brother Klee had felt the sword move to meet Andrixine's need. Lord Edrix stared a moment when they confessed that they had stolen away to marry early—then burst out laughing loud enough to make the forest ring.

Despite the dead bodies, the mood was light as they returned to the castle. Lady Arriena pretended dismay when she was called to come hear what Kalsan and Andrixine had done.

"Well, I'll have you know you'll just have to endure the ceremony tomorrow all over again," she said, shaking her head, eyes sparkling to make a lie of her frown. "With all the preparations we've made and the guests expected tomorrow—" Then she laughed and hugged her daughter, kissing both cheeks. A moment later she shocked Kalsan speechless by hugging and kissing him, too.

He was still speechless as everyone began to disperse to return to their beds. Lady Arriena hooked her arm through her daughter's and led her away. Kalsan stared, knowing something was wrong in the picture but forgetting for a moment why Andrixine shouldn't go without him. Then he remembered, and he was more confused than ever. Should he go after her? Should he protest? It wasn't like he could ask advice, could he?

Then he turned and saw Lord Edrix watching him with amusement and sympathy in his eyes. Kalsan wondered if he could ask his new father-in-law what to do. Before he could decide, his brother and two sisters and their spouses descended on him, demanding to know what had happened.

The women thought it all terribly romantic, and his brother and brothers-in-law gave varying approval. Two hours later when he finally reached his too-large room, Kalsan didn't know what he should have done. He only knew he felt very lonely.

Until he saw the dark shape curled up on one side of his bed, asleep. He stood many long moments over her with the lamp in his hand, smiling until he thought his mouth would ache for days. Andrixine's hair was still damp from bathing, freed from her warrior braids. She looked small, wearing a thin, white cotton gown that hinted at tempting curves and shadows. Kalsan peeled off his shirt and boots and lay down on top of the blankets. It felt very right to stretch out next to her, spoon fashion, and wrap an arm around his wife.

"Kal?" she whispered sleepily, stirring at his touch.

"Sshh. Go back to sleep."

"Mother is...the wisest...woman...in the world," she said on a sigh that turned into a yawn.

"Thank Yomnian for that." He pressed a kiss against the back of her neck.

"Tickles." A sleepy laugh escaped her and she turned over to face him.

"Go back to sleep." That was the last thing he wanted, however.

"Kiss me?"

"You'll be sorry." He grinned, his heart suddenly racing at the sparkles that filled her eyes.

Andrixine curved her hand around the back of his neck and kissed him. It was the best possible answer he could have wanted.

PART FOUR
Sendorland

Chapter Eighteen

FOUR DAYS LATER, while out in the eastern fields of the estate, Andrixine saw the king's messenger, waving the king's banner of a black hawk on a green field, approaching down the long, straight trade road to the castle. She and Kalsan had come out with several others to choose which horses to take when they left in the morning for Cereston.

Andrixine knew she shouldn't be surprised to see the messenger. King Rafnar knew about her marriage and her intent to come to Cereston to report to him. It was pure good luck—or perhaps Yomnian's staying hand—that let her and Kalsan have this much time together before appearing in public. The king had likely only sent his messenger as escort.

What surprised her was the troop of twenty warriors in the king's own livery of deep green and black, and a flag flying above them with a silver sword on a dark blue, starry field. The flag of the Sword Bearer. Andrixine managed to keep a calm face, despite her discomfort, when the messenger rode straight to where she waited with Kalsan, Derek, Brother Klee and Jultar, and knelt after dismounting.

"Hail, Sword Bearer," the man said for the fourth time, as he rose from kneeling. He extended the slim pole carrying her flag. "Who rides for the Bearer?"

Derek slid off his mare and darted forward. Andrixine let a smile crack her solemn mask, proud of her brother's poise. He showed the effects of several intense hours of lecturing from Brother Klee, silent, quick, and he remembered to bow to the messenger before he took the banner.

"Greetings to you all from King Rafnar," the man continued. "He welcomes you and asks Yomnian's blessing on you and bids you hurry to join him."

"Does the king send for us for a reason?" Brother Klee asked from his place on Andrixine's left.

She bit her lip against a grin when the messenger went pale. If she hadn't been overwhelmed by other considerations, the thought of Rakleer, alive, would have intimidated her, too.

"Envoys have come from Sendorland, suing for peace."

"That doesn't make sense," Andrixine said, looking first to Kalsan on her right and then Jultar beyond him. "All the signs point to war."

"Envoys have come, speaking of land they claim was stolen from them in the past," the messenger said.

"Do they ask for compensation, or the land itself?" Brother Klee asked.

"That hasn't been spoken in my hearing."

"We should hurry, shouldn't we?" she said. "We're almost ready to leave, anyway."

"Tomorrow," Kalsan muttered. She hoped her face didn't look as red warm as it felt. In his voice, she heard her own longing for more time to grow used to being married. And more privacy.

The messenger hurried back to his own horse to remount. He rode at the back of their group, next to Derek. The king's soldiers followed close behind. Derek proudly held up her banner as he rode, and Andrixine wondered how long it would take for his arm to get tired.

"Hurry, yes," Jultar said as they crossed the wide fields where the horses had been pastured. "If the Sendorland envoys know a new Sword Bearer has appeared, tutored by Rakleer, perhaps they will change the tone of their negotiations."

Andrixine and Kalsan traded knowing grins.

"Lesson time," she murmured.

"Indeed," Brother Klee said. He glanced over his shoulder at the messenger. "Sendorland avoids envoys as a waste of time. The self-righteous always believe that what they want is merely their due, and they have the right to punish anyone who refuses them. When they do send diplomats, it is to make *demands,* not to negotiate. They demand and make threats and paint themselves as righteous victims. They ignore the truth when it suits them—and it suits them often, as history shows."

"Then this is a trick?" Kalsan asked. He glanced at Andrixine, frowning. She could guess his thoughts.

"Is it possible they have visionaries and they know the Spirit Sword is moving again?" she asked. "Maybe they mean to distract us from noticing something else?"

"If so, they are likely in terror," Jultar said. "Remember their prophecy that says a woman with a bright sword will bring disaster on them."

"If they had any sense, they would give up now," Kalsan said, trying for laughter.

The attempt fell flat, and they all nudged their horses to go a little faster. The sooner they were prepared, the sooner they could leave.

Duty called.

THEY SET OUT before noon and that night camped by a trickle of river so small it had no name. Andrixine was glad of Kalsan's warmth against her, his arm tight around her, despite being so self-conscious about lying next to him where everyone could see.

Toward morning, her dreams congealed into a vision that woke her with a choked shout. She tried to sit up and struggled, kicking and twisting, when Kalsan held her.

"Sshh," he whispered in her ear. "It's all right. It's only a dream."

"No." Her voice cracked. "Not a dream." She tugged an arm free and wiped sweat from her face. "Alysyn is—where's Brother Klee?"

The holy man was awake, sitting before the fire. Andrixine settled down next to him, grateful for the knowledge that he had sensed her dreams and foresaw that she would need his help.

"I saw Snowy Mount under attack. Soldiers pour through a crack in the mountain, coming with fire against the walls. They fight and kill, but they don't finish the job." She shook her head, frowning as the vision grew clearer. "The scholars and healers aren't their targets, but obstacles. They tear down the walls, but they have another target, someone inside." Andrixine shuddered. Kalsan slid an arm around her. "It's Alysyn. They want her. Because of me," she finished on a whisper.

"What do you say we should do, Sword Bearer?" Brother Klee asked, voice and gaze neutral. He spoke as a teacher, prompting her to consider and judge for herself.

For a moment, Andrixine resented his calm. She wanted to scream at him to tell her what to do. Then she thought of the implications of this attack. A tiny, nasty smile cracked the agonized mask of her face.

"They think they're making a surprise attack. They'll send a small force against peaceful scholars, sure that no one can resist."

"But we'll be there, won't we?" Kalsan asked. His grin was vicious. "They'll never know what hit them."

"No," Brother Klee said. "They must know what has happened. They must be taught it is futile to try to move secretly against the Spirit Sword, and dangerous to try to harm the Bearer."

THE KING'S MESSENGER balked at the news they would not continue to the capital. He grew pale when Andrixine gave him a message for the king.

"But—Sword Bearer—to command the king—" He shook his

head. Color rushed back into his face in his confusion. Andrixine suspected he had never been at a loss for words before.

"She does not command the king. Yet," Brother Klee added after a pause for emphasis. "It is her right as Bearer to counter the king's instructions. She asks his Majesty to join her in battle against Sendorland. She borrows the soldiers he has sent to accompany her. There is a vast difference."

"Yes, sir," the man said, regaining some poise. He turned back to Andrixine, his face still stricken.

"Don't you understand? If we let them win this first skirmish, they will believe themselves capable of winning the war." Andrixine shuddered at using "skirmish" for the attack aimed at her sister. "We must show them they can do nothing, plan nothing the Spirit Sword cannot enable us to counter." Standing in her stirrups, she pointed to the west, toward Snowy Mount and the mountain barrier between Reshor and Sendorland. "We are going. If it pleases the king, ask him to join us."

She dropped into the saddle, hard enough to make Grennel grunt. Andrixine nudged him, and he leaped forward as if starting a race. Kalsan stayed at her side from the start. Jultar and Brother Klee, with the Oathbound and the king's soldiers close behind in formation, trailed out behind them, leaving the king's messenger staring after them with his mouth hanging open.

Chapter Nineteen

KALSAN WAS ALMOST disappointed to see the unmarred walls and open gates of Snowy Mount with the afternoon shadows stretching out dark and long before them. Their band had covered the distance in seven days of hard riding, cutting through forests and across plains, ignoring trade roads and villages and inns. Each night he held Andrixine close, wrapped in their blankets by the campfire. He watched her for signs of distress, wracking his brains for the right words to say when she needed help. She remained calm, speaking reasonably, discussing terrain and battle maneuvers. Kalsan saw the haunted look in her eyes in unguarded moments, though. He saw when she wiped surreptitiously at her eyes. She was silent during morning and evening prayers, and he knew her heart was too full to speak what weighed on her. He fell silent during worship times as well, and cried out from his heart on her behalf.

When she clung to him in the semi-privacy of their blankets and hid her face against his shoulder to let out a few tears in silence, he understood the importance of his duty. Andrixine, as Sword Bearer, guarded Reshor. He guarded *her*, heart and mind and body.

He wished for a little trouble, a little conflict to let her release the worry churning inside her. It almost would have been welcome to see some sign of trouble among the holy folk. No one rang a warning bell as they rode up to the open gates. The various men and women paused in their tasks and regarded them with only a little interest, no worry or relief on their faces.

Two soldiers with Faxinor triple-cross crests on their tunics saw them and came running from the stables. Then Sister Dainia stepped forward to help with their horses and called out to Brother Klee.

"Where is my sister?" Andrixine asked the guardsman Taran, after greeting him. "And Trilia?"

"No one can guess where the little miss is hiding," Taran said with a crooked grin lighting his dusky, white-bearded face. "Nurse is hunting for her. She has been since just before nooning." He glanced at Kalsan, then back to Andrixine. "Excuse my saying, M'Lady, but I thought you'd still be celebrating your wedding."

"We would, if the sword hadn't spoken," Kalsan broke in. "Have you been here long enough to know the defenses?"

"Defenses, sir?" He rocked back on his heels and stared at Kalsan. "I suppose—"

"I know them," Brother Klee said, joining them after conferring with Sister Dainia. "Come, we must meet with Lucius."

"Alysyn—" Andrixine began.

"Is fine." The holy man rested his hand on her shoulder. "The enemy has not arrived, and, if I am correct, will not for several more days." He gestured toward the central building. Andrixine frowned, but didn't resist when he led the way across the courtyard and inside.

"You said once..." Her frown deepened as she thought. "The sword gives you visions of what men plan, yes? The future if we don't intervene?"

"The sword showed you the plans as they were made. If the plans were made in the capital in Sendorland, they have even further to travel than we did. And, unless the army has changed its ways since I wore the Spirit Sword, it does not take only a few hours to arm and provision and assemble an attacking force. Even a small one, to fight some unprepared, unarmed scholars." Brother Klee's tight smile grew sharp.

Kalsan saw what sort of warrior he had been, generations ago. He thought of Andrixine wearing that expression in another hundred years, teaching the next Bearer. He shuddered.

"I think I know why and how they chose Snowy Mount and Alysyn," Andrixine said, when they passed through the wide, double doors and started down the cool, blue-tiled hallway. "Uncle Maxil. He came across the border when he escaped Faxinor. That's why we couldn't find him. He told them I was Sword Bearer. He told them how to hurt me by taking Alysyn."

"Then he can't know Feril is dead," Kalsan said.

"No." She shook her head. Her eyes narrowed as she visibly added that bit of information to her calculations.

"We can use that against him at the proper time."

"You make a good team," Brother Klee said. They came to a cross hall, and he gestured to the left. "May you, together, be a curse on your enemies and a blessing on your allies."

A few steps later Andrixine halted, holding out a hand to signal them to silence. Kalsan turned to her, worried, then puzzled when he saw the smile curl up the corners of her mouth. He hadn't seen her smile like that in days. Then he heard a little girl's prattling voice.

"No one would think to bother Lucius for Alysyn's whereabouts," Brother Klee said, eyes sparkling.

Kalsan felt a considerable brightening of the atmosphere as they continued down the hall. The door to the High Scholar's quarters stood ajar, letting them peek through the gap before announcing themselves.

Alysyn sat on the woven rug, moving carved wooden animals and describing what each one did and thought to the white-garbed, smiling man sitting on the hearth watching her. A decimated bowl of cherry conserves and muffins sat within her reach, with evidence of her snacking smeared on her face and her blue dress. Kalsan studied the little girl, seeing the Faxinor bones softened by baby fat. He glanced at Andrixine, startled by the sight of her face balanced between laughter and tears.

He felt a dropping sensation in his stomach, not at all unpleasant, when he remembered they were expected to have children. He wouldn't mind a little red-haired girl or two.

"Did you save any cherries for me?" Andrixine asked, pushing the door open.

"Rixy!" Alysyn crowed after staring at her sister for five long seconds, her mouth hanging open and all the toys dropping from her hands. She clapped her hands and sprang from the floor to fling herself at her sister.

"Poppet." She hugged the little girl, spinning them in a circle twice before settling on the bench next to the door. "Have you been a good soldier like you promised? You haven't been giving High Scholar Lucius trouble?" she added, giving the man a smile and nod in greeting.

"She has brightened our days considerably," the elderly man said, rising to meet them. "What brings you back to us so swiftly?"

"The sword has shown her trouble striking Snowy Mount," Brother Klee said.

"Ah." He turned a curious smile to Kalsan.

"High Scholar Lucius," Andrixine hurried to say, "this is my husband, Kalsan of Hestrin."

"Of Faxinor," Kalsan corrected her with a mocking frown. "We came all the way to meet you, little sister," he added, when Alysyn's eyes grew wide and she opened her mouth to blurt the question visible on her face.

"But Rixy—" The child shook her head, a pout turning her mouth into a rosebud.

"It's all right, poppet." Andrixine squeezed her sister until she giggled. "We're going to have a special party when you get home again, just because you missed the wedding. You'll like that, won't you?" She waited until the child's face relaxed into a smile again, then put her down. "Now, I want you to go find Nurse. She's been looking for you."

"Nursey?" Alysyn wriggled free of Andrixine's arms. "Where?" She darted out the door before her sister could answer.

"Has she truly been all right?" she asked, turning back to Lucius.

"A very good soldier," the man assured her. "Now, what has happened since you left us? I assume your mother is safe and your quest complete?"

"More than complete." Andrixine turned to Kalsan, her eyes bright for a moment. "We have much to tell you, and much to prepare for."

THEY JOINED BATTLE with the Sendorland soldiers—forty men, leading their horses because of the roughness of the terrain—at dawn three days later, in a ravine two hours' ride from Snowy Mount. Brother Klee had sent word to Maysford, and the blacksmith, Brick, sent out the call, putting the countryside on alert. A shepherd boy saw the invaders' campfire and sent word to Snowy Mount, giving the defenders the advantage of choosing their battlefield.

Andrixine sat astride Grennel on the lip of the ravine the invaders followed, looked down into the misty, rubble-strewn, bush-clogged bottom, and smiled. She didn't mind the chill of the night still soaking her bones or the bruises from rocks that had poked through her blankets and Kalsan's best efforts to make her comfortable. She didn't care the enemy outnumbered her warriors with the king's company still a week's ride away at best. She didn't mind the early hour—it was to their advantage. All that mattered was that the battle would go nowhere near Snowy Mount.

With the element of surprise, the early hour and knowledge of the terrain on their side, her warriors and the king's soldiers could meet and beat back, if not defeat the invaders.

The important question in all this was whether these Sendorland soldiers were spies, the leading edge of a larger force, or a lone band coming on the scholars' retreat in arrogant confidence. They didn't look threatening to her as they picked their way through the morning mist, their cloaks hanging heavy with damp, watching the ground under their feet, clinging to the reins of their horses. The horses slowed and held back, Andrixine noted. The animals were wiser than their masters, knowing ambush waited ahead of them, and unwilling to meet it.

A questioning whinny floated up through the heavy, chill air from the ravine floor. The light grew a little brighter, the air a bit warmer as the rising sun nibbled at the gray filling it. Another horse called from the ravine.

Silence grew thick and heavy with waiting and watching tension. Andrixine stood in her stirrups, waiting for the first sign the Sendorland forces saw her band. She rested her hand on the Spirit Sword at her hip, vibrating with a life that disturbed and exhilarated her.

There—a head lifted, eyes moving from scanning the unsure footing to study the sky. The face looked pale against a thin line of black beard. Even from a long bowshot away, Andrixine saw the man's eyes widen, and he opened his mouth to speak.

"Go back!" she shouted, cupping her hands around her mouth. "If you do not turn around, you will be destroyed!"

Shouts and curses and the screams of startled horses were her answer. The Sendorland soldiers continued forward. She looked to Jultar. Her war chief nodded, smiling grimly, and raised his sword.

"Down!" she shouted, drawing the Spirit Sword and raising it high.

The blade exploded with light. Her warriors leaped forward to force the battle exactly where they had chosen.

The invaders in the ravine scrambled to mount their horses. Risking their animals' legs on rough ground, they dashed toward smoother, open land beyond the ravine. As Andrixine wanted.

The ravine widened, and the ground sloped down to flatten into a plain perfect for battle. The rubble strewing the landscape was scattered far enough not to endanger their horses.

Grennel streaked down the slope to the fighting ground. This was what he had been bred for. Andrixine felt his eagerness shuddering through his straining muscles.

Her warriors—she could actually feel they were *her* warriors— raced at her heels in a clatter of hooves and chain mail, and arrows rattling in quivers. The ground dropped swiftly, bringing them to the plain moments before the Sendorland party broke out into the open. Andrixine turned Grennel to face them and saw the last shreds of mist evaporate as sunlight lanced over the edge of the ravine. She stood in her stirrups again, raising the sword, and let out the war cry filling her throat. Kalsan joined her, then the rest.

It bounced off the rocks, off the invaders, off the very sky itself. The first riders emerging from the ravine yanked hard on their reins, making their horses stumble to a ragged halt. Ten lengths away, Andrixine saw their faces clearly now—confusion, dismay, anger.

"This is your last chance to turn around," Jultar roared as their forces slowed. "There is nowhere you can cross Reshor's borders that you will not be met and stopped."

"You only have ten warriors behind you," a soldier called. "Why should we listen to you?" His voice cracked on the last three words as the twenty soldiers in King Rafnar's livery appeared behind Andrixine's warriors.

A Sendorland soldier blew a trumpet blast. Andrixine shuddered in dismay as the enemy dug their heels into their mounts and leaped forward, forcing the battle.

Behind her, Kalsan let out a shout and stood in his stirrups as his horse darted forward. The other warriors took up his cry, the soldiers echoed him and the ground shuddered under their horses' hooves.

After that, she was only aware of the shouts of men, the ringing clash of swords and the blue glow of the Spirit Sword in her mind as it guided her hand. Andrixine guided Grennel with her knees, clinging tight with her legs, swinging a spear with one hand and the Spirit Sword with the other. Her chain mail shimmered and chimed with every sharp movement. Her helmet sat light and hot on her head, absorbing the heat of the rising sun. She ignored it.

Horses slammed up against Grennel, threatening his balance. He turned and kicked and bit, protecting his rider, keeping her legs from being smashed between his and other massive, sweating bodies.

She knew Kalsan was there, fighting to keep close to her, constantly watching for the stray arrow or sword or an enemy coming up behind her. She felt his concern every time his glance touched her. Andrixine fought tears and didn't know if she was happy or sad—but she knew he was her life, higher than her vows, Faxinor or her family.

Fire touched her leg. She bit her tongue and turned, swinging the spear up and over. The man who had cut the shallow slice into her thigh stared, his eyes rolling up in his head to follow the arch of the spear down into his chest. A silent shriek opened his mouth as the momentum propelled the spear out his back. He twitched once, twisting sideways off his horse. Andrixine nearly dropped her sword to hold the spear and prevent it being yanked from her hand.

"Are you all right?" Kalsan shouted through the momentary calm around her.

"Fine." She looked around for another attacker, then touched her slashed trousers. Blood pooled from the slice in her muscle, soaking into the thick cloth. Swallowing hard, Andrixine pressed the flat of her sword against her violated flesh. Fire and ice raced through her body, twisting the breath from her lungs. Then it was over. Only dried blood and a slight swelling showed where she had been wounded. That, and the jagged cut in her clothes.

Then another soldier came at her, his spear raised, and she turned to face him.

The battle ended when all the Sendorland soldiers had lost their mounts. Two were on foot, staggering in retreat. The others were dead or trying to get back to their feet. Not one was unmarked. Those who still held their weapons dropped them with dull thuds on the churned ground at Jultar's order.

Andrixine slumped in her saddle, feeling the aches and stings, the bruises and sweat and strained muscles. The heat hit her with the force of a toppling wall of stone. Her hand cramped around the hilt of the sword. She doubted she could let go without prying her fingers free with a chisel. Her arm ached as she wiped the sword clean and sheathed it. She caught a motion from the corner of her eye and, turning, saw two horses and riders appear in the mouth of the ravine.

"Catch them!" Derek shouted from his vantage point on the ravine edge high above. He raised his trumpet to his lips and blew an ear-cracking blast as the newcomers fled.

Andrixine shook her head, feeling a weary daze settle around her shoulders. Brenden and Rogan darted across the churned plain, their horses leaping over bodies and gouges in the soil. Derek darted down the slope, urging his horse faster, holding on with one hand while he tried to keep blowing his horn. Andrixine knew she should try to stop him but she was too tired, too numb. If one of the wounded enemy tried to hurt him, her brother would learn caution and not at too high a price.

Somehow, she moved on. As leader, it was her duty to tally the cost of the battle, to count the wounded and dead and dying. A corner of her mind waited for the first sign of Derek's return as she slid off Grennel and walked across the torn battlefield.

Brother Klee appeared with five healers from Snowy Mount, dispensing salves, bandages, wine and food to the wounded on both sides. Andrixine felt useless as she walked with Jultar, inspecting damaged weapons and wounded horses, indicating a place to bury the dead and another place to set up a tent for those who needed more extensive help and could not be moved.

None of her warriors had died. She concentrated on that every time she saw a blood-soaked bandage. No one would lose a hand or leg or eye or arm. Xandar had the worst injury. A battleaxe had crashed down on his helmet, splitting it in three pieces and opening a thumb-wide gash across his scalp from forehead to behind his right ear.

Brother Klee had to shave all his hair away before he could clean, salve and sew the cut. Xandar complained of dizziness, but his vision was steady and he didn't lose the drugged wine he drank. He would recover.

Kalsan was bruised and filthy from falling when his saddle was cut from under him and he rolled through dirt and the remains of a slashed water bag. Otherwise, both he and Fala were unhurt, and Andrixine sent up a silent prayer of thanks when she found out. Kalsan took charge of the prisoners, supervising them as they dug graves for their fallen comrades. He let them wash and eat some bread and cheese before making them dig.

Then Derek's horn cut through the moaning of the injured, the snorting of tired horses, the sound of shovels in dirt and the dragging of bodies across torn sod. She turned, feeling a small surge of energy that came from relief, and knew how her mother felt when one of her children returned from an adventure.

"Andrixine!" Derek called as he darted from the ravine. He urged his straining horse faster, waving his horn and dashing to meet her. "Uncle Maxil is here!" the boy shouted over the thuds of his horse's hooves. He grinned, pale and spattered with dirt and darker spots she hoped would be someone else's blood. "We caught him and a Sendorland lord—they're furious!"

"I imagine." Andrixine turned to Jultar and gave him a questioning look.

The warlord's smile was all nasty satisfaction. "They came expecting to see their own soldiers winning."

Derek nodded, his smile twisting to mirror Jultar's. He had never liked their cousin, though he had admired their uncle's clever way with words. Learning of the plot to kill his sister had given Derek a taste of the bitter side of life.

Andrixine rested a hand on her brother's shoulder as she walked with him and Jultar to meet the four men coming from the ravine. Brenden and Rogan were mounted, leading the other two horses. Their prisoners walked before them with their hands tied behind their backs. As she drew closer, Andrixine saw their torn, dirty clothes, and she smiled. Good—her enemies had tried to fight and brought rough treatment on themselves. She hoped they were bruised as well.

Maxil of Faxinor looked away when the two small groups met. The other nobleman glared. He was dressed for victory, Andrixine decided, his flowing cape of royal blue lined with white better suited to a king's ballroom than a battlefield. His long coat was royal blue over a white shirt, his trousers trimmed in gold that just matched the shade of his short, curled hair. He focused his furious stare on Andrixine. His eyes reminded her of someone, though she was sure she had never seen that person look so self-righteously angry.

"Will you give your name?" Jultar asked.

"I am Lord Mordon Traxslan, advisor to King Drahas of Sendorland." Mordon kept his eyes fixed on Andrixine. "You would do well to let me go now, before your crimes grow greater."

"Is it a crime to defend our land against invasion?" Andrixine asked, unable to keep a touch of disbelieving laughter from her voice.

"You, woman, will keep your mouth closed in my presence!" the Sendorland lord snapped.

"This is Andrixine Faxinor, chosen of Yomnian, the Sword Bearer and our war leader," Jultar said with cold reproof.

"So you are Arriena's child." Mordon's lips twisted as if ill. "I knew I should have killed her in the cradle. I knew she was a lying whore like all women, from the moment she was born."

"Don't speak like that about my mother!" Derek blurted. He gripped his short knife and took two steps toward the man. Andrixine stopped him with a hand on his shoulder.

"So you are our mother's cousin." She smiled stiffly. "You tried to use her to harm our father."

"She is a filthy traitor, worthy of death," Mordon spat. He glared at her, and his shoulders hunched, as if he would tear his hands free of his bonds and lunge at her. Then he glanced at Maxil and his fury turned to an icy grin. "It seems treachery runs strong in both sides of your family, Sword Bearer. You'll find that the heresy of your demon blade will not protect you from Yomnian's justice."

"You are the villain here, not us. You are our prisoner, caught in the act of invasion, violating long-standing peace treaties." She kept her voice smooth, her face neutral. Weariness made that easier, not harder.

"You have no proof," he returned with a shrug.

"Confessions from the commander of your soldiers?" Jultar said. "The visions of the Spirit Sword, which brought us here? I think that proof enough."

"Visions. Spirit Sword. Women warriors. Faugh!" Mordon spat, barely missing Andrixine's toes.

Jultar backhanded him, and no one helped Mordon to his feet. He waited until the arrogant man wiped the blood from his nose and lips onto his sleeve. "What ransom can you offer for the return of your soldiers and your safe conduct to the border?"

Mordon drew himself up straight, split lips pursing as if he held something nasty in his mouth. "We have no gold, nothing to give in ransom," he said, his voice tight, eyes like coals, revealing how galling the words were. To invade enemy territory without the means of ransom in case his mission failed was the height of arrogance—or stupidity.

Chapter Twenty

AFTER FOUR DAYS of waiting for King Rafnar and his forces to arrive, Andrixine discovered boredom. It totally surprised her. She couldn't understand how she could be bored, with so much to do and everyone demanding her attention, her opinion, her decisions. They came to her at every hour of the day with reports on building up Snowy Mount's defenses, or information coming from Maysford, or new figures on the supplies of food and medicine, or scouting forays into the ravines and gullies around the valley.

Brick arrived from Maysford with two wagonloads of weapons and young men to offer their services to the holy folk and their vows to the Sword Bearer. Alysyn was on her way home to Faxinor and safety, so Andrixine didn't have her sister for distraction. Kalsan acted as her eyes and ears and voice, riding on inspection at all hours. Brother Klee put aside his scholar's robes to give instruction in the finer points of warfare to the young men from Maysford, so he had few hours free to teach her.

Andrixine longed to be free of questions and constantly spying eyes, just for an hour. Just to take a walk outside the suffocating walls of Snowy Mount. The forest beyond the fields and orchards of the retreat was reportedly clear of spies or intruders. Who would it harm if she vanished for a few hours just to clear her head and be alone? Yet, how could she escape unseen?

It took her two days to remember she had packed several dresses when she thought they were going to Cereston and the king. Among the fine court dresses was a simple one, nearly a peasant's costume, in hopes that Kalsan could keep his promise and take her exploring through the city when they weren't needed in court. With her warrior braids hidden under a kerchief that any proper, married woman would use, Andrixine knew she could escape undetected. Would it do any harm if she wasn't available for an hour?

The next afternoon, she had her chance. At lunch, they discussed a new training phase for the young recruits. That would involve all the warriors and soldiers and leave her free for a short time. Andrixine excused herself as soon as politely possible and fled the refectory. It was a matter of moments to skin out of her clothes in her room and tug on the white, snug-fitting bodice and green skirt and petticoats and tuck up her braids. She tied the matching green kerchief into place as she scurried down the hall.

The young soldier in the king's livery standing guard at the main gate barely nodded to her as she hurried by. He likely thought she was another village woman come to visit her man in soldier training. She bit her tongue to fight laughter until she had vanished around the curving walls and headed toward the short path to the forest.

She was barefoot to complete the disguise. The dust felt warm and soft under her feet and kicked up in little clouds. On the eastern side of the retreat's high walls, past the orchards and fields, stretched green, deep forest. She intended to enjoy herself, exploring in perfect peace and quiet.

The moment she left the shadowed safety of the walls, Andrixine felt another presence. Her neck prickled with the sensation, like a cold breeze had brushed it. She quickened her steps and checked to be sure her knife was secure on her belt.

A lull fell in the gentle breeze that made the leaves whisper. She heard a single set of booted feet thumping softly on the dusty little trail to the woods. One man, she could handle. She quickened her steps and moved off the trail to run on grass and not risk her bare feet on stones.

"Andrixine!" Kalsan called, laughing. "Wait for me!"

Her heart leaped in her chest for a few beats. She turned and waited for him, hands on hips, wondering if she felt angry or foolish.

"What are you doing out here?" he asked when he reached her.

"I needed to get away."

"That's the truth. You can't go anywhere without hearing battle stories or battle plans." Kalsan reached for her hand. He cocked his head to one side and smiled crookedly at her. "Where were you going?"

"To explore the woods. I doubt enemy soldiers would be hiding in it," she added, forestalling any protest he might make.

"I should hope not. I've done three patrols through there already." He nodded toward the trees. "There are several nice, shady spots there—private places—that I've been meaning to mention to you."

"Oh?" She let him tug on her arm to get her walking again.

"Not as nice as our place back at Faxinor, but rather charming." He chuckled and slid his arm around her waist. "I'm just curious why you didn't ask me along."

"You, I thought, had other plans for this afternoon." She leaned into the delicious comfort of his arm around her. It amazed her again how much she enjoyed such simple contact.

"My plans can go drown in the sea if they interfere with my more important duties."

"Such as?"

"Tending to the happiness and comfort of the Sword Bearer." He pulled his face into a somber mask of pompous dignity, drawing laughter from her. "That's much better. You've been too serious lately."

"I can't imagine why." They stepped into the shadows of the forest. The trees rose tall and thick around them, immediately cutting them off from view of the monastery's walls.

"I like to hear you laugh. What's wrong with that?" he asked, chuckling a little when she shook her head.

"I sound like a donkey when I laugh. It's from when I was so ill. And...it still hurts sometimes to laugh."

"I know. I can hear the pain. But I hear your strength and healing, and your determination to know joy despite it all. That's what's so beautiful about you," he finished on a whisper, drawing her close.

"Kal," she sighed, feeling herself melt as he brushed the lightest kiss across her lips. "You make me feel..."

"Hmm?" Kalsan drew back enough to see her face. Mischief and hunger sparkled in his eyes, making her blush. "What?"

"I don't have the words. Complete, maybe. That's the closest I can come."

"Flatterer." He shook her a little. "This moment, all I feel is lustful. Forgive me."

"No." She laughed when he blinked, startled. "You flatter me, my Lord Kalsan. And what's wrong with feeling lustful inside our marriage vows? I think this is a gift from Yomnian, too."

"My wise lady." Kalsan tucked a wisp of hair back into her kerchief. "Only you could see Yomnian's guiding in something so earthy." He nodded, drawing her close so her head rested on his shoulder again. "Maybe everything in this world is good in its proper place and time."

"The way Yomnian wanted it to be, before we sinned."

"Hmm. Yes. But I must tell you what is not in its proper place. This dress on the battlefield." He scowled when she could only laugh. "Every warrior will watch you and not fight."

"It's just for today, you know. To get out unseen."

"Why would you want to do that?" Kalsan brushed a soft kiss across her lips.

"I wanted to get away from everyone for a while."

"Even me?" he whispered, tightening his arms around her.

"No, but..." Gladly, she let him stop her words with kisses.

"But what?" he whispered, releasing her mouth for a few seconds.

"I don't remember."

Kalsan grinned and captured her mouth again. Laughter bubbled between them, and they clung to each other until the quiet of the forest took over.

"What we should really do is sneak back to our room and catch a few hours of sleep," he said after a moment. To give lie to his words, he tightened his arms around her.

"But?"

"But we are warriors, and though these woods were declared safe this morning doesn't mean they are now."

"We could have a pleasant walk, at the very least." She slid her arms between them and pushed. "Kalsan—"

He resisted, sparks appearing in his eyes. "Where do you think you're going, wife?"

"We have to patrol."

He grinned when she pushed harder. "Right now?"

"Yes, right now," she retorted, pushing with the heels of her hands planted square on his breastbone. Kalsan laced his fingers together behind her back, locking her tighter into his arms. "Sometimes, you are so—stubborn!"

"Thank you, my lady. The compliment is returned in double force." He kissed her nose, drawing a squeal from her.

A plan came to her. She continued pressing back, stretching his arms to their limit. She balanced on one foot. Kalsan sensed the change and looked down. She stomped hard on his booted foot. Her bare foot felt bruised, but Kalsan let out a yelp. His hold loosened for a moment. She threw herself against him and dropped to her knees, to leap and twist free and run.

Laughing, Kalsan raced after her. Andrixine stumbled on forest debris, bruising her feet more. She wished she had worn her boots, even if they did look ridiculous with her skirts. She skimmed over piles of leaves and darted behind trees, trying to throw him off her trail. Her heart hammered, and her breath caught in her lungs. It was hard to run when laughter tried to bend her double.

Kalsan didn't shout after her, all too aware of the possible danger in their play. Andrixine raced up an incline, gaining a few seconds. Kalsan raced up after her, arms outstretched. She heard multiple hoof beats and paused to discern the direction. Kalsan leaped, wrapping his arms around her. They tumbled down the incline, picking up bits of twigs and leaves and moss until they hit flat ground and slowed to a stop. They lay tangled together, helpless in shudders of laughter.

"You're a terrible man, my Lord Kalsan," she sputtered, and wriggled as he kissed the nape of her neck.

"Indeed he is," a tenor voice said, accompanied by hoof beats entering the clearing where they had landed. "Kalsan of Hestrin, don't you have anything better to do than tumble peasant girls almost under the king's nose?"

"That voice," Kalsan growled in her ear. He released her and struggled to sit up. "Vorberon, how nice to see you again."

Andrixine recognized the name. Kalsan had told her about the officious bully who used the king's authority like a club. Vorberon had tried to intimidate Kalsan during his short trip to Cereston to track her uncle, until he learned the young warrior was to marry the Sword Bearer. Her husband was anything but pleased to see the man now.

Andrixine rolled over and sat up. She brushed her hands over herself, making sure her clothes were straight and nothing exposed. After one look at the tall, broad-shouldered blond man in the king's green and black livery, she knew she wouldn't have liked him even if Kalsan hadn't told her about him. Not his cool, slightly scandalized tone of voice or the arrogant tilt to his head or the way his lip curled a little when she faced him. His gaze roved over her, noting the curves in her bodice.

"I assume we're almost to Snowy Mount," Vorberon said. He dismounted his chestnut gelding and strode over to the heap of leaves and twigs they sat in.

"Through the woods." Kalsan's voice tightened, sending a thrill through Andrixine.

"Hurry on ahead and tell them the king is coming."

"Isn't that your job?"

"It is, but you'll obey me." Vorberon held out a hand to Andrixine. She refused his help and stayed seated in the leaves.

"How close is the king?"

"Close enough that if you don't tell the High Scholar and the Sword Bearer he's coming, both sides will be upset with you," he said, tone light, a nasty gleam in his eyes.

"The Sword Bearer knows," Andrixine said, her voice breaking slightly from smothered laughter. Kalsan glared at her—then worked to stifle his own grin.

"What would a peasant slut know about the Sword Bearer?"

Vorberon snapped.

"Watch your tongue, Vorberon!" Kalsan leaped to his feet, fists clenched.

"No, you watch yours," Vorberon said, breaking out in nasty laughter. He gestured over his shoulder as four foot soldiers stepped out of the trees behind him. All four were the type of muscular hulks with minimal intelligence that weak men with much power kept around them. "What do you think will happen, Hestrin, when your wife learns about your betrayal?"

"My wife?" His voice cracked.

"His wife?" Andrixine wanted to laugh, but it chilled in her chest as she realized Vorberon threatened Kalsan. "You don't know what you're talking about."

"Not that I blame him for playing while he can," Vorberon said with a sneer as his guards stepped closer. They watched Kalsan carefully, especially the sword in his belt. "The Sword Bearer is manly enough she would look ridiculous in a dress."

"Oh, really?" Andrixine bit her lip against laughing. "You've seen her, have you?" She grinned at Kalsan, and saw he glared at Vorberon.

"I don't need to see her. Just look at the Sword Sisters—every one of them took up the sword because no man would have them. You, girl, will play with me, too, or your sweetheart could lose his head." Vorberon reached out and grabbed at Andrixine's arm.

"Leave her be!" Kalsan growled. He flung the courtier to the ground, making him tumble backwards.

The four guards attacked en mass. Kalsan ducked and rolled aside and leaped to his feet fighting. Andrixine turned to find a stout stick for a club, to help, but Vorberon's arms snaked around her from behind.

"Now we can have some fun." He chuckled, his breath hot against the back of her neck when she started to struggle. He had her arms pinned at her sides.

"Let her go!" Kalsan shouted and tried to break through the wall of men. Two held onto his arms, so he couldn't pull his sword free. A gloved fist hit his face and blood spattered.

Andrixine muffled a squeal when Vorberon shifted one hand to search her bodice. Hot fury flowed through her, fighting the chill of terror and memory. She freed one arm and found her knife. It flashed in the sunlight as she slashed down. Vorberon jerked aside so she only sliced his hip. That distracted him enough she could turn and twist free, and in the process bring a knee up into his gut.

Vorberon gasped and hunched over, one clutching hand swinging out and snatching at her kerchief. Andrixine slammed her doubled fists down on the back of his neck, and he crumpled like a puppet with no strings, yanking the kerchief free.

Kalsan shouted wordless rage. She turned to see one opponent sway a moment before falling flat on his face. That left three still fighting him.

Vorberon's sword lay in clear view. Andrixine knelt on his chest and yanked the weapon free. The man blinked and stared at her through tear-filled eyes.

"Move, and I'll gut you like the filthy pig you are," she growled as she got up, digging her knee into his chest one last time. She turned back to the fighters, the sword raised. Another man staggered back from the fight. He turned, saw her bring the sword within a hand of his chest, and froze. His face turned white in the forest shadows.

Hoof beats broke through the sounds of flesh thudding on flesh and men shouting in pain and anger. Andrixine stepped toward the combatants, hesitant to strike without warning. They were the king's men, after all. The man she held at sword's point broke and ran.

Riders appeared around the bend in the forest trail. One man shouted and pointed. The cry was echoed. She heard someone give blurred orders, and suddenly more men in livery and fighting leathers appeared, leaping off their horses to race up and separate the fighters.

Kalsan struggled several moments longer, until he realized the two men he fought were also being held. His face was bruised, blood trickling from his nose to clot in his new beard. He turned, searching until he found her. His eyes widened, and he grinned when he saw the sword in her hands, her warrior braids hanging free.

"Let him go," she told the two horsemen holding Kalsan.

"Not without the king's orders...Sword Bearer?" the taller, red-haired one ventured. The double cord of blue and silver binding her braids was a telling clue, she realized, even if she hadn't been threatening him with a sword.

"Where is the king?" she demanded. From the corner of her eye, Andrixine saw Vorberon begin to struggle to his feet with the help of more liveried men.

There was a commotion at the head of the column of riders. One man dismounted and approached. Andrixine studied him, noted his cloak and trousers, rich in color and weave, yet simple in cut; noted the fine make of his helmet and the dull silver gleam of his chain mail shirt; noted how some people moved out of his way and others followed in careful attendance. Dark red hair like banked coals, blue-green eyes, wide cheekbones and a nose like a hawk, Rafnar, king of Reshor was a striking man. He looked enough like his cousin, Commander Jeshra, that Andrixine would know him even without the other clues. The moment she thought that, Jeshra herself appeared from behind the king. She nodded to Andrixine, face somber but eyes dancing with laughter.

"Lady Andrixine Faxinor?" King Rafnar said, giving her a nodding bow, one power to another.

"Majesty." She curtsied—difficult with a sword. "Please tell your men to release my husband."

"Would you kindly tell me what happened?" He gestured for his men to do so.

"The strumpet tried to kill me," Vorberon said as two servants helped him limp to meet the king.

"My wife doesn't *try*, Vorberon. She succeeds," Kalsan growled.

"He ordered his men to attack my husband so he could rape me. Or rather, *try* to rape me," she countered. She didn't fight her chilly smile when Vorberon's face went pale and his mouth dropped open. Panic made his eyes dull.

"That is a serious charge, my Lady Faxinor." The king frowned, then turned to Kalsan who joined Andrixine and mopped at his bloody face with his sleeve. "Kalsan of Hestrin and Faxinor?"

"Your service, your Majesty." Kalsan managed to keep the growl from his voice. He bowed, but shallowly. Despite his torn, dirty clothes he looked more regal than two-thirds of the nobles surrounding them now.

"You serve me well by serving your wife so well." His stern face softened a little when Kalsan straightened and some of his anger faded. "What do you add to the charge Lady Andrixine has made?"

"Vorberon is a fool." Kalsan rested his hand on Andrixine's shoulder. "He saw us sparking and thought I betrayed my wife. After all, how can a woman warrior be lovely?"

"How indeed?" the king murmured. A hint of amusement touched his eyes. "Go on."

He appeared not to notice when chuckles rippled through the long column of soldiers and nobles fading into the forest shadows behind him. A good portion of that laughter was female, and Andrixine looked long enough to see many warriors with Sword Sister purple in their braids.

"He called Andrixine a peasant slut and then said my wife was too manly to be a woman. Then he demanded that Andrixine...entertain him. He set his men on me when I defended her. We never really had a chance to explain the truth," he added, shrugging. Andrixine felt the shaking in his hand that rested on her shoulder, and knew he held her to hide it.

"Rape is punished by death. Attempted rape by castration," King Rafnar said. "What do you say in your defense, Vorberon?"

"Your Majesty..." Vorberon shuddered. He turned to Andrixine, opened his mouth to spill the pleading in his eyes—and stopped short when he saw his sword in her hand.

"Stupidity and arrogance shouldn't be punished so drastically," Andrixine said, surprising herself with her words. She turned the sword and offered it to the servant supporting Vorberon. The man's hand shook as he reached to take it.

"Indeed not, Lady Andrixine." The king smiled. "We do have more serious matters to discuss." He offered her his arm.

"Very serious, Majesty. We have already fought a small force from Sendorland, and the men we captured say more will appear any day now."

"Then it seems we have arrived just in time."

THE ECHOING, STONE-PAVED refectory at Snowy Mount became the king's council chamber. Andrixine sat at King Rafnar's right hand, the sheathed Spirit Sword resting on the table before her. The tables had all been moved to form a disjointed oval, with Jultar, Brother Klee, High Scholar Lucius, Kalsan and the members of her war band near the head table; Commander Jeshra and Commander Caleen of the Cereston Sword Sister Chapter House, with their seconds, and the king's counselors and warlords sat further down. Sword Sisters stood along the walls and before the doors as guards, dressed for battle. They watched Andrixine as if she were the only person in the room.

She sat still and listened, weighing the news the king's men had brought. She didn't need the sword's gift of visions to see Reshor would be in trouble if they listened to the blandishments of the Sendorland envoy. He had come to the king speaking of peace, of holding back the raider bands that crept through the barrier mountain range, in exchange for the return of land Sendorland had lost generations ago.

Andrixine knew the envoy would claim Lord Mordon had acted without King Drahas' knowledge or approval. From what her mother had taught her of Sendorland, Lord Mordon would not dare move without the king's knowledge. The envoy was there to delay Reshor's preparations until his own military had the advantage.

"Yomnian, guide me. Work in me. Work through me. I am your servant," Andrixine whispered. Beside her, Kalsan held her hand under the table.

The Spirit Sword's glow brightened, flickering with white and gold. Kalsan noticed and turned to watch. Then the counselors past him saw and reacted.

Prompted by a silent voice in her mind and by stories of previous Sword Bearers, Andrixine stood and raised the sword, scabbard in one hand and hilt in the other, stopping the king in mid-sentence.

"Majesty, will you listen to what the Spirit Sword says?" She almost smiled when the king nodded, eyes widening. Almost smiled, but for the certainty she would not like what she saw.

Andrixine slid the blade free, raised it to point to the ceiling and closed her eyes. Silently, she prayed what Brother Klee had taught her, to calm and open her mind. The light grew stronger, piercing her closed lids. She could almost feel the fearing wonder of the counselors around the table.

Screaming horses raced past. Blood spattered everywhere, turning the grass black. Smoke filled the sky. The sun was red like blood and sitting low on the eastern horizon, cradled in a stony pass she knew well from scouting trips.

"Dawn," she gasped. Andrixine blinked hard to clear her eyes of the vision as the blade's light dimmed. "Sendorland attacks at dawn. We must stop them here, or not at all." She turned to the king, unashamed of the tears in her eyes. Her head ached, echoing the pained thumping of her heart.

"To arms," King Rafnar said, standing. No one but Andrixine's own warriors moved.

"Why do you hesitate?" Commander Caleen shouted from halfway down the room. She stood and saluted Andrixine. "The Sword Bearer has spoken!"

"YOU ARE ANGRY," Brother Klee said.

"I don't have time to be angry." Kalsan tested the point on the spearhead he had just sharpened. He flinched and sucked on the new bleeding pinprick in his thumb.

"You have been miserable since you returned with the king." The holy man sat on the bench facing Kalsan and reached for another whetstone and a waiting sword.

"Did the sword show you that?" Kalsan flinched when his voice echoed around the stone room. It had once been a creamery, before Snowy Mount expanded and the dairy moved elsewhere. The room had most recently been used for training Andrixine back to health, and now Jultar had taken it over as a weapons room.

"I don't need the sword, merely strong eyes and concern for those around me." Brother Klee delicately wiped the whetstone along the blade three times before speaking again. "Andrixine told me what happened."

"Did she tell you I nearly let her get raped?" he growled, then hissed when the spearhead shifted in his grip.

"That isn't how she sees it."

"My lady is too generous. I was useless."

"You were outnumbered."

"Vorberon is a bully. I should have known he wouldn't try anything without someone to back his hand."

"You did very well, incapacitating two of four strong men in a very unfair fight."

"While Vorberon put his hands on my wife!" Kalsan flung down the spearhead. "If he had managed—"

"He didn't."

"I wanted to kill him just for frightening her."

"Isn't that rather drastic?"

"She is my life!" Kalsan caught his breath, hearing his voice echo around the room. "Just the thought of her being hurt tears into me worse than a sword. If she—she is my life," he repeated, fading to a whisper. "I hate that sword because it takes her into battle."

"The sword protects her and heals her."

"She'll be in danger the rest of her life. I'll spend my life protecting her, worrying about assassins and getting separated from her in battle and..." He shook his head. "I don't know how to explain this terror I feel for her."

"You love her," Brother Klee said, a faint smile quirking the corners of his mouth.

"I've loved her since before I met her." Kalsan slumped on the bench. "I dreamed of her before we met. She ruined me for all the sweethearts I had made along the way. I knew I had to find her. And then I found out Drixus was Andrixine, and I needed her—I wanted her." He shrugged, a lopsided grin only making him look more miserable. "I love her. What perfect timing. I'm too much a coward to tell her I love her now, after this afternoon."

"Only brave men can speak of love?"

"Love is rare."

"Then it should be nurtured, not hidden from the light." Brother Klee finished sharpening the sword and slid it into its scabbard. "Tell her. Now. Before she rides into battle and you spend the whole of it regretting *not* speaking to her," he said with teasing exasperation. He gestured at the door. When Kalsan hesitated, he leaned forward and yanked him to his feet. "Go!"

Feeling foolish but relieved, Kalsan bolted. He ran to the main hall, down the many branching passageways to the guest wing. His imagination gave him speed, and he pictured how he would tell her.

He would take her into his arms and kiss her breathless. He would tell her on a whisper, then repeat it, kissing her between each word, until he saw the belief in her eyes.

Two Sword Sisters in full armor, spears in their hands, blocked the door to the room he and Andrixine shared. Neither were among the Sword Sisters who attended Andrixine at the wedding. Kalsan felt a chill as he approached down the long hall. Neither woman looked at him. He felt like a spirit, unseen and unheard—or worse, something below their notice. They had watched Andrixine with devotion fire in their eyes from the moment their three units were presented to her in the courtyard. He hadn't cared then, but now it bothered him.

"No one goes in," the tawny-skinned woman on the right said, when Kalsan reached for the doorknob.

"This is my room." He smiled to cut any embarrassment she might feel at her mistake.

"No one goes in," her partner repeated, black eyes gleaming through her helmet. Her spear shaft flashed out, rapping Kalsan's hand when he grasped the doorknob. Her dusky skin reminded him of a particularly nasty cat his sisters favored.

"This is the Sword Bearer's room, and no one enters," the first said.

"The Sword Bearer is my wife." He tried to make his tone calm and reasonable despite his stinging knuckles. What did it take for these women to understand?

"She confers in private with the commanders," the catty one said. Her eyes sparkled in malice.

"She doesn't keep secrets from me." Kalsan reached for the doorknob again. When she tried to crack his knuckles a second time, he was ready and yanked the spear from her hands.

"You'll do no better with a spear," the tawny one said, laughter threatening in her voice.

"Leave, little boy," the cat crooned and rested her hand on her sword. "The Bearer doesn't need you. This afternoon proved that well enough."

Something shriveled inside Kalsan. Did the whole army know about his miserable showing? He felt like he had as a little boy, when the village bullies had taunted him. He couldn't fight because they outnumbered him and his tongue wasn't quick enough to return their insults.

"We are here to serve the Bearer and guard her honor and body. We see to her needs. We dispose of useless equipment to save her the bother," she continued, her voice cracking.

She laughed and took a step closer to Kalsan. He held his ground and refused to raise a hand. She *wanted* an excuse to strike him down, he realized. One wrong move from him, and she could strike and claim self-defense. Andrixine might not believe—but would he be alive to know that?

Kalsan stood straight and struggled to stop the cold fury building in his chest from reaching his voice. "I doubt she knows your plans or your chosen duties."

"What you think doesn't matter, little boy."

"You will let me through to speak with my wife."

"You have no right to order us," Tawny said, a chuckle making her voice rich.

"I have to earn the right?" Kalsan gestured down the hall. "Then we'll go to the courtyard and prove who is more worthy—in a *fair* fight," he couldn't resist adding. The catty woman flinched at the implied insult.

"I can beat you easily with half the weapons you'll need," she growled. "Lissan!" She glared as her partner stepped back and pounded on the door.

It opened two seconds later, while the three in the hall glared at each other. Commander Caleen was a tall, gray-haired woman in leathers with the flame insignia of an Oathbound commander on the collar of her shirt.

"Why do you disturb us, Lissan?" she asked, her voice mellow— and threatening with its very pleasantness.

"This man claims he is the Bearer's husband and has the right to enter," Lissan, the tawny one said.

Caleen looked Kalsan up and down, her eyes pausing on the spear still clutched in his hand. She glanced over at the catty woman, noted her missing spear, and her gaze lingered on her angry face.

"My Lady, there is a problem," the commander said, stepping back into the room. She closed the door.

"Kalsan?" Andrixine flung the door open a few seconds later. She looked puzzled when she saw the guards at her door. "Why are you two here?"

"Lissan and Darsa are part of your honor guard," Caleen said. "I told them to let no one disturb our conference."

"But I need my husband here." She shook her head with a little sigh of exasperation. "Kalsan is my partner. He—he is my eyes, my voice where I cannot be."

"I tried to tell them," Kalsan couldn't resist saying. He stepped up to the door and paused long enough to hand the spear back to Darsa. She glared at him.

"Sisters." Andrixine took a step out the door so she could see both guards. Her gaze fastened on Darsa. "My husband is never to be denied my presence, is that understood?"

"Yes, Bearer," Lissan said. Her partner flushed and nodded but said nothing.

Kalsan felt a tiny shiver of apprehension when the door closed. He was inside and his opponents outside, but he still felt their gaze piercing his body, sharp with dislike.

The next hour went too quickly. Andrixine and Kalsan acquainted both Sword Sister commanders with the landscape around Snowy Mount, the maps made by their scouts in the last few days, the weak points in the defenses, places where the enemy could sneak through. They tallied the warriors' skills and talents and decided where they would be best placed.

From there they went on to meet with the king for one final conference before heading out into the night. The pass in Andrixine's vision split into two after several hundred yards. She would lead the Sword Sisters in defense of one, and the king would take charge of the other. Between them, Sendorland would be halted and forced back.

Kalsan never had a moment alone with Andrixine. He refused to speak the words that burned on his lips while others were near enough to hear.

Chapter Twenty-One

A FINE MIST FILLED the night air, obscuring what moonlight filtered through the shifting clouds over the mountain range. Andrixine shivered and pulled her cloak closer. Absently, her fingers stroked the embroidered edges, reading in the darkness the flame-sword-leaf emblem of Sword Sister Supreme Commander. She had been awed and flustered when Jeshra and Caleen had presented her with the full regalia—cloak, trousers, shirt, mail shirt and leggings, metal-bound boots, gauntlets and crested helmet. She remembered the naive days when she longed to be a simple warrior among the Sword Sisters. She had tasted battle, watched men bleed to death or die with their heads half-hacked from their shoulders. She didn't want to be party to anyone losing their lives this coming day. Wearing the clothes and armor of the Sword Sisters laid a claim on her, made her responsible for each woman injured or killed that day. She wished she could vomit and ease her churning stomach.

Andrixine stood on a ridge, looking down the rocky pass where Sendorland troops would spill through at dawn. Commander Caleen stood next to her, waiting and watchful. Somewhere in that darkness, navigating by faint moonlight, Kalsan and Commander Jeshra and one hundred Sword Sisters found hiding places to lay an ambush and block the retreat of the Sendorland forces, while more Sword Sisters plunged down and trapped them in a pincer move.

She wished Kalsan stood with her on the ridge, sharing warmth and a few last moments before battle called them. She shivered more, remembering that moment in the doorway to their room, seeing the hatred in her guards' eyes toward her husband.

"A problem, my Lady?" Caleen asked. She had an enviable talent for speaking so quietly only the person next to her heard.

Behind them, Derek slept undisturbed, propped up against a rock, Andrixine's banner draped over him like a blanket. She knew her brother would be heartily ashamed at falling asleep during the watch, but she knew he needed his sleep if he was to stay alert and alive during the battle. What had ever made her soften and grant her brother's request to ride to war with her?

"No. Yes," she corrected. She would feel better doing *something*, no matter how petty. "Those two at my door."

"Lissan and Darsa."

"I don't want them there."

"I admit it is superfluous, posting guards in a house of holy folk." A touch of humor made her voice warm. "And...you are newly married."

"Besides that." Andrixine felt her face warm. She hadn't even considered the loss of privacy. "They are hostile to my husband. I won't permit that."

"If you will permit me, Lady—"

"That's another problem. If we're to work together, I'd much prefer you use my name." Andrixine was relieved to see the older woman smile.

"Thank you, Andrixine." She nodded. "There are several things you should know, which would explain Lissan and Darsa, and others like them. We heard your marriage was hurried and for convenience. To fulfill your duties as heir, to provide you the closest possible guard to your honor and person." She paused.

"It was, but only at the start. My husband was my oath-friend before he asked me."

"Asked?" Caleen shook her head, negating the request for more details. "Jeshra's chapter house is filled mostly by noble daughters who come to the Sword Sisters because they *want* to serve, because they hear Yomnian's call. The chapter house I command in Cereston is filled mostly by common-born. Many come to us to escape marriages that are thin excuses for slavery. They don't have the options and training of we noble daughters. They marry to escape unhappy homes or to take the burden off their parents, and the men they marry take advantage of that. Many come to us escaping husbands who see them as tools, animals who need their spirits broken. Or, they have grown up seeing their mothers and aunts and sisters abused and want nothing to do with marriage. The Sword Sisters provide refuge and a place where they feel valued. We were...distraught to think the Sword Bearer was trapped in an unwanted marriage."

"They hate Kalsan because of their own pain," she whispered.

"Our advocates at court could help free you," Caleen offered.

"I made my vows to Yomnian, as well as to Kalsan. I am learning if I put Yomnian's will first, everything necessary for my happiness will be provided. Caleen, I am very happy in my marriage," Andrixine said, putting emphasis on each word.

"I understand."

"Please make sure that anyone who feels as those two feel also understands." She wrapped her arms around herself, chilled with more than the mist soaking through her cloak, slicking her hair, filling her lungs with damp. "If you must, tell every Sister that anyone who attacks my husband attacks me."

"That is rather drastic."

"They'll be drastically punished if they do anything to harm Kalsan. Yes, my marriage was compulsory, but I am happy. My life has been a whirlwind since the sword chose me, but Kalsan is my center of calm. If anything happened to him..." She wrapped her cloak more tightly around herself. "How soon until morning?"

"Not long."

Andrixine nodded and turned to stare into the misty dark plain spreading below her feet. Somewhere out there, Kalsan worked his way into position for attack. She needed his arms around her, needed to know he was safe. He had suffered no more than bruises in the first battle. Andrixine knew she would feel in her own body every cut, every broken bone he suffered.

IN THE MIDDLE of the churning sea of charging horses and flashing, slashing swords, Andrixine knew the exact moment the Sendorland soldiers realized *women* warriors faced them. It was almost a collective gasp of horror. The din of battle continued, but there was a sense of silence, of pulling back. The men of Sendorland were trained to consider women weak, undisciplined, immoral and easily broken—yet these women warriors had already cut a bloody swath through their ranks. Sendorland soldiers were trained from the day they entered the military to a fine edge of terror at the thought of a woman wielding a sword. What paralysis took them when over three hundred women warriors battered at them with arrow, spear and sword?

The retreat began piecemeal. She saw one man turn and run—or try to, hemmed in on all sides. The woman he had been trying to brain with a battleaxe shoved down into him with her spear, taking him high in the chest. He crumpled, suspended half-erect in death with the spear stuck in the ground. Andrixine turned away, nauseated more by the feral battle lust clear in the woman's eyes than by the way she killed.

Some soldiers went berserk, battering, hacking and stabbing at anything moving within sight. They endangered their fellow soldiers. More than once Andrixine saw Sendorland soldiers take down one of their own, purely in self-defense. She tried to believe they had brought it on themselves with their superstition and repression, but it still chilled her.

The Sword Sisters moved forward, gathering momentum. They forced the Sendorland soldiers backwards through the pass they had entered at dawn, leaving a trail of bloody, broken bodies.

Kalsan had vanished, Andrixine realized with a choking sense of panic. He fought his way to her side when she came charging down into the pass, and he had led his troops up behind Sendorland in ambush. He stayed within reach, fighting behind and beside and before her as the sun slowly crawled to zenith. More than a dozen times she turned, hearing a sword whistle as it arched toward her, and saw Kalsan intercept the blade with his own, following up with a stab of his long knife. Each time he made sure the man was dead, then turned quickly to find her. Each time, the light in his eyes changed from battle sternness to worry to relief in a heartbeat. His smile had been as brief and sweet as a parting kiss. With a salute to her, he turned back to the battle. It had never truly separated them until now.

How long had he been gone? She nearly didn't see the foot soldier leap at Grennel's stirrups. Andrixine kicked, but it was too late. She slashed down with the Spirit Sword. It blazed and the man opened his mouth to shriek mortal terror—the sound cut off before it began. Grennel snorted and darted forward, lashing out with his hooves, taking down another enemy before the man could see them coming.

Suddenly, all she saw were fleeing backs, the yellow and black Sendorland tunics spattered with blood, torn and slashed and muddy. Andrixine tugged on Grennel's reins to stop him when he shifted into a gallop. Her stallion might be willing and eager but she needed a moment to breathe. Where was Kalsan?

Turning Grennel, she surveyed the battlefield behind her. There was Derek, whacking at a retreating Sendorland soldier with his short sword and the splintered pole that once carried her standard. She grinned, relieved that her brother was still on his feet, and delighted that the banner was lost.

The fight moved further into the narrowing pass, the tide heading back to Sendorland. Sheer rock walls streaked with trickling springs and tiny pockets of grass reached to the sky on both sides, framing the near-zenith sun. Andrixine surveyed the destruction that had been at her back all this time. She grinned, knowing a moment of triumph at simply having survived. Then the sticky mask of grime on her face made itself felt along with the aches in her shoulders, the pulled muscles in her thighs from guiding Grennel, the sticky-dry spatters of blood on her arms, clotting her chain mail and leathers.

A tiny knot of fighting several hundred yards away, near the left rock wall caught her attention. Andrixine watched two Sendorland men emerge from the mass of flashing swords and run. Two Sisters darted after them, drawing their arms back in perfect unison to fling their spears. Both men went down with matched cries. Andrixine couldn't feel anything, not even approval of their skill. How long had this battle gone on? It felt like all her life, not half the day.

The fighting disintegrated. Another Sendorland soldier stumbled out of the commotion and slowly crumpled to his knees, clutching his chest. Three Sword Sisters followed him and paused to watch him die, then headed down the gap after the retreating enemy. Other Sword Sisters moved away, with stumbling and dying enemies in their wake. Only two figures remained fighting as the dregs of the battle vanished around the bend in the pass. Andrixine felt her heart miss a beat— Kalsan was one of those warriors. She urged Grennel closer.

Kalsan had lost his cloak. His overshirt had been slashed half off, exposing chain mail dulled with blood and dirt. He held his ground, matching every thrust and lunge of his opponent with sword blocks that even from halfway across the battlefield, Andrixine knew were only a fraction of a second fast enough. He tired. She imagined she felt the heaviness in his arms, the aches of bruises, stings of tiny cuts, sticky blood gluing his clothes to his body. Yet he smiled, his teeth bared, a white slash against the grime blackening his face.

He tripped, sprawling backwards over a corpse, and his helmet tumbled off, the strap broken. She swallowed a scream, staring as Kalsan somersaulted to his feet, spun and slashed at his opponent's momentarily exposed neck. The soldier went down and didn't get up.

Andrixine closed her eyes against the hot pressure of tears. How many battles could she endure, seeing scenes like that? How much fear could she feel for him without growing ill? What good was a Sword Bearer who couldn't keep her mind on the battle because her heart rode with another?

"Why do I have to love a warrior?" she whispered.

Silence on the battlefield. It sent a chill up her back and prickled her sweaty scalp. Andrixine knew there were dying and wounded crying in pain all around her. She could smell the blood, the spilled guts, the sour metallic smell of pain. Yet there was only silence.

Her chain mail was too heavy. Her helmet threatened to crush her skull. She reached up and yanked it off and hung it by its chin strap from Grennel's saddle. Andrixine opened her eyes as she tugged down the coif of chain mail and let the chill breeze soak into her sweat-slicked hair. She tugged off her gauntlets, smiling wearily at the bruises on her stiff hands.

Kalsan stood watching her, framed against moving shadows. Slowly, she raised her sword in salute. He smiled, raised his sword and bowed, revealing a dark shadow creeping up behind him.

"Kalsan!" Andrixine screamed warning before she recognized what she saw.

A Sword Sister crept up behind him, spear raised in both hands. Kalsan straightened, spinning on one heel. He swung up with his sword, catching the spear shaft and deflecting the blow to one side. The momentum pushed him off balance and he went to his knees.

Three more Sisters leaped on Kalsan. Andrixine dug her heels into Grennel, making the stallion shriek. He darted across the battlefield, breaking bones and kicking aside wounded and dead bodies.

Seconds slowed to hours, her muscles mired in ice as Andrixine watched the warriors swing swords and spears and fists at her husband. She saw him kick and punch in defense. Two more Sisters joined the battle, hiding him from her view.

A shrill, throat-tearing cry filled the air as she leaped from Grennel in mid-gallop and threw herself on the struggling knot of bodies. The Spirit Sword burned, its blue light turning red. Andrixine heard a woman scream, felt hot blood run down the blade onto her bare hand. A body crumpled like a rag doll.

"Mercy!" another woman shrieked. "Sword Bearer, we only serve—" Her words vanished in a gurgle as the sword entered her chest.

"No!" Lissan appeared from nowhere and flung herself at Andrixine, trying to pin her arms. "Please!" She gasped as a knee caught her low in her chest. She fell, retching, and wisely stayed down.

A howl like a crazed animal split the air as one Sister flung herself down on Kalsan's prone, unmoving body. Darsa's helmet was gone, letting her hair stream down her back, thick with sweat and filth. She had no weapon but a knife and she raised it to plunge into Kalsan's back.

"For you, Sword Bearer!"

Andrixine sliced off her hand. The knife went flying from the lax fingers. Andrixine took half a step back, held her breath and raised the sword. She bared her teeth against the terror in Darsa's dusky face.

Fire raced up Andrixine's arms. The Spirit Sword blazed red and yellow, hiding the blade. The air left her lungs as she felt her skin begin to shrivel. She screamed and flung the sword far from her and went to her knees, her head pressed to the bloody ground, her arms over her head.

Bearers who fell from their vows were killed by the sword.

The silence congealed around her. Andrixine braced herself for the final flash of destruction.

Twenty struggling heartbeats passed before she realized she wasn't dead. Death, after all, didn't include aching muscles and weariness, filthy, sweaty clothes and the reek of blood.

Andrixine raised her head. She was alone with Kalsan and the dead bodies, and Grennel keeping faithful guard over her.

And the sword, quiescent now, lying in a tiny patch of grass ringed by muddy, churned hoof prints.

"Kalsan," she whimpered.

Her muscles protested as she crawled to his side. She turned him over. Tears blurred her vision when she saw the blood trickling from his mouth, his pale face, the ugly red splotch at his temple from the blow that had felled him.

But he still breathed. She knelt and cradled him close, his head on her shoulder, and closed her eyes. She had no idea what to do besides hold him. She was too numb to even pray, though she knew she should. A voice whispered in her heart that this time, Yomnian would not listen.

She ignored everything and everyone. Grennel stood guard, head hanging, his tail not even moving. A few soldiers on both sides passed by, but were too intent on fleeing the battle or rejoining it to come over to investigate. Derek found her and came close enough to see Kalsan in her arms. Her brother wisely stayed silent and soon left to look for help.

Brother Klee found them a short time later as the healers from Snowy Mount descended into the pass to tend to the injured and take away the dead for burial. Andrixine slowly grew aware of someone watching her. Just as slowly, she raised her head.

"Andrixine, where is the sword?" he asked, his voice gentle, pity wrinkling his face.

"No." She clutched Kalsan tighter and felt him flinch. He moaned, and the sound cut through her chest.

"You are the Sword—"

"I won't!" Andrixine would have stood if not for Kalsan's weight holding her to the ground.

"I know what happened." Brother Klee knelt next to her and rested a hand on her shoulder.

"Why didn't it kill me?" Her voice cracked. Her fury at him, at his insistence on her duty, softened into tears that pressed at her skull and squeezed the breath from her. "It has to kill me. I—what I did—" She shook her aching head and hid her face in Kalsan's filthy hair.

"Obviously, it still wants you as its Bearer," the holy man observed after a few seconds of silence.

"What if I don't want it?" She caught her breath when she thought she felt Kalsan's arm move.

"Andrixine!" Brother Klee nearly sat backwards in shock.

"They tried to kill Kalsan because of me. To free me." She swallowed hard to hold back the sobs filling her throat. "If I must choose between the sword and Kalsan, I take Kalsan."

"It isn't that simple, daughter."

"He is my life!" She raised her head and glared at him, meeting his stern, caring gaze until he had to look away. She closed her eyes and tasted her own tears as she kissed Kalsan's forehead, his wounded temple, his lips. "He is my love," she whispered, and knew she imagined the sudden rise in Kalsan's chest and the hiss of indrawn breath.

"Yomnian must come first, daughter, or even the purest love will turn to poison."

"I know," she whispered. "I want to serve—but why does Kalsan have to pay?"

"Who says he is paying? Is he dead?" Brother Klee managed a tiny, crooked smile when she jerked her head up and stared.

"No." The word slipped out almost against her will.

"Trust Yomnian, child, or you will know a far greater sorrow for the rest of your life."

She could only close her eyes and let a few more tears slide out, scalding her skin and creating a trail through the dirt crusting her face.

Brother Klee moved away. She heard his boots squelching across the torn ground. The wind whispered in her ears. She felt Kalsan's pulse against her lips when she kissed his temple. Her mother had always cured terrible childhood wounds with a simple kiss. If only she could do that for Kalsan now.

"Andrixine." Brother Klee came back to stand before her. "Look at me." When she refused to raise her head, he took a handful of her dirty hair and tugged.

"No," she whispered, as she opened her eyes and faced the sword only inches from her nose. It glowed a soft blue. Once, she had taken comfort from that pale light.

"Take the sword."

"It will kill me."

"If you were found guilty, you would already be dead."

Exasperation touched his voice—that she could take. What stung was the hint of laughter. What did he find amusing about her pain?

"Take the sword," he repeated, and waited while the voices behind them grew stronger, accompanied by the cries of the wounded as they awoke or were moved. "You swore to serve Yomnian when there were far greater sorrows at stake, Andrixine. Why do you falter now? Take the sword and trust in Yomnian. Do not make me force your hand open."

Her stiff hand opened. She held it out gingerly, expecting any moment the fire would enfold her. Kalsan's eyes flickered open, and she didn't see. He took a deeper breath and watched Brother Klee put the hilt into her clasp. The former Sword Bearer had to close her stiff fingers around it.

The light flickered as if underwater. Andrixine held her breath, waiting.

"Now heal your husband," Brother Klee said. A gentle smile softened his lips. He turned his back on them and walked away.

"Can you?" Kalsan whispered. He winced and moaned when Andrixine jerked and nearly dropped him. "Careful!"

Tears blinded her as she helped him up. Kneeling face to face, she flung her arms around him. Kalsan's arms trembled but held her tight. She let the sword fall to the mud and welcomed the ache of his bruising kisses. She tasted the blood from his split lip, felt the sticky blood on his scalp as she tangled her fingers in his hair and held him close.

"Let me breathe, love," he whispered on a weak chuckle. "You are my love, you know."

"Kalsan—" She couldn't resist him when he pushed her back to arm's length.

"I thought I'd die before I could tell you I loved you." He dabbed the blood from the corner of his mouth with the shredded remains of his sleeve and swallowed hard against whatever thickened his voice. "Andrixine, I heard you—"

"You *are* my life." She clutched at his shoulders. "My oath-friend, my lover, my husband—my one love."

"You'd turn your back on the sword for me?" The incredulous look widening his eyes started her giggling. She couldn't understand why tears followed. "Promise me, Andrixine. Promise you'll never put me ahead of Yomnian. I love you too much to let you endanger your soul for my sake."

"But—"

"Promise me?" Then he gathered her close, holding her until they could hear the flapping of the wings of the first vultures descending on the aftermath of the battle.

"I promise," she whispered and felt a hardness in her chest suddenly dissolve.

Through the haze of weariness and relief, Andrixine remembered the sword and Brother Klee's words. Still hesitant, she slipped free of Kalsan's arms, reached for the sword and lightly pressed the flat of the blade to his wounds. Cool blue light flowed over her hands like the blood that had flowed before.

Epilogue

HOW LONG HE lay awake, listening to the soughing of the night wind as it threatened to become a storm, Kalsan couldn't be sure. Something had awakened him, a brightness, a sense of movement in the room. He sensed no danger, no trouble, so he lay still, enjoying the peace.

The summer had been long and hard. There had been few actual battles in the mountains dividing Sendorland from Reshor, but the rigors of keeping the armies ahead of attempted invasions had been draining. Still, the effort had been worthwhile because now Reshor had peace. At least, peace through the fall and winter.

Just last night, he and Andrixine had ridden through the gates of Faxinor castle, weary and brown from a summer spent outdoors, eager for the months of rest that winter would give them. Kalsan speculated that two weeks enduring the twisted paths of court life had been harder for Andrixine than the worst of pitched battles. He had been delighted for her when King Rafnar released them to go home.

Kalsan hoped the fall and winter would last forever. Spring would come too quickly, with news from the guard posts scattered through the mountains, trips to Cereston to meet with the king, and court politics to navigate. There would be new envoys from Sendorland to face, to listen to and try to decipher what was a lie and what was a concession to the truth. For now though, his most important duty was to make sure Andrixine rested and relaxed and enjoyed life for a change.

He woke a little more and realized that the bed was empty next to him. Kalsan rolled over to look for Andrixine.

She sat in her thin shift in the window seat looking out over the inner gardens. The Spirit Sword rested on the cushion next to her. Eyes half-closed, she wore a faint, sleepy smile.

"Love?" He slid out of bed and padded across the cool stone floor to settle down next to her.

She smiled a little wider and snuggled into his arms, and gently stroked the handle of the sword. In reaction to her touch, it flared once with pale blue light. Kalsan knew what that meant.

"A vision?" A sudden bright pink in her cheeks intrigued him and drove away the fear that they had to leave on another mission. "A good vision?"

"Very good." She turned in his embrace and cupped his bearded cheek with one hand as she gazed into his eyes.

"Tell me?"

"What do you want to name our firstborn?" She held still, face bright with laughter, waiting while he digested the news.

"You're pregnant?"

"Twins." She chuckled when he gaped and his arms tightened around her. "Boys. Both will be my heirs."

"Better than letting them fight over the inheritance." Low laughter bubbled up as they kissed. "Are you happy?"

"Very. They both look like you."

"Flatterer," he growled, and shook her a little. He kissed her long and deeply.

"Kalsan?"

"Hmm?" He was more interested in the smooth curve of her lips, but the slight catch in her voice snagged his attention.

"One inherits Faxinor. The other inherits the sword."

"How?" he managed to ask through a choking fear of the future. "When?"

"I hand it to him when your hair is silver." She smiled through sudden tears. "We'll be together a long, long time, my love."

~ * ~

Michelle L. Levigne

Michelle Levigne has loved fantasy, quests and adventures since discovering Chronicles of Narnia in Sunday School. She has a long apprenticeship in writing fan fiction, including Star Trek, Highlander, Stingray, Starman, Beauty & the Beast and The Phoenix. Her first professional sale was in conjunction with the Writers of the Future Contest, with the story "Relay," in Volume VII. Heir of Faxinor was her first full-length sale, and she is delighted to have it adopted into the Hard Shell family. Please visit her web site and explore all the words of her imagination at: www.MLevigne.com

Printed in the United States
132973LV00001B/43/A